THE HOUNDSKEEPER

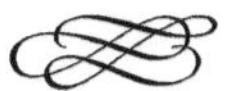

EVELYN GRIMALD

*For all the writers of romance out there:
You taught me about love and about humanity. For that, I
thank you from the bottom of my heart.*

CHAPTER 1

*P*ercival Northwood was dying. He knew it, and his doctors had confirmed the matter. Some parts of him were still regretful about the situation, but overall, he felt relief. His life had been a long one. It had often been a happy one. It had also been a lonely one. All that was left now was to settle his affairs and take himself to the seaside so that he might die in peace and dignity.

He pressed his hand against the pane of glass, looking out over the vast lawn and gardens that encircled the house at Belleview estate. It had been a foolish thing to have stubbornly kept this house and all its inhabitants when he had no kith nor kin with which to share it or to leave it. Had it been selfish to keep everything for himself? He thought perhaps so. But when he looked out the window of the library to the figure running in and around the three dogs there, he couldn't find regret.

Even as Northwood watched, the kitchen lad he had sent to run this particular message stopped the running figure. From this great distance, he could barely see that the person was a woman. She was scandalously dressed in breeks, a shirt, and an old worn vest, and was obviously a lithe and athletic person. She showed no care for the dirt and grass that smudged her clothes, only for the panting dogs at her side. Her hair hung over one shoulder in a long brown braid. It was the same colour as the earth upon which she ran. The woman and the lad exchanged information, with him pointing back to the house—and Northwood—and the woman gesturing to her dogs. Finally, the lad won the day.

She huffed and brushed off some of the dirt upon herself before stalking over to her boots and tugging them onto her stockinged feet. The lad watched, obviously admiring her. Northwood chuckled; he wasn't surprised. Eleana was a pretty lass, with her wild looks, skin touched golden and freckled by the sun, and the hounds always at her side looking up with adoration and loyalty. She was like Northwood's own daughter, had he been so blessed, and he still admired her, unconventional as she was. The kitchen boy was no exception.

Eleana made more gestures with her hands. Two of the three dogs wagged their tails and dutifully went off to the kennels, a long stone building near the stables. She watched for a moment, making certain that they did as they were ordered, then gestured to the third dog. It shook itself, black and white fur shining glossy in the sun. Then, with a stretch, it trotted over to Eleana's side, head pressed against her leg. Eleana touched the dog's head lovingly, then turned towards the house.

Both the dog and lad trailed in her wake. Northwood was not certain which was the more eager to follow.

Once Eleana had been lost to the interior of the house—and likely a berating from the housekeeper for trailing dirt on her newly cleaned floors—Northwood shuffled over to his chair by the fireplace. It was a warm day and yet he still felt chilled. His fingers were always cold these days. They seemed to become more numb as time wore on. With it becoming more and more difficult to stand or to walk or to even sleep, he knew that it was time. It was past time, but sentiment had caused him to prolong this moment for as long as possible.

Foolish.

Northwood shook his head, tucking a blanket around his legs. This whole ordeal was foolishness. What would society think of him now, the great Percival Northwood, once one of the most powerful people in the country, wielding political and financial influence like a knife, now reduced to the reclusive wretch whose pleasures came from spying on his Houndskeeper as she played. He had forgotten who he was and what he had once been. That was the only reason he found this task as difficult as he did. That was all. Not sentiment. Not attachment. Not… anything.

He had just resolved himself to this when a knock came on the door to the library. Northwood cleared his throat.

"Come," he said imperiously.

The door opened silently, admitting a dog and Eleana. The dog looked up at his mistress, pleading. She flicked her wrist and he ran over to Northwood. In spite of himself, Northwood wound his fingers through the dog's silky fur with a smile.

"Hello, Hunter." he said, tousling the dog's ears. The creature replied with a lick to his hand before returning to Eleana's side. Northwood swallowed back the disappointment at the loss before pointing to a chair opposite him. She sat, expression happy. Hunter lay at her feet, tail wagging. "One of these days, that dog is going to run to someone *without* your permission," Northwood said. He coughed slightly before continuing. "What will you do then? Marry the man?"

Eleana rolled her eyes, though she smiled while doing so, and flapped her hand dismissively. She leaned forwards and laid a hand on Hunter's head, as if to reinforce the fact that he was a good, obedient dog.

"Oh, I know you're considered one of the best Houndskeepers in the country, but even you cannot deny Hunter if he wanted to run off." Northwood rasped. Eleana shrugged, but she didn't seem willing to argue the matter. He shook his head, coughing again. Eleana was immediately up and gliding over to the sideboard where a pitcher of water was kept. Northwood would have preferred the warmth of brandy, but his alcohol drinking days were long behind him. He gratefully took the glass Eleana offered, guiding it to his mouth with shaking hands. She watched until Northwood had proved that he could take a sip without her help, then sat back down in her chair.

She spread her hands in a supplicating gesture, eyebrows raised in curiosity. Northwood took another sip of water, suddenly unwilling to tell her what he had called her there to tell.

"Eleana, I did not call you here to talk about Hunter. Or any of the other dogs, for that matter," Northwood said unnecessarily. He hadn't been down to see the dogs in ages. Eleana's mouth tightened. "I am… I have sold Belleview."

It wasn't what he had meant to tell her, not by any means, but it was all he could manage. Even that was difficult. Eleana's face paled until her dusting of freckles seemed unnaturally dark. She shook her head fervently, the loose strands of hair that had escaped her braid flying about her face. Northwood would have put up a hand to stop the protest, but he wasn't certain that he had the strength. But when Eleana slipped out of her chair and came to kneel by his side, he did pull his hands away from hers.

"There is nothing to be done," Northwood said sharply. "You know as well as I that when I inherited the estate, my family's money was nearly at its end. It has been many years since then and… it is time to sell. That is the end to it."

It was true that the money had been nearly gone, but Northwood was not uncanny in the matters of finance. He had brought his family's estate back from the brink of ruin and gone on to do much, much more than that. But Eleana, who had lived on the estate for all her twenty-two years—either as daughter to one of the workers or as Houndskeeper herself—would have known nothing of Northwood's reputation or his affairs.

It was perhaps easier to lie to her this way, he reasoned silently. He did not want to see the way her brown eyes would fill when he informed her that he was dying. He did not want to see her pain. If that meant it was better to spout falsehoods and untruths about the situation, then so be it. Northwood would lie.

He did, though, allow his cold, wrinkled fingers to touch Eleana's hand. She felt warm and strong. Northwood felt a tremor in his throat and forced it down. This was just the foolish sentiment of an old man. Wasn't it?

Eleana shook her head desperately, her fingers grasping at his. Northwood pulled them from her grasp after a brief moment, swallowing thickly. "You'll be more than fine with the new master. He has purchased the entirety of the estate and promised that he would not sell it piecemeal. The tenants will be cared for. You will be cared for. He is, apparently, wealthy enough to make such promises and I do not doubt him. And," here Northwood forced himself to smile, "he is far younger than I. He'll be able to go riding and hunting and you can finally put those hounds of yours to use."

Eleana pulled back from Northwood's conciliatory manner, glaring. She jabbed herself in the chest with a finger and then pointed to Northwood. Northwood would not pretend to mistake the gesture.

"You cannot come with me, child," Northwood snapped, voice suddenly containing a remnant of the commanding tone that was his right given status and station. He softened slightly as Eleana sank back on her knees. Hunter came up and thrust his head beneath her elbow, sensing his mistress's distress. Northwood shook his head. "Your place is here. Your father gave you this post and chose to move to town, to better give you a chance to live. *Here.* Your hounds are here. Your life is here. And I have nothing to offer you."

Eleana bit her lower lip, then sighed, her breath unsteady. She pressed an open hand over her heart and looked at him before reaching out and putting her other hand on his heart. She tried to smile, but that, too, was unsteady. Northwood knew, though he had never seen that particular gesture from the woman, that she was saying "I love you." He reached out and stroked her hair gently, brushing a loose strand behind her ear.

"Dear one, you are the closest thing to a daughter I have ever had. And I would only want the best for you. Stay. Live."

Eleana opened her mouth in a silent plea and Northwood wanted nothing more than to draw her into his arms. Instead, he straightened in his chair and turned his head away so as not to meet her desperate gaze. "Go. What's done is done. In one week, your new master will be here, and I expect you to be on your best behaviour. I will be gone in the morning."

Eleana pulled back at his sharp tone. Northwood saw the flash of anger in her eyes, as well as the hurt he'd inflicted. With the grace of youth, Eleana rose to her feet and strode from the room. She needed no gesture to bring Hunter to heel; the hound followed dutifully behind. Hunter looked back at Northwood. Eleana did not.

But that was for the best, Northwood mused. If she had looked back, she would surely have seen the glistening in his eyes. What good would sentiment do him —or anyone—now?

CHAPTER 2

*E*leana Tarell would have happily ignored forever the fervent activities of the Belleview estate after Northwood's departure. The carpets were dragged out by beleaguered footmen and beaten by frantic maids. Silver was polished. Every surface was dusted. The garden was pruned and cleared to the point of distraction. The kitchens were barely quiet, with people coming in and out at all hours to snatch what food they could. A week was hardly enough time to move from a comfortable estate belonging to a powerful, but old, man to a grand house that was the envy of the neighbourhood.

It was hardly enough time for Eleana's anger to cool, either.

She found herself more in the way than otherwise, and even if she had been needed desperately, she was not certain she would have offered her help. Instead, she tended to her dogs just as before. She bathed them.

She cleaned their kennels. She exercised them. When she wasn't stomping from the kennel to the house, she was wandering the vast forest that surrounded the estate.

Eleana had grown up on Belleview; she knew its grounds and its tenants intimately. But before, where she had been a cheerful presence, always free with a wave and a smile, she was now almost invisible. She plodded through the forest paths, Hunter and one or another of the dogs at her side, doing her best to stay away from people. She shied away from the community dinners of the household staff, instead eating in her small cottage adjoined to the kennels. She retreated into herself and into her dogs, preferring them to all other company.

She told herself that she wasn't upset when no one bothered to ask after her. Then Hunter would nudge her with his nose, hoping that she would throw a stick or pet him, and all would be right with the world.

After all, none of her dogs had ever willingly left her like so many people had.

Eleana continued in this way for the entire week preceding the new master's arrival. She even managed to conveniently forget that the man was set to arrive that day, instead choosing to be out in her most comfortable walking clothes, Hunter and a larger-boned scenting dog named Baron at her side. Eleana had walked nearly seven miles and it was now midday. She was brought back to the house with Hunter and wondered if she could snatch something from the kitchens without anybody the wiser.

Eleana wandered up the drive, Hunter and Baron sniffing at some grass and then playfully nipping at one another behind her. A noise caught her attention and Eleana jumped off the gravel drive, the dogs leaping back as well. Eleana gestured sharply and the two dogs fell in at her heels just as a grand carriage came up and past them. It was stately, well-made, and obviously expensive, just as the two matching white horses with their gleaming brass tack that pulled the carriage were of the finest stock. There was a black stallion tied to the back of the carriage and even Eleana, who knew nothing about horses, was impressed with its stride and sleek appearance.

The carriage passed and its significance struck Eleana. It must have been the new owner of Belleview. How could she have forgotten that he was meant to arrive today? Eleana looked down at her clothes. She wore men's breeks, patched at both knees and belted tightly around her waist with a worn leather belt. Her shirt was of coarse linen and while it was loose enough to hide the outline of her corset, it was far from decent for a woman of any class to be wearing. Only her brown hair, freshly washed the night before and tied neatly into its braid, could be of any pride to her.

Sniffing, Eleana stuck her nose into the air, hiding a smirk. If the new master didn't like her appearance, he could very well go soak his head. She was a little embarrassed that Northwood's legacy would include her personage looking like this, but the remnants of Eleana's anger was enough to soothe that wound.

She knew and understood Northwood's reasons. If there was no way he could stay due to poor investments, then there was nothing to be done. Besides, he had been right. Eleana's life was here. She could never have left her father or the hounds who were in her care. She had never even been off the estate in her life except to go visit a few of the other neighbouring estates when training dogs or dealing with hunts. But... to have left things like that? That was cause enough, Eleana thought, for her anger.

She sighed and patted her thigh, bringing both dogs to heel. Then, determination pushing her forwards, she climbed the hill to go face the great house and Himself.

The household—all those who were clean enough to be seen, anyway—were standing outside, arranged in neat lines and wearing their finest uniforms. The housekeeper, Mrs. Graham, had paid particular attention to her appearance, Eleana was amused to note. She had even gone so far as to put on her mother's brooch. The men stood with their shoulders tall and proud and their backs straight.

Mrs. Graham caught sight of Eleana as she walked up the drive and her eyes widened. But the doors of the new owner's carriage were opening and there was nothing that Mrs. Graham could do now to shoo Eleana away. Eleana did, though, reinforce her command for her dogs to heel as she walked closer.

The man who emerged from the carriage did not

seem to notice Eleana when she walked up the drive, but she noticed him. She scowled at the fact that he was precisely what he should have been. He was young, perhaps no more than thirty. He was of average height for a man, with fitted black breeches and leather boots. His shirt gleamed a fair white where it showed above the collar of his dark jacket. A blue silk cravat hung around his throat, marking the fact that his clothes were both expensive and in good taste. As Eleana drew closer, however, she saw that more than fashionable, he had obvious charm.

It came in the form of the pensive, thoughtful, almost sat look on his face. His features were pleasing, and his dark hair lay across his forehead in waves. For all of this, though, it was plain that the man was distracted, distraught even. He looked around him but did not seem to see the splendour of Belleview.

Eleana paused at the top of the hill, some distance away from this spectacle of greeting. Her dogs waited at her side, picking up on her tension and pressing close to comfort her. She watched as Mrs. Graham sketched a curtsey. The housekeeper's voice trembled, but it still carried far enough for Eleana to hear.

"We welcome you, sir, to Belleview and hope that you shall be happy here in your new home..." Mrs. Graham's words seemed to startle the man out of whatever line of thought he had been pursuing and he started as if in shock. Cautiously, he gave the waiting staff a half-smile, the expression making him seem all the sadder since it didn't quite reach his eyes.

"Thank you," he began, voice soft and deep enough for Eleana to have to strain to hear. "I am Lord Richard Byrns, second son of the seventh Marquess of Farley. My… my family has long been without an estate and I am pleased to be able to make Belleview my home. I believe we shall get on quite well. You shall have to keep reminding me of your names for a while so that we can get acquainted. And please, if you wish to know something, ask. I want us to understand one another."

There was a slight pause, then a young maid—little more than a girl—stuttered, "P-please, m'lord, is there no mistress?" The maid's voice seemed to strike this Lord Byrns and he shuddered visibly, closing his eyes and taking a slight step back, bumping into the carriage directly behind him. Eleana watched emotion play across this new master's features. He took a deep, visible breath, then faced the maid without emotion.

"No," he said. "My late wife died of lung-rot one year ago. I moved here from the city to get away from her memory and the demands of society. Never speak of her again." By the time he finished speaking, his voice was trembling with anger, his fists clenched at his sides. No one said anything further and all turned away slightly, as if afraid to meet his eyes.

This new master took a deep breath, then stepped forwards as if to make amends for his anger. He stepped far enough from the carriage for a great black form to fly from it, body trembling with excitement and tail wagging. Eleana recognised the breed of dog immediately; they were a popular cross between a hunter and a fighter, their more-pointed muzzle larger after the fighter blood in them. The dog was all black, slim and well-muscled, and had obviously been cooped up in that carriage for far too long.

"Smoke, come." the new lord of Belleview commanded, but the dog was already racing off to go and investigate Eleana and the other two dogs.

This new dog was obviously not as well trained as Eleana's hounds. A few of the young servants moved, either to intercept or flee, but it was too late. The dog was already lunging for Baron, either in play or aggression. Eleana noted the slightly horrified posture of this new lord, but that was all. In the moment when the dog came close enough to Eleana to touch, she turned from woman to wolf.

Eleana didn't have time to order her dogs away, so she flicked her wrist and trusted them to stay where they were. The black dog tried to lunge around Eleana, obviously excited. While he was probably just wanting to play, he could have just as easily been trying to attack and assert his dominance. But on the Belleview estate, there was only one alpha and that was Eleana. In a flash of motion, she dropped to her knees. She curled up her lips, showing her teeth to the black dog, eyes locking with his. Smoke's own lip curled, and his hackles rose.

"Smoke, no," came the cry from the wayward dog's master, but he was too late. Eleana kept her stare with the dog and advanced, snapping her teeth as she did so. Smoke growled and it was obvious his instincts were telling him to attack, where training was telling him to stand down. Here was a human, acting like a dog, trying to claim dominance. He should assert his own claim. But nor could he attack a human. In his moment of indecision, Eleana lunged forwards, one hand slamming into the dog's shoulder, the other putting pressure on its muzzle. Smoke's paws slid out from beneath him and he fell to the ground on his side.

Eleana swung her leg over the dog and, keeping her eyes locked with his and a hand at his throat, rolled him onto his back, staring him down. Smoke, startled and suddenly afraid, whined, flashing his teeth in a sorry grimace of submission while he broke eye contact and whined again. Eleana kept her teeth bared and leaned down, putting a slight pressure on the dog's throat, her teeth nearly touching the black nose. Smoke whined again and showed her the whites of his eyes, obviously accepting her position as alpha. To seal the bargain, Eleana opened her jaws and bit down gently on Smoke's nose.

In another flash, it was all over. Eleana let Smoke up and got to her feet while the black dog danced around her, his tail wagging and his ears half-perked. Eleana held her hand out, an obvious gesture which even those with no understanding of dogs could tell meant 'sit.' Smoke sat, wagging his tail the entire time. Eleana smiled, pleased with the dog, then twirled her fingers at Hunter who trotted up and exchanged sniffs and tail wags with the new dog. Next came Baron, and once Smoke remained friendly with both dogs, Eleana flicked her wrist and the dogs went off, running around the yard in play.

Then, it was time to deal with the master. Eleana turned to him, taking in his astonished expression and caring not at all. She stalked up to him, fury radiating off of her. Fire burned in her eyes as she stopped just in front of him. Her brown eyes locked with Lord Byrns and he blinked, staggering backwards a step.

Eleana pointed her finger at Lord Byrns' chest, her strength making him rock on his heels slightly. Then, she gestured angrily to the dogs running around, rolling and playing, and touched her own head. She spread out her arms in an accusing sweep and glared. Lord Byrns backed up another step and held up his hands, inadvertently granting his own submission to Eleana's alpha position.

"I didn't know that Smoke would do that. I tried to have him trained in the city but finding a good Houndskeeper is difficult. I'm sorry, ah-"

"Eleana," Mrs. Graham cut in, stepping out of her place in the array of servants to approach the bewildered lord and the furious Houndskeeper. "She is the Houndskeeper here at Belleview. Best Keeper in, well, the whole country probably. Trains her dogs to respond to her silent commands as well as vocal commands."

As Mrs. Graham approached, Eleana glared once more at the new master and strode away, commanding Hunter and Baron to heel and sending Smoke to his human, but no longer his master.

RICHARD BYRNS STARED after the wild woman that had berated him soundly without a single word. She was fire and energy. He had found himself without words at the unconventional manner of dress, the irreverent way with which she treated him, and even her eyes. He kept his shocked gaze on her as she walked, powerful and straight, across the lawn to, presumably, where the kennels were. Richard tugged at his vest in a desperate attempt to regain some of his composure.

Perhaps coming to Belleview had been a bad idea.

"She… she does not like me much, does she?"

"Eleana?" Mrs. Graham peered after the retreating girl and pursed her lips. "I don't think she much *likes* anyone apart from her dogs. I mean, she can be right friendly enough if she puts her mind to it, but… well, not that she'd *tell* you if she thought otherwise, after all."

"Why not?" Richard asked, angry at his own curiosity and the motion behind it.

"She cannot speak. She's mute. Hasn't said a word in… well, ever. I don't know if she was born that way or if she grew up that way, but that's how it is. She trains her dogs in complete silence, with her fancy finger twists and wrist bending and such. Mr. Northwood, as he was master to her, once offered to get a professional sign-teacher here to teach Eleana, but she would have none of it. She communicates well enough when she needs to by using her hands and such.

Having a conversation with her, a real one mind you, is as rare as butterflies in winter, but it is a beautiful thing." Mrs. Graham looked at the new lord before shaking her head. She turned and in a flurry of activity, Richard found himself inside, ensconced in what appeared to be the library. He held a glass of scotch in his hand while his belongings were sorted out.

The tour had been brief but insightful, nonetheless. There were three separate wings—one entirely for the servants—and more space than one man could ever possibly need. But it had been what he'd wanted; to get away from the city and to be alone in his thoughts, mourning his wife and wallowing in his own misery. The servants had obviously seen his grief immediately and steered clear. Even the affable Mrs. Graham had made the tour as quickly as possible and left him alone in the library, the head butler—a short, round man called Hayes—close behind her.

Richard drained the scotch in one quick gulp and poured himself another. He was on his third, nursing it in a char beside the fireplace that had been laid but not lit. It was a warm enough day that the fire wasn't necessary, but part of him would have liked it all the same. At least it would have given him something to stare at while he meditated on what he could not avoid.

One year, almost to the day, it had been since his beloved Christina Byrns had died, leaving him alone, bereft, and full of self-loathing. Richard had wanted for so long to do nothing more than to get away from the close and pressing society of the town and escape to the country. Perhaps he could die at a young age and leave this estate behind for his cousin to inherit as a testimony to the family.

But then he had come here and met a wild woman who looked like she belonged in the woods, a creature of myth and legend and magic.

When she had touched him, jabbing him with her finger, it was like a bolt of lightning had come down from the heavens and struck Richard in the chest. His entire body had tingled at her touch. He felt his thoughts straying towards her, the way she had handled Smoke, the way she had handled *him*.

Richard had felt love before. He had loved Christina with every possible moment. This immediate, absolute, and consuming love, which filled his entire body and began to enthral him? This was something entirely familiar and yet different from what he had known with Christina. This was complete in a way that could never have been. He loved Eleana, the Houndskeeper of Belleview estate. He had loved her the minute she came into his world.

And he hated her for it.

CHAPTER 3

Richard Byrns hadn't known that it was possible to be in an even worse mood than he had the night before, but stalking into the breakfast room with Smoke bouncing around him did just that. How could he be so interested and pleased with a place such as Belleview and yet want nothing more than to hate it, too? Richard scoffed and shook his head, opening the door. He did not miss the irony of the fact that he felt such things for the mysterious Eleana, either.

The breakfast room was pleasantly furnished, with cheerful yellow wall coverings and tall windows that let him look out over the grounds. The table was large enough to seat a whole household of guests but was set ominously only for one. There were two people already in the room, the straight-backed Hughes and a younger—and taller—footman. Both wore formal expressions and stepped forwards, ready to serve.

"Good morning, m'lord," Hughes said imperiously, nodding his round head at Richard.

"Er, yes. Good morning." Richard replied. He stepped towards the spread of food on the sideboard and was intercepted by Hughes.

"Mrs. Graham and I were wondering whether or not you took the paper," Hughes said. "In case you were interested, I have sent for the Times and the Chronicle."

"Ah, thank you," Richard muttered. "But… I don't think I'll… The Times is fine, I suppose."

"Very good, m'lord," Hughes said with a nod. He jerked his hand at the footman who nipped forwards and snatched the Chronicle from the table. "Young Lewis here is happy to serve you whatever-"

"Oh, I prefer to serve myself," Richard interrupted. He was not blind to the widening of Hughes' eyes, nor of the blush that crept up Lewis' face, but he was able to resolutely ignore them. "I have made do on my own for some time, and there seems to be no reason to change that."

Hughes seemed to consider this, exchanging a glance with the unfortunate footman. "Ah, of course, my lord. If you have need of us, just, ah, ring."

Hughes indicated the bell pull beside the door and, bowing slightly, ushered Lewis out and closed the door firmly behind them with a click. Richard scoffed again at the ridiculousness of the situation. Yes, his station and status usually required that he acquiesce to the care of the servants. He was supposed to let others do for him; it was his privilege and his right. But in the year since Christina… Richard's grief had been great enough that he never spoke to the servants, nor allowed them in the same room as himself. He had wanted to be alone, and they made certain it was kept that way.

He sighed and tugged on the grey vest he wore. As if moving through a fog, he dished out eggs and sausage onto fine china and buttered some toast. The tea he drank was more to his taste, though, especially after he doctored it with a few drops from the silver flask he carried in his pocket. Richard looked at the door, wondering if Hughes was waiting outside for him to call. Probably not. He was alone, once again.

Smoke whined and put his head on Richard's lap. He chuckled slightly, the sound weak, and scratched the dog behind his ears. "What's the point, eh boy? I'm not hungry. I haven't been hungry since… since she died. It's like a hole opened in my chest and is trying to consume me. Only everyone else is trying to get me to stay alive. And now I've made an enemy of the household. Well, that's alright. I don't need them to like me, do I? I have you and I have my drink and I have my thoughts. Isn't that enough?"

Richard looked at Smoke, taking in his happy and expressive face. The dog's tongue darted out to lick his chops. The act didn't make Richard feel any better. He sighed.

"Who am I kidding?" he muttered. "You're only here for the food. Well, have at it."

He took the plate before him and set it on the ground. He did smile slightly at the sight of Smoke going for the sausages without abandon, whole body wagging with his pleasure. Had he ever been so pleased to see something?

Eleana, his mind answered immediately. Richard shut off that line of thinking and slammed his teacup onto the table. He was slightly disappointed that it didn't shatter.

The door to the breakfast room opened quietly and slammed shut, making Richard jump in his plush chair and turn. He had wrapped his hand around the fork remaining on the table, but his fingers released it involuntarily as he saw who was standing there. As if his mind had conjured her, Eleana had appeared in the room. She stood there, fury written plainly on her features, the placid Hunter at her side.

Richard took the time—unwilling, he silently cried—to note her appearance. Her clothes were neater and of finer quality than those she had worn the previous day, but she was still dressed as a man. The sight of her figure so plain to behold, so open, nearly made Richard blush. He pushed his thoughts towards the anger that arose in equal measure as the pleasure he felt at the sight of her. He loathed himself for this weakness, and he loathed her for making him feel it.

He had hoped never to see her again after their startling encounter the day before. He had lost what scant sleep he usually cobbled together trying to puzzle her out and decide what it was he really felt. He had instead decided that they would never cross paths again and he would be able to ignore her. After all, he would be spending most of his time in the house or riding around the grounds. What need did he have to see the kennels? What need did he have of kennels at all? Smoke was the only dog he needed.

Yet here she was, standing there like a vision from a dream, fire and fury and fey. All he could do was let slip the words, "What are you doing here?"

She did not appear to hear him. Eleana's attention was focused on the black dog leaning over the plate of food on the ground. To his credit, upon her entering, Smoke had immediately backed away from the plate, thereby granting the right of food to his alpha. Eleana ignored Richard's presence entirely and swooped in, snatching the plate from before the dog and depositing it unceremoniously on the table.

Richard threw his napkin on the table and rose, his chair scraping backwards as he did. "What are you doing?" he snapped, drawing to his full height and glowering down at Eleana.

Eleana started, blinking up at him with surprise. Her attention had been on Smoke. Richard took a step forwards, not sure whether he wanted to draw near to her or to intimidate her.

"You have the nerve to come in here and interrupt my breakfast just to take away food from my dog? I did not summon you and I do not want you here." He lifted his chin firmly, making his preferences clear. Eleana turned, a slight glimmer of something—possibly fear—

in her eyes when she returned to reality. But the glimmer was gone quickly enough to make Richard doubt that he had ever seen it there, whatever it was. Eleana curled her lip as she had done yesterday while declaring dominance over Smoke. The fierce expression in her eye gave Richard pause. He frowned. "Answer me. I am lord here and I want an answer."

The snarl of dominance turned into a look of disgust. Eleana jabbed herself in the chest with a finger and pointed to Smoke before doing a strange series of twists and twiddles with her fingers. At the movements, Hunter crouched down and leapt into the air, twisting around fully once before landing lightly on his feet. Eleana indicated to her hound with both hands. Hunter looked back calmly, as though he had done nothing significant. Eleana put her hands on her hips, glaring at Richard.

He could see plainly that she did not like him. That much was no mystery. Practically from the moment Smoke had gone running from his control, Richard had seen that she did not like him. She blamed him for Smoke's behaviour, possibly for his purchasing Belleview, and for who knows what other offences laid at his feet. Richard grasped the silver flask in his pocket for a reminder of something solid. He wanted her to like him, yet if she did that, this would be all the more difficult. So, he simply watched her gestures with wide-eyed astonishment, trying desperately to understand the peculiar language of the Houndskeeper.

Richard licked his dry lips and brought his teacup

to his mouth. Finding it empty, he cursed quietly and filled it from the flask, not even thinking about the result. He brought the cup up and drained it, feeling a sharp burn at the back of his throat from the alcohol, and a similar burn in his chest from Eleana's eyes.

"I don't know what game you're playing at, but I demand that you make yourself clear. What are you doing here? And who gave you the right to take away food that I have given to my dog? The impertinence is appalling," Richard said, his voice quickly rising in tone from soft annoyance to harsh anger. At least, he hoped it was anger rising in his chest and not something else equally strong and passionate.

At the tone of his voice, Hunter took a step forwards and lowered his head, hackles raised and a growl rumbling deep in his chest. Smoke whined, putting his ears flat against his head and tucking his tail close.

Eleana jerked at the sounds coming from the dogs. She stared, shocked, at the black and white dog at her side. Almost frantically, Eleana made a circular drawing in the air with her fingers between Richard and herself. Hunter looked at his mistress and put his ears back slightly, obviously confused. Eleana made the circle again before blindly reaching behind her and grabbing Richard's hand, holding it as a friend would. She refused to look away from Hunter's gaze.

She must have been completely oblivious to not notice what her touch was doing to him, Richard thought. Did she not feel the sparks that tingled on his skin where her hand met his? Did she not feel that same swelling in his chest and that urge to step forwards, between her and the wary Hunter? While he did not completely understand what was going on, he understood enough to surmise that Eleana was explaining to Hunter why she did not need his protection. She was marking Richard as a sort of pack-mate, if not a friend. But the way her skin grazed his, soft like meadow grass and yet worn and calloused, sent shivers up his spine. He wanted nothing more than for her to keep a hold of his hand and yet there was that deep dislike there, too.

Eleana released him when Hunter sat and Richard immediately recoiled his hand, trying with difficulty not to rub it clean on his vest. He set his jaw. "Will you please explain to me what is going on?" he asked, trying to keep control over his voice, trying to keep the surge of emotion that was equal parts anger and desire, down.

Eleana repeated her gesture towards herself and suddenly Richard felt as though he was playing some sort of ridiculous parlour game. "You," he repeated dutifully. Eleana responded with a nod. She gestured to Smoke before looking at Richard for confirmation. "Smoke," he said, already weary of this game. He wanted to be able to understand her, or better yet, hear her speak. That seemed to be another impossibility in his life. Eleana twirled her fingers and Hunter rose, turning in a circle. "Tricks," Richard said drily. Understanding dawned on him. "You want to train my dog to do tricks?"

Eleana grimaced and tucked a strand of hair behind her ear. Richard could tell that neither of them were pleased with that particular translation. He felt more the idiot for this entire situation and it was plain to see that she thought him equally stupid for not being able to understand her as well as her dogs. Eleana sighed, the sound so loud for her normally silent state. It was enough to startle Richard, which made her smile. He clenched his teeth.

Eleana put her hand before her mouth, fingers facing outwards, and twiddled them while pointing at Richard, her movements slow and precise. She waited while he stared at her in obvious confusion, his brows lowered and his expression one of complete dismay. Eleana frowned and tried again, opening and closing her mouth as if talking, all the while pointing to Richard. It took him a few moments to figure out what she was doing.

"What I said? You want me to repeat what I just said?" he asked desperately. Eleana clapped her hands in victory and nodded. Obliging and desperate, Richard did as she asked. "You want to train my dog to do tricks," he said, his astonishment at Eleana over-coming his dislike for a brief moment. She pointed at him, obviously pleased, before holding her hands far apart then close together again. Eleana repeated this process until Richard figured it out. "You want me to shorten what I just said?" Richard asked, running a hand through his hair, suddenly exhausted.

Eleana nodded, exchanging a glance that Richard read as contemptuous with Hunter. The dog watched the goings on with as much calm and poise as ever. She waited, hands pressed together, a pleasant smile forming on her face as one would with a child who did not understand his lesson.

Richard realised at last what Eleana had come to the breakfast room for. "You want to train my dog."

She nodded, seemingly ignoring the dry way her new lord had addressed her. Turning towards the door, Eleana twitched her fingers at Smoke who then took his cue from Hunter and followed along.

She was at the door, looking triumphant and tired and more than a little beautiful, when Richard uttered the one word that sent a bolt of fury racing through the both of them. "Why?"

Eleana turned, eyes blazing and face set in a mask of polite disbelief. Richard saw his mistake and grew pale at the undertaking he had just ventured upon. Did he really wish to go through all that again? No. Did he really want to try and translate a whole phrase, a whole explanation when a single, simple question had taken so much time? No. Did he want to watch this person wave her arms about, looking at him as if he were an idiot or a fool? No. Did he want her to stay so that he could try and learn her language, to try and understand her, to determine who this Eleana was, really? Yes.

No!

Richard set his face in a polite mask while he warred with himself. He was still grieving for his wife —whom he *loved*. Therefore, he could *not* be in love with this insolent person. As such, his immediate dislike and even hatred of her was founded merely upon her attitude and not the fact that she made him feel unfaithful and wrong.

Eleana took his silence as a response; she turned to open the door and paused in surprise. She clicked her fingers, causing Hunter to give a soft whoof, much to Richard's confusion. The relief that swept across Eleana's features became clear, though, as Mrs. Graham swept in, looking surprised.

"Eleana, dear, whatever are you doing in the house? And in the breakfast room, no less," Mrs. Graham exclaimed, hurrying into the room. At the sound of her voice and the image of her solid presence, Richard sank into his chair, a measure of stress leaving him.

"Madam, thank goodness," he said, draining the last of his flask into his teacup and not caring one jot about the witnesses. Mrs. Graham took a tentative step forwards. Richard lifted the cup and emptied it with a swift tilt of his head. "I require your assistance."

"Whatever you need, m'lord," Mrs. Graham said respectfully, giving a slight nod to Richard. Eleana stepped into the housekeeper's line of sight and started moving, her frantic motions catching the attention of Richard and making him forget to speak.

Eleana pointed to him and then to her mouth, fingers twiddling all the while, and then to her head while she shook it back and forth. Mrs. Graham stifled a chuckle. "Of course he doesn't understand you, dear. What did you expect? He has only been here a day." Eleana threw her hands up and blew a huff of air, exasperated. That much Richard could discern. Shaking her head slightly, Mrs. Graham turned to the new lord of Belleview. "What seems to be the trouble?"

"She burst in here, unannounced and unasked for, and took the plate of food I had set down for Smoke. Then she goes on a tirade when I ask what she was doing here. She says she wants to train Smoke and I asked why. I just want to know why she thinks that my dog needs to be trained. he's already been with the finest Houndskeepers in the city," Richard said, addressing his speech to Mrs. Graham as if Eleana wasn't even there.

The slight Houndskeepers frowned and folded her arms, then immediately unfolded them, waving her arms about and flicking her wrists, indicating Smoke on occasion and then herself, once covering her throat with her hands and baring her teeth. Mrs. Graham folded her hands in the pleats of her skirts. "She says that she needs to train your dog because his training is insufficient. He would not have attacked yesterday had he been properly trained," Mrs. Graham replied. Eleana gesticulated further, slowly becoming more and more calm with the presence of someone who actually understood her. "As Houndskeeper," Mrs. Graham continued the translation. "It is her duty to make certain that all dogs at Belleview are safe and well-trained. She does not care if you trained Smoke your-self; if he is not properly trained, he must be trained."

"That's all well and good-" Richard started and was immediately cut off by Eleana's motions. How did someone who could not speak at all manage to inter-rupt another person? Especially someone whose class, power, and finances were so much above this, this whelp of a woman?

Mrs. Graham blushed slightly but nonetheless lifted her chin and dutifully translated. "And she says that if she ever catches you feeding human food to a dog again, she will personally, ah, put you in the kennels and leave you there until you are trained. Meaning no offence, m'lord."

Eleana smiled at Mrs. Graham and gave a mocking bow to Richard before spinning on her heel and marching out of the room, the two dogs trailing after her.

Richard stared at her retreating form before she disappeared, then turned back to the table before him. He clenched his hands on the arms of his chair, jaw tight. A frown made its way onto his face. "That woman is the most disrespectful and insolent person I have ever met. She does not even seem to regard me as the master here. She must learn her place," he snarled, more to himself than to Mrs. Graham.

"Oh, no, my lord, please!" the housekeeper said, moving to stand where Richard could easily see her, alarm plain in her visage. "Please don't discharge her! El is spirited, yes, but she cares about her dogs—and

Belleview—more than anything. And if she were forced to leave Belleview, it would likely kill her!"

"Don't be ridiculous," Richard scoffed. Truthfully, sending Eleana away had not even occurred to him. He had thought merely to ignore her. But the thought of being separated by more than a few walls and doors was appealing. If he sent the troublesome Eleana far away, she would not be able to influence his thoughts away from the memory of his wife. He had only known her for less than a full day, so there was no reason why he should not forget her. If she were as good a Houndskeeper as was kept being pointed out to him, then she would easily find work. Richard nodded, settled. "She must learn."

"Sir, at the risk of sounding impertinent," Mrs. Graham said, her voice no longer pleading but dry and flat, "Belleview is the only home that girl has ever known. She is safe here with people who love her, and dogs who would do anything to please her. So what if she hurt your pride, coming in here to train Smoke without being summoned? Eleana does not like you because you purchased Belleview and Mr. Percival Northwood was like a father to her. She takes some time to get used to, but you will get used to her. And besides, if you discharge her, then you will have to hire a whole new household of servants. I guarantee you that."

"You dare," Richard hissed, narrowing his eyes at the housekeeper. Mrs. Graham drew herself up, her figure imposing and eyes flashing.

"I dare. Frankly, you can drown yourself in your grief and your drink and I do not think that one person here would care. You certainly haven't given any reason for us to respect you. But if you think of getting rid of someone who is part of the foundation of Belleview, then you will find that we care. We care a great deal," Mrs. Graham said. She did not bother waiting for a response but instead turned on her heel and left the dining room. And so, just as so many times in the past, Richard found himself once more alone in a houseful of people.

Richard took a deep breath, surprised at the animosity that came from the people around him. All for the sake of protecting a sprite of a Houndskeeper, and a woman at that. He should dismiss the entire lot of them. He reached for the teacup and frowned to find it once more empty. He did not usually drink so much, and certainly not so early in the morning, but recent events were enough to drive any sane man to drink. Richard stood and walked over to the cut glass decanter sitting on the sideboard for luncheon. He poured himself a full glass and took a deep drink, revelling in the wave of heat that washed over him. It made everything hurt less.

"Well, Christina," he said, glancing reverently towards the ceiling. "I did what you always wanted me to do. I bought an estate in the country. Though I doubt that you would have wanted us to live here all the year round. Yet here I am, away from all that frivolous nonsense that you were so good at and that I never understood. And people don't seem to like me much, just like it was in the city."

Silence met his words. Richard laughed softly to himself, the sound more mocking than happy. He took another sip then regarded the glass, walking over to the window.

"Look at me. I'm a drunk and I have alienated everyone within a day, just by being wealthy enough—and stupid enough—to buy this pile. And there's this girl, Eleana. She's the Houndskeeper, here, and she thinks that Smoke isn't trained properly. Just like you were always saying. I guess you were right about those city Keepers not being worth the money I paid them."

Richard stopped talking as he looked out the window. He surveyed the garden and blinked. He looked just beyond the beds of carefully cultivated flowers and cultured half-hedges into the open law and saw three spots. One stood in the middle, human and impossibly feminine, while a smaller black form raced around. The third sat calmly, looking on. She really was masterful at her work, already getting Smoke to jump and sit on command, heeling and staying, coming and going. She seemed to be so happy with the hounds, kneeling down to praise often, her movements graceful and magical. She was happy; what right did he have to take her home away from her? For that matter, why could he not get to know her, to try and get on her good side? She was beautiful.

Whirling, Richard threw the now-empty glass against the wall, watching as it shattered into many pieces. He was hoping that it would make him feel better, but he felt only a sick feeling rising from his stomach. "Damn it, Christina!" he cried, doubling over to try and keep the agony from ripping through him. "Why do you have to be gone?" he sobbed. "Why did you have to die? And now I can't even remember you properly because this… this woman, this mysterious creature who can't say a word, she seems to have captured my mind and my heart with just one look. I *swore* to be faithful to *you*, forever more, and here she comes into my life and makes me break that vow with just one look. I wish you were here, Christina. You always knew what to do."

Richard fell to his knees, bending until he was almost prostrate on the ground, his mouth stretched in a grimace of agony and grief, tears falling freely.

"Why must you be dead?" he asked again, his voice tearing through the room in a scream. "I don't know what to do." His voice now came out in a whisper. Then he said no more, simply crying as he tried to come to grips with the presence of his grief and that of Eleana, making him love her when he did not want to love.

Mrs. Graham stood outside the door, brought back by the crashing of the glass against the wall. She had heard every word and thought about going in and cleaning up, as was her duty. Maybe offering what condolences she could. She did not have to like Lord Richard Byrns to feel pity for him. She also knew that no man should have to go through such humiliation as knowing a perfect stranger had witnessed his lowest moment. So she said nothing, straightened her dress, and walked away to deal with the servants' lunch.

She oversaw the final touches of the meal, nodding her head briefly at the greeting of the cook. Normally, Mrs. Graham would have happily relayed all that she had seen and given her very firm opinion on the matter, but something held her back. She watched instead by the door when Eleana approached the house, having been summoned by the luncheon bell. The two dogs followed at her heel, looking up at her with admiration.

Eleana smiled at Mrs. Graham as she entered, then leaned down and scratched Smoke's ears. The black dog wagged his tail, tongue lolling. Eleana released him and made a gesture to go find his master. Smoke hesitated, looking up at Eleana. The Houndskeeper made the gesture again and this time, Smoke did run off back to Lord Byrns.

Hunter remained, settling at Eleana's feet while she ate in her chair by the door. "So, dearie," the head cook, a big boned woman with a bright blue bonnet on her head, asked with a smile. "How do you like the new dog?"

Eleana grinned and held her hand, thumb towards the ceiling, fingers curled in. She lowered her hand when the cook laughed and rubbed her hair affectionately. Mrs. Graham felt herself also smiling at Eleana as she sat in her place at one end of the table.

"Of course he's a good dog," Mrs. Graham said. "Every dog is a good dog around you. Now, just you wait before everyone else gets here to eat that bread, or there will be trouble."

Eleana smiled, then dutifully waited with her hands in her lap for the others to file in, chatting softly and taking their places. Mrs. Graham watched Eleana eat her soup heartily, smiling and laughing with the others. The housekeeper thought of the new lord of Belleview in that cheerful room, his heart bleeding on the floor. A part of her went out to him; she was certain that Eleana spared not a thought for him, and was that not the problem entirely.

It took one miserable week of moping about before Richard finally realised that his life could be quite a bit worse. And suddenly it was. This came in the form of one of his least favourite requirements in the life of a gentleman: social obligations. He had wandered the house throughout the week, ostensibly looking at the decorations and the furniture, marvelling at some of the woodwork and the strength of the stone walls and ornamentation of the leaded glass. But the decor could no more entice him than could going out to ride his horse or taking a tour of the grounds. His mind, his heart, were torn asunder, conflicted, and all he could do was try and numb the pain with drink.

No one had bothered to stop him.

In fact, Richard had very little contact with the other inhabitants of the house at all. Every morning, Eleana came to fetch Smoke for training, but she never stayed long enough for a conversation. She remained, to him at least, frustratingly silent. The others stayed quite out of his way, letting him serve himself as he had requested, or remaining silent when receiving their orders. Richard was alone with his thoughts.

On the day officially marking his one week's residency at Belleview, society impressed itself, though. He had just finished breakfast and was mildly surprised that Eleana had not yet come for Smoke. Not angry, per se, but surprised. Seeing her was enough of a torment and a joy to suitably ruin his day no matter the circumstances. But she had not yet come. Perhaps she deemed Smoke well enough trained. Certainly, the dog was much more behaved than ever before. But surely one week's time was not enough to remedy the mistakes of the city Houndskeepers?

These thoughts kept Richard's attention vaguely occupied while he finished his tea. It was only at the slight coughing from behind him that Richard realised he was not alone. Hayes stood there by the sideboard, his round face fixed in an expression of imperious solemnity. His hands were clasped behind his back and he did not look particularly pleased to be there. Richard winced inwardly; they had not had any further disagreements since that first day, but nor did he imagine the butler would ever like him well.

"M'lord, you have visitors," Hayes said formally, not looking at him. Richard, for his part, stared and looked at the butler incredulously. Hayes made no move to rescind his statement.

"Of course," Richard muttered. "I come out of the city to get some peace and am still obligated with the burdens of society." He looked at Smoke mournfully. The dog wagged his tail.

"Shall I send them away?" Hayes asked, turning to leave. Richard sighed, standing from the table. He did not look down its length, refusing to note its emptiness.

"No, that is quite alright. I shall see them in the main parlour," Richard grumbled. He threw his napkin onto the table and followed the butler. "Come," Richard said to Smoke. The dog rose to his feet without question and followed dutifully along. He stared in surprise for a moment. It seemed that the rumours were correct about Eleana. She seemed to train dogs with her own silent commands as well as with the voice of another.

Richard followed Hayes to the main parlour and waited ten beats for whomever was visiting to be led into the room. He reminded himself to stand straight and be polite, things that Christina was continuously telling him to do, a teasing smile on her lips. Then, the door opened, and the visitors followed Hayes into the room.

The parlour was a light room, the wall coverings reminiscent of the breakfast room in colour and the pictures all charming and fantastical. The furniture was of high quality, even if it looked as though it had not been used in a while. It was a woman's room, to be sure, and the arrival of two men perhaps too aware of their masculinity seemed a stark contrast.

They were both older gentlemen, though one had hair of white and the other grey. Their clothes were elegant and well made in the current fashions, and they carried themselves proudly, looking at the room around them with interest, just as they looked at Richard with interest. The white-haired gentleman was portly, his frock coat unbuttoned, revealing his girth. The other man was only beginning to show signs of a sedentary lifestyle that often came with age. They paused at their entrance to the room and bowed formally, which Richard returned.

"Lord Byrns," the white-haired man said. "I am Sir James Martin, of the Haverford estate. This is Mr. Samuel Vaughn, of Welton House. He owns the property adjacent your alfalfa fields, if I am not mistaken."

"Ah, indeed," Richard said. He had alfalfa fields? "It is a pleasure to meet you." Such a pleasure that he would be increasingly obliged if they would say their piece and depart.

Instead, they sat on the couch opposite the one before which Richard stood. He copied the motion, as was expected. Mr. Vaughn spoke first, eyes darting around the room. "We came to welcome you to the neighbourhood and to invite you to a ball which Sir James is holding this next week. It will be a wonderful way to get properly introduced to the neighbourhood. What better way to get acquainted than over a game of cards and a drink? I imagine that there should be many charming young ladies willing to dance, too, if you so desire."

"I, ah-" Richard started, trying furiously to think of a polite way to refuse. Social engagements had always been more of a duty to him rather than a pleasure, and he hadn't come to Belleview to be introduced to charming young ladies. In fact, he had come for quite the opposite reason and was already having difficulties with a certain young—

There was a brief knock on the door, and it swung open to admit Eleana to the room. Richard swallowed nervously. What would these gentlemen say to the presence of such a woman? Her scandalous dress and position as Houndskeeper could perhaps be well tolerated amongst the workers and tenant farmers of Belleview, but those members of polite society were often far more judgemental.

Eleana started at the sight of the company but gave a swift curtsey. It was an odd sight to see, given her breeches and shirt. The two visitors blinked, then Sir James roared with pleasure before Richard had a chance to make excuses. "Eleana! My dear, how are you? And how are you enjoying your new master?"

Eleana shrugged, a sly grin on her face, then pointed to Smoke. Sir James chuckled. "Of course you're training his dog. We've just come to introduce ourselves and invite Lord Byrns to the ball at Haverford. The servants will be having a sort of celebration of their own—those that are not to be working, that is —and I have no doubt that they would be pleased to have you come."

Eleana looked alarmed and held her hands up

before her, waving them as she shook her head. Richard wished it would be so easy for him to refuse his own invitation. Mr. Vaughn frowned. "Nonsense, girl. It will be grand fun, I am sure, and there have already been preparations for a small feast for the servants. Bring your Hunter, too. I am certain he would like the attention. Besides, you can also check on the Haverford dogs."

Eleana started to refuse again, but a stern look from Sir James stopped her. "You will come. It is my pleasure that you should come," he said. Eleana fidgeted with the end of her braided hair, looking uncomfortable. She flashed a desperate look at Richard. He blinked, surprised. She must have been quite desperate to ask *him* for help.

Sir James seemed to realise that he had been neglecting Eleana's master and quickly ducked his head in respect. He might outrank Eleana and therefore expect her to follow his commands, but she did belong to Richard's estate. "Of course, with your permission, Lord Byrns."

Richard hesitated. He did not want to go to this ridiculous ball in the first place, but there was no polite way for him to be able to refuse. Such rules had been ingrained in him since birth. The more reasonable part of him said that he did not wish Eleana to suffer, and she obviously equated the ball with suffering. But the part of him that lashed out at her wanted her to realise that he was the one with the power. He controlled her livelihood and she could not defy him without consequences. Richard gave a slight smile to his visitors. "We would both be delighted to accept your invitation."

Eleana looked at him with dismay. She then summoned Smoke to her side and barely stayed long enough afterwards to listen to any details regarding the ball. She whirled to the door and stormed from the room. Richard frowned and looked at the two men to see what they would think of her foul mood.

Sir James, though, just chuckled. "She always was a headstrong girl. A good girl, for her station, but stubborn. It will do her good to learn her place."

Richard's stomach tightened at the words. He had forced Eleana to bend to his will. While he knew that his station often merited such things, he could not often think of a human being reduced to such submission. Nor was she to blame for his anger at her. This unreasonable love was his own burden. And yet, he could not help but believe that it was her fault for making him feel unfaithful towards his wife.

Richard forced down his conflicting emotions to address the two people before him, as was his duty. "How did you come to know her?"

"Eleana?" Mr. Vaughn asked, looking at the door she exited as if she still stood there. "She has trained nearly every hound in the neighbourhood. Her work is exceptional."

"She helped me find a suitable bitch for one of my hunters just this last year," Sir James added. Richard gave a slight nod, uncertain how to proceed with the conversation. He was beginning to get a headache and did not want to think further on Eleana.

His guests seemed to sense his reticence and, after exchanging a few more words on how Richard was enjoying Belleview, claimed excuses and departed. Richard leaned back on his couch and stared at the ceiling, wishing for another drink. He was about to rise and go to the library for his usual tumbler when Hayes walked in.

"Will you need anything else this morning, m'lord?" Hayes asked.

"I suppose I had better figure out the appropriate attire for a ball," Richard muttered. The butler seemed startled.

"M'lord?" he asked. Richard was not blind to the way Hayes looked him over to determine his state of sobriety. Hayes seemed even more confused at discovering a lack of drink. Richard simply threw a wan smile at the butler and stood.

"I have been coerced into attending the Haverford ball next se'ennight. I don't remember if I have anything appropriate from the city," he explained, then wondered also if Eleana had anything to wear besides trousers and work shirts. He turned towards the butler and frowned. Hayes would no more know if Eleana owned dresses than would Richard. "Would you please fetch Mrs. Graham?"

Hayes blinked, startled at the uncharacteristic behaviour. Then, he bowed slightly. "Of course, m'lord." He turned and was just about to shut the door behind him when he heard, "I hate balls." Hayes smiled; that was better.

Richard did not leave the parlour to fetch a drink, waiting as he was for Mrs. Graham. Instead, he stood at the window, his thoughts quickly losing the dullness that came with alcohol. As such, he felt every stab of guilt for being cruel to Eleana. He was finally able to realise that he really did not dislike her for making him think and feel as he did. It was himself that he loathed for being weak minded. He had loved Christina. It had never been a throbbing passion between them, but more of a love that grew with time until it filled his entire being. Then, she was gone. Now, he had taken one look into the eyes of a furious woman and became overwhelmed with a type of love that he had never felt with Christina. And he felt sick for feeling it.

He did not realise that tears were slipping down his cheek and that his sight was blurred with water until Mrs. Graham came in with a querulous, "M'lord?"

Richard hurriedly wiped his eyes and turned to the housekeeper. She started in shock and opened her mouth. Richard spoke before she could. "Do you know if Eleana owns a dress appropriate for a servant's celebration?" With clipped words, he explained that he had been invited to the Haverford ball and that Eleana was to attend the servant's celebration. Mrs. Graham blinked and licked suddenly dry lips.

"Well, I don't know, m'lord. She hasn't had a reason to wear a dress for, oh, some two years now. If you wish, I can give you her sizes," Mrs. Graham said. Richard shook his head.

"No, just get something made up for her. And make it nice. I do not want people to think that I cannot afford to clothe my servants," he said. Mrs. Graham nodded and started to leave when Richard sank into one of the couches, looking piteously at the design in the rug. Mrs. Graham sighed. She looked up to the ceiling for a moment, then marched over to Richard and, without asking permission, sat beside him.

Richard recoiled slightly when she reached out and grabbed his hand. Mrs. Graham fixed him with a stern look and he immediately complied. "I have a boy about your age, out at sea, so don't think I don't know how to deal with you. Now, no blathering, you're going to tell me what's going on," she ordered.

"What?" Richard demanded, drawing himself up. He was her lord, her master! He was nobility and she just a housekeeper. He should not take orders from her. Mrs. Graham tightened her mouth in a distinctive look and Richard sighed, all thought of arguing with her gone.

"Speak up, lad," she ordered, her tone comforting and matronly. Richard took a deep breath and began to talk. He talked about his wife, how they had met, how he had come to love her, how he felt, their difference, their similarities, and most importantly, how she died.

"The lung rot was harsh," he said, throat tight, staring fixedly at a spot on the couch. "She had been feeling slightly ill for months, as if she had a lingering cold. But she was fine! She went about her life as normal. We even went to a ball and I danced with her nearly all night. The next morning, I went out to visit a friend and when I came back, she was so sick. The lung rot had finally gotten to her. The physicians could do nothing and so I sat there and watched her die." By the end of his speech, he was sobbing, unable to prevent himself.

He hated that he was so weak as to cry. Never before had he considered himself able to cry more than one or two tears. Not even at his father's death had he done more than swallow the pain and let two drops slide down his cheeks. But after his wife's death, he had been unable to repeat the process.

Mrs. Graham pulled him in and let the man cry on her shoulder. She made comforting noises and rubbed his back gently, waiting until he had settled before pulling back. Richard looked at the rug again and gave one sharp laugh of pain. "And the thing is, just before she died, she said she wanted me to be happy. She wanted me to remember her when she was gone and for me to be happy," he said before burying his head in his hands, despair plain at the obvious contradiction.

Mrs. Graham must have seen that he wouldn't be talking much more and so she finished the story for him. "And so, you left behind the city and all the things that would remind you of your Christina. You bought Belleview so that you could have a place to get away from everything. Then you should be pleased, distracted, and yet able to remember your wife. What is so terrible here?"

Richard turned his head to look up at the house-keeper, his voice hoarse and nearly silent. "I made a vow to be faithful to her."

Mrs. Graham looked at him, brows drawn together. "I don't understand. How could coming to Belleview make you unfaithful to your wife? Unless there were someone... oh," she said, understanding dawning on her. "Oh, my."

"The moment I saw her," Richard said by way of explanation, voice torn with agony and guilt. "She is so completely unsuitable! She's a... a... servant! A worker! What use would she be as the wife to an [earl]? Society would shun her. She would hate me. And... And she isn't Christina!"

Mrs. Graham was silent for a moment before she reached out and put her hand on Richard's shoulder, making him turn to look at her. "Your wife is gone," she said simply and softly. "And she wanted you to be happy. You are not being unfaithful to her by loving another woman. You are fulfilling her dying wish. As to remembering her, what better way to do so than by loving?"

Richard was silent, no longer able to cry. He searched Mrs. Graham's face before turning to look in front of him stoically, thoughts churning. The house-keeper stood and walked to the door. She looked back at him once more.

"I cannot justify this to you, nor can I deal with whatever burden you are carrying. You must do that yourself. But it seems to me that you have grieved long enough. Now it is time to do as your Christina asked and be happy." With that, she was gone.

DURING THE NEXT FEW DAYS, no more was spoken between Richard and Mrs. Graham about what had been said in the parlour. Nor did he speak further with Eleana when she came each morning to train Smoke. It was only three days before the Haverford ball when he was forced into a confrontation in the form of the dress which he had ordered for Eleana. He had forgotten about the matter entirely until Mrs. Graham deposited the box in his hands and swept off, refusing his pleas to deliver the box to Eleana in his place.

Thanks to her meddling, none of the other servants would oblige him either, though he must have asked the whole house. They were all conspiring against him, it seemed.

After a nervous luncheon, he finished off a glass of scotch and stood, carrying the dress box under his arm. Richard straightened his waistcoat and cravat, tugging at the lapels of his frock coat. He glanced at a triumphant Mrs. Graham when she held open the door into the gardens. He marched out into the cultivated space, wondering why he hadn't been there before. The groundskeepers certainly did a wonderful job and the smell of the flowers was tantamount to peace. Or as much peace as a man walking towards his doom could have.

His pace had started out determined, but as Richard neared the end of the gardens and approached the open yard where the kennels and Eleana were, his steps slowed. By the time he was close to the Houndskeeper, he was walking at a crawl. He got within twenty yards of Eleana and stopped, transfixed.

She was standing on the lawn near the kennel door, her hands at her side, and three different dogs before her. Hunter and Smoke sat off to the side, watching the proceedings with interest. The dogs standing before Eleana, Richard realised, were all a similar build: slim and pretty, but not quite as long-legged as the racers, nor compact enough for a lady's dogs. These were not hunters nor fighters, so what could they possibly be? He was about to walk forwards and interrupt the training session when Eleana flicked her wrists in a complicated twist. The dogs flew into action.

Their russet pelts were all similar, though one had spots of brown and another some cream while the third was solid. But as the dogs raced around in circles, the patterns synchronised. They leapt into the air and became one colour. These dogs, Richard realised, were tricksters. Show dogs. They were trained solely for the entertainment of an audience and it was rare that Houndskeepers trained them at all, since many saw them as useless. The way that Eleana had trained these dogs, running and leaping and doing complicated twists in the air, there was no doubt that these dogs were far from useless. They were beautiful. Their mistress' smile proved that she knew it, too.

The set ended and Eleana fell to her knees, petting each of the dog and praising them with smiles and hand gestures. The three tricksters wriggled all over with pleasure and it didn't take long for Eleana to be buried under a pile of dogs. Hunter and Smoke stood, tails wagging. They waited a heartbeat before rushing forwards to join the pile. Occasionally, Eleana's face appeared, laughing, then became covered again as one of the hounds moved to lick her. Eventually, she shoved the dogs off her and signalled something. The dogs raced away, chasing each other across the lawn. All except Hunter who had spotted Richard and whoofed softly to Eleana.

She started and stood, a slight blush covering her cheeks as she brushed off grass and dog fur. Richard turned his head away slightly, also embarrassed to be caught admiring her as she worked. He walked forwards until they were close enough for a comfortable conversation, remembering belatedly the errand he had been made to run. "I-"he started before coughing and clearing his throat. "I didn't mean to disturb you," he said.

Eleana blinked, peering at him as though he had said something strange by being so polite. She waved away his apology and shrugged her shoulders. She pointed to him and herself.

Richard furrowed his brows for a moment. Then, tentatively, "What do I want?"

Eleana grinned and nodded. He had gotten her question in one guess, an improvement from the first day he had arrived. There was a lapse as Richard waited for her to continue before he realised that she had been the one to ask him the question. He fumbled with the dress box at his side and knew immediately what he had to do to make things right.

"I am sorry that I forced your hand regarding the Haverford ball," he admitted. Eleana's expression, which had been sharp after her grin of a triumphant translation, grew astonished. "I was cruel, and I thought it would make me happier not to be the only person suffering. I hate balls."

Eleana widened her eyes melodramatically and huffed her agreement, making Richard smile slightly. Maybe it was just him, or maybe Eleana was making things easier, but he wasn't trying so hard to understand her. He could tell that she was saying, "Me, too," when she had exaggerated her features just then. And he was pleased, if not surprised, to have something in common with her.

"Well, as an apology, I had Mrs. Graham order a dress for you to wear," Richard said, holding out the dress box. Eleana made a face but took the box. "Unless you'd rather wear breeches?" Richard asked, feeling stupid for presuming that she would wear a dress. Perhaps the other servants in the neighbourhood were as unconcerned with her attire as Mr. Vaughn and Sir James. Eleana shook her head and then bit her lower lip, thinking.

She set the dress box on the ground and tugged with one hand at her breeches, smiling. Then, she grabbed hold of a pretend dress hem and lifted it slightly above her feet. She put on a frightened and whining face and danced on her toes, pretending to howl in fear as she moved about. Richard laughed, the sound loud and true. It was the first real laugh he had given in a very long time.

"I know what you mean," he said. "And you're right. Many ladies do act like that and men expect women to be… something else because they wear a dress. All the same, it is sometimes nice to dress up for something. And you just have to prove everyone wrong when wearing a dress. Make them see you."

Richard leaned over to pick up the box and hand it to her. When he looked up, he realised his mistake. Eleana was fairly gaping at him. He mumbled a quick excuse and bowed slightly before turning and hurrying across the yard, mortified.

Eleana signalled Smoke to follow his master even as she stared after his retreating form. What a strange encounter!

Had he really come out to the kennels just to apologise to her and give her a gift? Strangely, there was something about him that was nicer and more pleasant than before. Eleana wondered what had gotten into his head and shook her own, flicking her wrist to call her dogs to her, the dress box under one arm. She put the tricksters back in the kennel with a hambone each as praise, then went to her adjoining cottage and sat on the small bed.

Hunter walked over and put his head on her knee, looking up at her with his large, sad brown eyes. Eleana dutifully scratched his ear and shook her head. She didn't know what to make of this Lord Byrns. He was beginning to understand her, which showed promise towards his intelligence. But why in the world was he being so civil towards her? Every other previous encounter had been full of anger on both sides, or they actively ignored each other. Now he was giving her gifts of apology. And the fact that he had talked to Mrs. Graham about ordering it meant that he had foresight.

Eleana sighed and scratched Hunter's ears once more before giving him his own hambone and reaching for the strings on the dress box. She threw it open and stared. He did realise that this was just a servant's celebration, did he not? She wouldn't actually be attending the ball with him. The dress was certainly grand enough, she felt, for the ball, though some small part of her knew that it was far simpler than the great dresses ladies often wore.

Eleana pulled out the dress and fingered its fine fabric. It was a lovely, tightly woven cotton in a shade of light blue that reminded her of cornflowers. The neckline was rounded, and the sleeves were gathered at the peaks in the most current fashions. The skirt was long, flowing from the under bust to brush the ground. There were bands of embroidered flowers along the hem. Eleana held up the dress to herself and was astonished at the gift. It was perfect, and she certainly wouldn't feel like a silly lady while wearing it. She would be beautiful.

Almost reverently, Eleana hung the dress on the back of the door to her bedroom, letting her fingers trail over the fabric before she turned from the room and moved to the kitchen. She knew she should go out and start giving baths to some of the fighters she was training as guard dogs, ones who had gotten bits of mud all over them the day before. Instead, she just sank down into a chair at her small table, a feeling of pleasure bubbling up through her. She smiled, almost involuntarily, and wondered absently what had brought about this change in her new master.

Eleana shook away the slight pang of guilt for her sudden good-will towards Lord Byrns; she was not being disloyal to Northwood. He had said to be on her best behaviour. And, Eleana swallowed, it was unlikely that she should ever see him again. That was not the way the world worked. Why should she not like her new master? Whatever animosity Eleana had built up towards Richard during the first week or so of his life at Belleview was pushed aside by the gratitude for this gift and the pleasure at having been apologised to. She wanted to know why he was suddenly acting differently, but a part of her didn't care. That was the part that seemed to be winning.

CHAPTER 5

*E*leana's joy in her dress began to wane as soon as she started to question the motivation behind the gift. It was certainly a beautiful dress and she had no desire to return it with a shrug of "no, thank you." But the thought persisted: why had Lord Byrns given it to her? Was he trying to bribe her? Buy her affections? After all, she had made it clear from the very beginning that she did not like him. But she had not heard of similar gifts to the other servants, which would indicate that he was trying to rise in their affections. That meant the focus was solely on her.

She had heard stories told around the servants' table with whispered voices and sly eyes about wealthy men who would buy girls of all classes pretty things. They would say nothing at first, just let the gifts speak for themselves. Then, they would claim to be desperately in love. They never were, and by the time the girl realised it, she was ruined and good for nothing but being a man's mistress, one that was bitter and lonely.

Eleana had known more than one girl from the nearby village bearing a man's child out of wedlock and being shunned as a result.

She did not know if this Richard Byrns were capable of such despicable guile. Perhaps that was not what he had intended in the first place. The merest drop of doubt, though, was enough to make her question his motivation and vow to herself that she would not fall into any of his traps to try and get his approval. She hadn't liked him when he first arrived and every subsequent meeting—aside from the last—had confirmed her suspicions.

So, for the next few days, Eleana took pains to avoid Lord Byrns. She would fetch Smoke as quickly as possible in the mornings and return him just before luncheon. Then, she would spend her time in the kennels doing cleaning or traipsing through the forest with Hunter and a couple of other dogs at her heels. If Lord Byrns tried to search for her to give her more gifts or to talk to her or to watch her train, he would not find her.

Then, inevitably, came the night of this ridiculous ball. Eleana knew that she would have to ride at the back of the carriage which would deliver Lord Byrns, and therefore she would have to be ready before he came out. Not to mention that she would have to coax Hunter to ride along in the back as well, a thing he hated almost as much as she did. Eleana was fully prepared with the knowledge of the unpleasant evening she was going to have as she finished her chores early and begged a light dinner out of the cook.

While she nibbled on a crust of bread with some cold meats, Eleana spied Fey, the head maid to Belleview, doing some mending in the kitchen. That would, perhaps, solve one problem. Fey was only slightly older than most of the other young girls who acted as maids, but she had trained to be a lady's maid. This gave her both skills and status amongst the others. It meant that Eleana had only rarely traded words with the woman, a gap in acquaintance she was feeling deeply now.

Tentatively, Eleana approached Fey, pleading in her eyes. "Eleana!" Fey exclaimed, looking up from her sewing with some surprise. "Do you require assistance?"

Eleana bit her lip and gestured to herself as if she were wearing a dress, her hand sweeping down and out. Then she reached up and touched her hair and finally clasped her hands together in a pleading motion. Fey looked astonished. "Of course I'll help you! Do you have hair powders? Pins?"

Eleana winced and shook her head. She'd never bothered with such things, just washing the dirt from her hair and braiding it rather than applying the powders and pomades that so many women favoured. And pins? No!

Fey smiled and set her sewing aside. "I'll fetch a few things and meet you at your cottage."

Eleana let her shoulders sag in relief. Fey left and

Eleana went out to her cottage, a hand resting on Hunter's fur to try and draw courage from him. It had been months since she had worn a dress—and that was just to a local wedding in the village, nothing requiring such finery. Now she faced something grand and beautiful and, whatever the motives in the giving, she wanted to do it justice.

Hunter whined when Eleana stripped off her shirt and breeks. She undid her working stays and pulled out something far more elaborate, gently boned with reed rather than the cording she normally wore. Fey arrived just as Eleana was lacing up the front and laughed at the sight.

"No, you mustn't have your chemise quite so high! You'll strangle yourself," Fey said, taking the lacing from Eleana and readjusting the chemise before doing up the laces. "There. Better? Good. Now, the petticoat."

Eleana dutifully stood still while Fey helped her put on the petticoat and then the dress itself. It felt so strange to wear so many layers and not be wearing her breeches, but Eleana decided that she could move in the dress well enough. And the little slippers she wore were fun to walk in. When she caught sight of herself in the handheld mirror that Fey presented, though, Eleana fell frozen, stunned.

Her hair was not yet done. Her face had not yet been powdered or painted. She was still herself. Yet… the person looking back at her was a lady. Maybe not in status or class or anything else, but she was a lady none the less.

"You look lovely, Eleana. The dress compliments your hair and your freckles perfectly. Where did you find such a thing?" Fey asked, smoothing out a blue woollen shawl one of the other maids had offered.

Eleana blushed with pleasure. She pointed out the window towards the main house then back to the dress. Fey's jaw dropped. "You mean to say that Lord Byrns gave you that dress?" Her voice had gone quiet and Eleana was a little surprised to see admiration along with approbation in the eyes of the other woman. She nodded.

"Why?" Fey asked.

Eleana shook her head and shrugged. She bit her lip and pointed at Hunter then twirled her fingers, ending with another shrug.

Fey clucked her tongue and tucked a stray blonde curl under her cap. "I doubt that very much. Men are not accustomed to giving dresses in thanks for training a dog."

Eleana hunched her shoulders. That was what had her worried.

Fey closed her eyes. "Well, the damage is done and as long as you tell no one else about the matter, let that be that. Now sit and I'll do your hair."

Eleana tried not to let her thoughts wander towards Lord Byrns while Fey powdered, combed, and pinned her hair up into a semblance of beautiful fashion. It was all she could do not to tear the dress off, no matter how beautiful, and go nowhere near the ball. But he had accepted the invitation and she was nothing more than a Houndskeeper. Eleana would go.

"There," Fey said finally, holding out the mirror once again. Eleana saw an elegant woman, her face framed by a few strands of hair, her neck long and slender. "Now you just need some bauble and the transformation will be complete, like Cinderella. I can ask around, if you like?"

Eleana shook her head. She reached out for a small box on her dressing table and opened it. Inside was a single pearl drop on a length of green ribbon. "It's beautiful," Fey gasped. "I've never seen you wear it. Your mother's?"

Eleana nodded. She had never known her mother, but the box had been passed into her hands by her father on her twelfth birthday. Since then, hardly a week passed without her touching the delicate necklace, but she never wore it. Maybe it would bring her comfort against the ordeal still to come.

"Do try to enjoy yourself," Fey urged when Eleana stood and wrapped the shawl around herself. "I know that you don't care for such things, but these balls are meant to be enjoyed. Dance! Eat something! Smile! And ignore that Lord Byrns, if it makes you feel better."

Eleana grinned and nodded eagerly. That would make her feel better. She twined her arm with Fey's and, Hunter walking dutifully along at her side, walked to the main house with pride. She was greeted in the servants' hall with smiles and compliments. Even

Hayes reached out and kissed her hand, making her blush.

Mrs. Graham nodded firmly at Eleana's appearance. "You'll do. Make our house proud."

Eleana nodded and was escorted with quite the entourage to where the carriage was pulling up. She waited with the driver for Lord Byrns to come out, the pause in activity as she waited enough to set her stomach to churning.

It had just grown dark by the time Lord Byrns emerged, looking solemn and yet undeniably handsome in his buckskin breeches, shining boots, dark blue waistcoat and jacket, and white shirt and cravat. He looked formal and regal, his dark hair swept across his forehead in a black wave rather than the horsehair wigs that many would be sporting. He did not, Eleana noted, look particularly pleased to be dressed so formally, either.

RICHARD WAS NOT PLEASED. He had grumbled and pushed away the assistance of his personal valet—at least, the man assigned to him by Hayes as valet—the entire evening. He preferred to dress himself, even if that meant choosing a wool coat and linen shirt rather than the silk and cotton that would be expected of him. He had allowed the poor man to help with shining his boots, but both seemed to view that as a mere grudging nod to station. Richard was, there was little doubt, more irritable than usual. He could not forget the fact that the last time he had attended a dance, a ball, a party, his wife lay dying the next day.

Richard sighed as he walked out the front door and saw the carriage already waiting. He had hoped to delay this for as long as possible. Still, he straightened his shoulders and started down the steps, the heels of his boots clacking on the stone. Then, he stopped, spying a figure waiting off.

If Hunter had not been standing at her side, Richard would not have recognised Eleana. She looked so different from the woman who had trained Smoke and who had seemed to delight in arguing with him. She looked like any lady of class, though her dress was not up to the standards of society for a well-born lady. She was elegant, and her earthen beauty was emphasised. The way her neck curved, the hair swept away from it, made Richard's heart stutter. He realised after a moment that he had stopped moving and hurriedly finished his descent.

"You look lovely," Richard said gruffly when a footman opened the door to the carriage. He noted a single shining pearl drop at her neck and briefly wondered if a former beau had given it to her. That thought would do no one any good, so he pushed it aside. "Shall we go?" he asked, trying not to dwell on the woman standing beside him, imperious in her silence and yet so innocent and wondrous.

Eleana gave an indifferent shrug her shoulders and gestured to Hunter. The dog looked at her with sad eyes and sat, obviously pouting. Eleana stared him down and gestured again, this time more forcefully. Hunter sighed and leaped lightly onto the back of the enclosed carriage, sitting on the small bench meant for attendants. Eleana nodded her head in approval and sat beside her dog.

"What are you doing?" Richard asked, furrowing his brow. Eleana swept her hands over the seat and gave him a look that intricately detailed his idiocy. What did it look like she was doing? "No, you must ride inside. I do not want you to fall off," he insisted. Eleana narrowed her eyes slightly and shook her head, putting her hand on Hunter. Richard sighed and gave in.

He was already having a difficult enough evening. Now Eleana, when he thought he had made amends, refused his offer to ride inside the carriage. Richard reached inside his jacket and pulled out his flask just as the footman closed the door behind him, the carriage suddenly darker than before. He opened the flask and put it to his lips, breathing a sigh of relief as the warm liquid burned down his throat and dulled the pain.

The ride to the Haverford estate was not longer than half-an-hour, but by the time the carriage arrived, the dread that had been building in Richard seemed almost ready to burst. He did not want to be there. He would be forced to go through the terrible routine of introductions and be obliged to dance with young ladies to whom he was introduced. He would have to listen to polite conversation and intelligent remarks. He would have to play cards, but not too much or be considered a degenerate gambler. He hated this.

The carriage door was opened by a footman of the Haverford estate and Richard climbed out, looking displeased at the number of carriages and people about. Had the whole county been invited? He noticed a moment later that Eleana was standing near him, a look of loathing on her face while she gazed at the house and its guests. Richard was surprised; he had known that Eleana did not want to go, but he had not expected her hatred to be so open or obvious.

He opened his mouth to say something to her just as Eleana signalled to Hunter and strode off towards the back of the house, to where the servants' celebration was likely being held.

Richard was left alone.

There was nothing left for him but to walk up to the house. He tried not to lose his patience at the number of people and finally made it through the queue to where his host, Sir James, and his wife—a small, plump woman some fifteen years younger than he—stood.

Sir James beamed at his guest. "Welcome to Haverford. My dear, may I introduce Lord Richard Byrns of Belleview. Lord Byrns, my wife, Lady Marianne Martin."

Richard bowed as low as befitted his rank and took the hand of Lady Martin, being very careful to only grasp it slightly. "Charmed."

Sir James seemed pleased with the introduction and

continued. "I have one son, married, and a daughter, Miss Amelia Martin. I shall have to introduce her to you over the course of the evening."

Richard smiled as best he could and tried not to grimace. "Of course," he said, and though his reply was the only one he could politely give. It seemed to please his host and hostess more than he liked, as well. He had known that this would be the likely result of the evening, but he had not realised how unpleasant it would be. He was a widower and wealthy, not to mention that he was the second son of a Marquess. He would be looked upon as a most eligible match for the daughters of many currently present at Haverford. He would have to be careful not to pay any one person too much attention or it would become immediate gossip.

Richard wished Christina were here. She would have known exactly what to do.

As a guest and not introduced to anyone in the house apart from Sir James and Mr. Vaughn, Richard was obligated to stay near his host and wait for further introductions. He hated every minute of it. The mindless pleasantries were not nearly distracting enough, and his thoughts kept turning to Eleana.

He was introduced to Amelia Martin and many other young girls. Politeness and duty brought him to dance with many of them over the course of the evening, though never more than twice and those not following each other. Eventually, he was able to claim tiredness and stand in a secluded corner, a glass of red wine in his hand, his grief and distress nearly palpable.

It would only be an hour or so before he could leave without offending his host. Perhaps he should have gone into the game of cards. Or perhaps he should have gone to see how Eleana was doing.

"No," Richard hissed at himself. It would be idiotic in the extreme to do such a thing. Not only for himself, as he was trying to ignore her, but people would notice. They would say that he was paying more attention to his servant than his host and things would go very, very poorly from there. The gossip would last for weeks and while Richard could bear it, he would not do such a thing to Eleana.

Resolutely, Richard finished the last of his wine with a quick tip of his head and put the empty glass on the tray of a passing servant. He wandered through the rooms of the house, manoeuvring his way through the people that seemed to fill every vacant space. At last, he spotted Sir James.

"Ah, Lord Byrns, there you are!" his host exclaimed, smiling gaily at Richard and, by drawing Richard's attention, bringing him forwards to the group of people standing around him. There were three other gentlemen, including Mr. Vaughn and two ladies, one of which was Miss Martin. "We were just discussing hunting. Do you hunt?"

"Occasionally," Richard admitted, thinking of the pleasurable feeling of being on a horse. It was as close as a person could get to freedom from burdens. "It has been a while since I have had the opportunity for hunting."

"It is understandable, what with you having lived in the city," Mr. Vaughn said, deliberately avoiding discussing the one topic Richard knew they would love to dissect. Richard inclined his head politely, secretly amused that these people would be afraid of bringing up the death of his wife when they so obviously wanted him to marry one of their daughters.

"I find it so abominably cruel," Miss Martin said, giving a slight smile to Richard. One of the feathers in her hair tickled his nose and he fought not to sneeze. "I don't think that I could possibly kill an innocent creature."

"You disapprove of hunting, then?" Richard asked, trying to keep a light tone in his voice rather than the irritation he felt. Miss Martin immediately blushed, thinking that she had said something wrong and that by declaiming hunting, she was lessening her chance of catching his fancy.

"Not necessarily, no. I imagine it is a great sport. I just do not think that I would have it in me to kill something such as a rabbit, fox, or stag," she replied, trying to amend her previous statement. Richard inclined his head in acknowledgement but did not say anything further. Miss Martin fluttered slightly, trying to decide on relief or fear for what her statement had wrought on Richard. He tried harder not to sneeze.

"We were thinking of putting together a hunting party soon," Sir James said, ignoring his daughter's distress in favour of masculine conversation. "Of course, you must come. We shall have our horses and bring our hunting dogs and perhaps make a weekend of it. I imagine that you haven't had much chance to make note, but it is widely known that Belleview has the best hunting dogs in the county."

"I shall have to remember to investigate that claim," Richard said absently, wondering when he could politely extract himself from the conversation and make his way back to Belleview, where his bed and the solitude of his house awaited him.

"Is Belleview very beautiful?" Miss Martin asked, obviously trying to win her way back into the central conversation. The other gentlemen looked on with curiosity, and it was plain that they wondered what this young Lord thought of his new home.

"I have not had the chance yet to see the entire grounds, but what I have seen is wondrous, indeed." Richard said with a nod, realising fully the truth of his words. It was perhaps the only thing said this entire evening that he had meant with all his heart.

"Belleview is certainly grand," Mr. Vaughn agreed. "But I do not think that I could give up Welton House. I have grown too comfortable there for change."

"I should very much like to see Belleview," Miss Martin said. "I have heard so many stories about it and I wonder what is true or not."

"I would tell you what is true, but as I have not heard the stories, I cannot say," Richard said, blatantly ignoring the invitation that Miss Martin had so obviously desired. The conversation then turned to some local stories about people and estates and how people had a penchant for gossip and Richard allowed his thoughts to wander. He could not help but be curious again as to what Eleana was doing. He thought of his bed at Belleview and how tired he was of parties.

ELEANA, on the other hand, was kept far too busy to think of Richard. Since her thoughts did not trend that direction and she still disliked him, any time she did have to think only allowed for thoughts of Hunter or of the room before her. The servants' hall had been converted and, as the evening was a pleasant one, some of the festivities spilled out onto the lawn. There was a general area cleared for dancing and at one end of the room were tables and chairs and a long table laden with food.

The servants of various households throughout the county had come to this once-per-year event and were wearing their best. Some were dressed as elegantly as Eleana, while others wore their newest clothing that did not yet have patches. Most of the people Eleana did not know, but the other Houndskeepers of the larger estates welcomed her and petted Hunter. She was introduced to footmen, to stable hands, and kitchen maids, even to a butler not helping with the Haverford ball.

"Eleana," an older man said, holding a large glass of ale. He sat in the chair beside her and watched the people prepare for the next dance. Byron was head hostler at Haverford, a friend of her father's, and his only sign of trying to mark the occasion was the vibrant blue necktie at his throat. "I know you dislike parties," he chuckled, fixing her with the knowing glance of one who had known her all her life. Eleana ignored that look and smiled, instead. "How about a dance to liven things up, me girl?"

Eleana laughed and tried to refuse. Byron ignored her protests and swung her out of her chair. She barely had time to signal Hunter to stay put before she was whisked around the dancing area. The dance was lively and the music high and Eleana found herself pleasantly exhilarated. She did not have enough time to even catch her breath before another person whisked her away for another dance.

She did not have to talk to anyone. She did not have to be stared at for being unusual. She could just toss her head back and hope she did not lose all of Fey's hairpins. Dancing was, by far, the best part of these events.

Eleana was kept spinning around the floor, breathless and smiling, for a great while. First, she was handed from Byron to a young footman from a neighbouring estate, then to one of the Houndskeepers, then to another hostler, a huntsman, on and on. Eleana did not know how much later it was that she finally managed to excuse herself and collapse in her chair, Hunter wagging his tail eagerly at her appearance. She reached down to pet Hunter and smiled, thinking that perhaps Fey was right. She *should* enjoy herself.

Eleana had resolved to go and fetch some of the food when a sharp, cutting voice caught Eleana's attention. She turned her head slightly, looking for the source, dread building in her stomach. "I don't know what she is thinking, putting on airs. I mean, truly, does she think that we will believe that she is a respectable maid like the rest of us?"

"I wonder where she got the dress. I heard that she wanders around in men's clothing, *and* in a position that was meant for a man. Houndskeeper!" Another voice joined the first, taking up the line of conversation. By this time, Eleana had spotted the speakers, two girls about her age with their hair done up elaborately, their dresses nice but out of fashion with gatherings of fabric at the hips. Suddenly, Eleana felt overdressed and out of place, and she knew what they were going to say next.

"*Houndskeeper*, indeed! Which *hounds* is she keeping, do you think? I wonder how many have seen her out of those men's clothing she wears." The first speaker caught Eleana's eye and gave a cruel smile. "Isn't that right, Eleana Tarell?"

Eleana shook her head sharply. The girl put a hand to her ear as if waiting to hear a response. Eleana struggled with her fury and shook her head again, rising to her feet. The girls laughed, the sound repulsive.

"Silent as night. That's how they like it, isn't it Eleana?" the second girl snarled viciously. "Silent and obedient."

Eleana's hand flew to her throat as if she could will her voice into being. Tears stung her eyes. The room that had been full of people to dance with, a few people she knew and liked, warm and friendly—it was suddenly too loud, too hot, too close. She turned away from the chairs and tables and lurched forwards, trying to reach open air. The people seemed to be closing in and she could hear the sharp sound of that vicious, devious laughter.

Hunter caught wind of Eleana's distress and, loyal and loving, stepped before her to push his way through the crowd. People stepped aside for the black and white dog whose teeth gleamed ivory in the light, as silent as the mistress who followed him. Finally, Eleana managed to make her way outside and she quickly ducked away from the people, hiding around the corner of the house where no one would come looking for her.

Eleana bit her lip as her chin wavered. She sank to the ground, throwing her arms around her faithful dog, crying piteously and never once making a sound. Her distress was apparent. She kept hearing the girls' laughter ringing in her ears. This was not the first such insinuation that had been made against her. Most who said such things were just talking to make her upset. They might have been jealous of her dress or her good fortune at being Houndskeeper, or perhaps she was just an easy target. But their words stung all the same.

And so Eleana cried and wallowed until it was time for her to meet Lord Byrns back at the carriage. She appeared swiftly and without announcement, her face washed clean of the powder that had been streaked by tears. Her dress had been painstakingly rubbed clean of any dirt. Her eyes, still red, were fixed on the ground.

"You look pale," Lord Byrns commented. Eleana shrugged, yawning. Lord Byrns seemed to accept the excuse. This time, when he insisted Eleana ride inside the carriage, she did not argue. Hunter lay at her feet and she stared out the window.

Richard never did ask about her evening. He would never understand that in her moment of distress, she had not come to him as a lover would, but had stood alone, independent and used to being on her own but for the hounds and dogs she raised. Richard was not the white knight to her that he so wanted to be. He was nothing more than the cold and distant and sometimes cruel master, standing far apart from her.

CHAPTER 6

Two days following the disaster at the Haverford ball, Richard received an invitation. He was sitting at his writing desk, taking care of business regarding his own investments and anything regarding Belleview. He did his best to enjoy the morning sun in the library while it lasted.

"A letter for you, m'lord," Hayes announced, making Richard jump slightly, ink spotting his letter. He hadn't noticed Hayes walk in. Richard quickly reached for the blotter, but in vain; he would have to start again. Hayes said nothing, only extended the silver tray with the message.

Richard sighed and tore it open. It was from Mr. Vaughn, who was now inviting Richard to join him and several companions, namely Sir James and a Mr. Darlington, amongst others, to a hunting party. The grounds at Welton House were large enough for a two-day trip which would take place the next week. The longer, overnight trip was a slight surprise, but the part which really shocked him was the last paragraph:

IF YOU FIND *yourself too busy to join us on our excursion, then I beg use of Eleana and her hounds singularly. She is the most accomplished hunter for many towns around and under her control, our hunting dogs are much more manageable. She is quite a talented woman. Should you wish to accompany us, of course she will come, in any case. There is no need to provide a horse for her.*

RICHARD LOOKED up from the letter to ask Hayes what was meant by it, but the butler had vanished. That meant he must go and tell Eleana of the hunting party and her role himself. Richard quickly scrawled out an acceptance—driven by curiosity rather than a desire to see any of the people attending—and left it with the pile of outgoing post. Then, he promptly stood and took the letter out to the yard.

Richard stopped in shock at the sight that met him. Eleana was up to her elbows in water, a large tub with a wet dog inside looking at her forlornly. As he drew closer, Richard recognised the massive Baron and was startled to realise that the elkhound which was so friendly at any other time was snapping and groaning in an attempt to move away from the rag she was using to clean him.

Eleana glared at Baron and grabbed his leather collar, dragging him through the tub towards her, the hound protesting every step of the way. He kept his tail thrust between his legs in fear. She poured a bucket of water over him, washing away the last of the suds that clung to his fur before letting go of the collar. Immediately, Baron leaped out of the tub and was about to run off when Eleana snapped her fingers. The hunter cowered but did not resist as she towelled him dry and sent him off to lay in the sun with four other dogs, including Hunter and Smoke.

Richard walked closer and nearly turned away in embarrassment when he realised that Eleana was soaking wet and that her shirt clung to the corset she wore beneath her shirt in a most revealing way. Instead, he just coughed uncomfortably and averted his eyes. "I received a letter about a hunting party next week at Welton House. Mr. Vaughn requests your services and has invited me along. I thought to accept."

Eleana frowned. Richard handed her the letter, ignoring the fact that she was dripping wet. Eleana took it, but she merely glanced at the paper before returning it. She nodded.

"What did Mr. Vaughn mean by not needing a horse for you?" Richard asked, watching with fascination as Eleana walked over to a different group of dogs and grabbed the collar of a fighter, his large brown body powerful and his skin slightly wrinkled. Scars covered his muzzle. He would be quite the guard dog for the estate, Richard thought. The creature, though powerful, could not resist Eleana's pull and her authority when she dragged him over to the tub, picking the dog up and dumping him into the water. The fighter whined and tried to escape, but Eleana kept a firm hold of his collar. She knelt down, heaving a sigh of frustration which the dog seemed to ignore.

Richard waited for Eleana to answer his question about the horses, but Eleana had her hands full, literally, and did not seem inclined to answer.

He could tell quite plainly that he wasn't going to be able to coax more conversation out of the Houndskeeper, what with about seven more dogs to bathe: a mix of fighters and hunters, even a few racers. Richard was a bit surprised at the number and variety of dogs. There were hounds as well as dogs and, when he ducked his head inside the kennels, he saw that there were several others including a female nursing pups. Few estates kept such large kennels, and Richard wondered whether part of the estate's vast income was due to Eleana. He imagined that it was.

Richard left the kennels feeling quite out of his depth, and he narrowly escaped getting splashed when the fighter was let free of the tub with a spray of water. Richard stood nearby while Eleana dried the dog and brought forth the next one, quietly admiring her strength and perseverance. He would have been exhausted with the amount of work she seemed to manage by mid-morning.

He wanted to say something or perhaps walk forwards and help her, but something in the back of his mind kept him from doing so. Perhaps it was the way Eleana ignored him—that is, quite obviously—or perhaps it was the way she seemed to be so capable alone. She did not need his help and from the scowling look on her face, did not seem want it, either. So, he did not pursue the question she had left unanswered and simply stated that he would come by later to talk over the details of the hunt. After that, he walked back to the house.

* * *

ELEANA SUFFERED through the bathing of the remaining hounds and dogs before dumping out the tub of water and dutifully rolling it back to its spot behind the kennels. Once finished, she went for a bath of her own. She soaked in the cool water long enough to feel clean, then washed her hair and put on a simple dress and overskirt that was belted tightly at the waist. The overskirt was a nondescript brown and the bodice of the dress a rust red; it was the only other dress or skirt she owned besides the one that Lord Byrns had given her. Eleana shrugged on a knitted shawl and pulled on her boots, dancing around the eager Hunter as she did up the buttons. Hunter knew precisely what this sort of dressing meant.

Eleana grabbed a small basket, glaring at her eager dog. She huffed, stalking out the door of her little cottage. She had made it halfway across the yard to the main drive when she was stopped by a young kitchen maid. "El, wait!" Eleana turned and the maid ran up to her, holding a parcel wrapped in brown greaseproof paper. "Cook said to give this to you. It's his favourite," she said with a smile.

Eleana blinked in surprise and held up the package to her nose, grinning at the scent of lemon bread. She nodded her head in thanks and allowed the woman to pet Hunter's head before turning again towards town, the parcel now stowed safely in her basket.

The walk into town was quiet and uneventful, apart from Hunter roving and frolicking along the roadside. No matter how Eleana called him to attention, Hunter would not obey. Of course, she did not try terribly hard. Considering where they were going, she knew they both had a right to be pleased.

The closest town to Belleview, that was not shared by the several estates nearby, was called Hartwell and was the largest under the Belleview banner. It housed small cottages along the main road and was large enough for a public house and a square opposite. The house that Eleana wanter, however, was on the far end of town. It was a small space, one with a well-cultivated garden and a surrounding stone wall growing green with moss and ivy. Eleana reached the small gate and Hunter looked to her eagerly, tail wagging enough to split the air with a whistle. She sighed and gave the command; he barked once, loudly and with excitement.

The door to the cottage opened just as Eleana closed the gate behind her and she was attacked at the knees by a small, squat dog, his fur long and grey and his tail cropped. He was a ratter, an old one at that, and went by the name Colonel. Eleana knelt down to pet the dog while the owner of the cottage walked down the path wearing a worn pair of buckskins patched at the knees, a green knit sweater under an equally worn coat, and a limp blue neck-tie at his throat. He was older, that much was made plain by his grey hair and the wrinkles on his face. But he wore none of the extra weight of age and moved as vigorously as if he were in his prime.

"Well, I wondered when you were going to come," he said, leaning down to greet Hunter and giving Eleana a sly look. She grinned and shrugged. "You know it isn't nice to leave off seeing your old da for so long."

Eleana played coy and made like she didn't know what he was talking about. Her father straightened and she moved forwards, wrapping her arms around his middle, her entire body tense with excitement. Her father, Joseph Tarell, laughed and slung an arm around her shoulder, leading her into the cottage. Meanwhile, Hunter and Colonel left for the garden to play.

"Now, you tell me about Belleview's new lord. Second son of a Marquess! Grandest sort we've had in this area for quite a while. He's been the talk of the entire town and I've been hounded at because my daughter works up at the house," Joseph said, taking Eleana's shawl and pushing her along towards the kitchen. She unpacked the basket of her parcel and the other foodstuff she had brought and made a face at the line of conversation.

"Oho, he's that bad, is he?" Joseph asked, hanging a kettle before the fire to head for tea. Eleana considered this before tilting her head up as if looking down on her father. Then, she pretended to reach for a glass and drain it, tilting her head back rapidly. This made her father solemn. "A drunk. Damn. Is he mean?"

Eleana shook her head and pulled her brows together, her face exaggeratedly sad.

"I see," Joseph said, understanding exactly what sort of man Lord Byrns was, at least as far as hid drinking was concerned. The lord of Belleview drank to get rid of his pain, and sometimes that was worse than being a mean drunk. There was a lapse in the conversation. Eleana could see her father watching her carefully, gauging her thoughts on the lord of Belleview. He came away with a thoughtful expression.

Eleana blinked, a slight blush of annoyance and embarrassment now painting her cheeks. She changed the direction of their conversation, more out of self-preservation than anything.

She wasn't quite certain how she felt about Lord Byrns and she did not particularly want to figure it out with her father probing her. Not to mention that there were certain events—like the ball at Haverford—that she would rather forget entirely. Many such conversations with Joseph had not ended well. So Eleana made as if she were holding a gun and swept it across the room, then pointed to herself.

"Mr. Vaughn's hunting party? Yes, I heard. I believe they've gotten another lord down from the city for the season to join them. Apparently, they wish to make an event of it, including packing tents for an overnight stay. Who knows why they would prefer to do that rather than sleep in their own beds, but there's not accounting for what the gentry will do. Still, I imagine you'll enjoy yourself. Will you take Baron out?" Joseph asked, ever the indulgent father. Eleana knew he saw right through her change in topic, but he did not pry.

Eleana nodded, then held her hands out as if a tree, her fingers draping downwards.

"Willow as well? Isn't she your newest hunter?" Eleana nodded again. "What about Absalom? He's a good, stout old dog. Best sniffer out of the ones I've trained," Joseph said, his smile nostalgic. He had been the Houndskeeper at Belleview before Eleana. She knew that he had given her the post to save her from a lifetime of service inside the house, trapped and away from her beloved hounds. Belleview was her home; it was where she had been raised and she was certain she could not be happy anywhere else. Sometimes, though, she wondered if her father missed it.

She flapped her wrist in indecision about Absalom and started to open the paper on the parcel the cook had given her just as the kettle began to boil. Joseph grinned at the sight of lemon bread and hurriedly poured out the brewing tea. Eleana never let him have any treats from the cook before. She preferred to offer at least one cup of tea and something remotely approaching a proper meal, which she had packed in the form of shepherd's pie, begged from the larder. They settled in over the food, taking drinks and eating happily.

Conversation flowed as easy between them as between the best of friends. Eleana was closer to her father than just about any other person; they had developed her language together and often spent hours talking over everything and nothing, over important events in her life and trivialities.

Tea lasted for a good hour while the two ate and conversed, then Eleana packed her basket and was helped into her shawl even as she helped Joseph into his coat. They called their respective dogs to them and began the walk through the town. Their amble was slower than when Eleana arrived, giving them a chance to enjoy the late afternoon sun and their last few moments together. They watched Hunter and Colonel scent out the area, tails wagging the entire time.

The edge of town where Eleana would leave her father came faster than either would have liked. As routine dictated, they stopped for a few moments. "Ella," Joseph said, looking at her with a smile. "I don't care if this new lord is a drunk lost in grief or if he seems to be the cheapest type of penny pincher. You give him a chance, alright? I know you're a good girl."

Eleana nodded emphatically and wrapped her arms around his middle again before pulling back and smiling up at him, ready to walk back to Belleview. Joseph rubbed his thumb over his daughter's cheek then gave a gentle shove to her shoulder. "Now you go on. Days off don't last forever. I love you, child, and I'll see you next visit."

Eleana waved and signalled Hunter to her side. The black and white hound gave a lick to Joseph's hand and exchanged farewells with Colonel before walking to her side so that her hand could rest on his head while they walked. The journey back to Belleview was as beautiful as before, but there was a slight melancholy in Eleana. She knew that it would vanish and that she would see her father again soon, but that knowledge did not stop her feeling a bit sad.

Belleview was quiet when Eleana returned, her basket now empty and Hunter at her side, yawning slightly. The sun was lowering until only its golden rays crested over the tops of the trees. Eleana quickly deposited her basket at her cottage and went out again, not bothering to change her clothes or even stop in to see the kennels. She just went out again, moving towards the forest, her legs sure and steady despite her heart faltering.

There were various paths through the forest, but most days Eleana chose to wander off the path and instead trust her own tracking instincts and Hunter to get her back to Belleview. Today, though, she moved towards the main path, the great trees above making shadows dance across her skin.

The forest was alive with life, the birds chirping high overhead and squirrels and rabbits quickly fleeing from her silent figure and her equally silent hound.

The undergrowth came right up to the edge of the path but did not encroach upon it, evidence that it was carefully maintained by the groundskeepers. Eleana followed the path, looking at the trees around her and not really paying attention to where she was going. Years of repetition had her turning at the exact point a small path veered off the main one.

This footpath was not maintained. Indeed, it looked more like a game trail rather than a proper path. But there was some evidence that it was used, if only in the fact that it had been worn in well enough to show dirt through the grass and plants growing up. The trees, immediately after stepping off the path, no longer seemed to sigh as a slight breeze moved through them. They became more menacing, more tightly packed together, secretive and whispering. She kept walking, Hunter only a few steps behind her, and the forest seemed to close up behind them.

Eleana pulled her shawl tighter around her, feeling like a spectre amongst the woods. She made no sound, even though she stepped over plants and life. Hunter's quiet breathing became the only sound while the birds fluttering about grew quieter and the signs of squirrels and other small life vanished. Then, abrupt and startling, the path stopped and opened into a small clearing.

Where the path had been left to the forest and not cut back, the clearing was just the opposite. It was well maintained and beautiful, the forest coming neatly to the edges, the grass which filled the clearing sweet smelling and soft. It was picturesque, or would have been, if not for the two tombstones that stood side by side, the stone crumbling and covered in moss.

Eleana knelt before the first, obviously much older than the second, engraved with the words *Bethany Jane Tarell*. She stared at the stone, trying to grasp memories from too long ago: a smile, a touch, a laugh. That was all she had left of her mother. Eleana meditated only a few minutes at her grave, but at the second grave, marked *William Renaulds*, she spent much more time. Hunter, who had waited by the side of the scene while she sat, now walked over to her and pressed his warm shoulder against hers, sensing her need.

Eleana pet Hunter absently and her memories were flooded with something much more than shadows and glimpses. This one was real, and he was gone.

She knelt there for quite a while, lost in thought. Only when the sun began to truly set and a cool breeze made her shiver did Eleana come to her senses. She pressed one hand to the name marked on the stone and the other to her heart and blinked back tears. Then, suddenly and hurriedly, she stood and walked out of the clearing, back along the path and to her little cottage, Hunter trotting along beside her the entire way home.

SUPPER WAS A TYPICALLY quiet affair for Richard. He wondered whether Eleana ate in her cottage or whether she dined with the other servants. He wished that he had someone to dine with instead of staring into the dimness where candles made shadows jump and where people should have been.

"Hayes," Richard said, staring into the amber depths of his drink and ignoring his food as was often the case. The butler stepped forwards, ready to do whatever was needed.

"Yes, m'lord," Hayes said, bowing slightly at the waist, his gaze not meeting Richard's. The two had come to some sort of truce over the last couple of days while Richard tried to settle into Belleview. He had even gone out of his way to let himself be served breakfast and supper, though he preferred otherwise. Still, he knew full well that Hayes expected him to lapse into whatever he had been before. Richard hoped that he wouldn't. He was becoming attached to Belleview, even considering Eleana's disconcerting presence, and he was hoping to get to know the estate better.

"What are the industries attached to Belleview?" Richard asked, his question startling Hayes. As he was looking at his drink, trying to divine something unknowable in its depths, he did not notice the momentary change in his butler's expression.

"There are many, m'lord. There are alfalfa fields, as well as the raising of sheep and a few cattle. Many of the tenants live in villages scattered over the estate and perform their own trades. There is a mill attached to the largest town, some two hours slow ride from here.

I suppose you shall have to ask the estate manager, Mr. Price, about the details," Hayes replied, stepping back into place since his master did not require any immediate service.

"Hm," Richard grumbled, bringing the cut crystal glass to his lips and sipping at the rich amber liquid inside. "And the closest town?"

"The closest town attached to Belleview is Hartwell, some half-hour's walk. The closest not attached is, well, you passed through Sedgeton on the way to Haverford, m'lord," Hayes said, stifling a smile. Richard glanced up at him, nodding thoughtfully. The butler coughed slightly and continued. "Shall I make plans for you to visit the nearest town tomorrow? I believe there is a nice town centre with much to entertain."

Richard paused for a moment at the gentle prodding. He finished the last of his fish and pushed the plate away, signalling the young footman to clear it. Richard sipped the last of his drink before nodding slowly. "Yes, I think that would be good. And please inform Eleana that I wish for her, Hunter, and Smoke to accompany me."

"Eleana, m'lord?" Hayes asked, his surprise showing through his normally stoic expression.

Richard hastily covered his slip, lifting his chin slightly. "Eleana seems to know everyone in the county, though she is such a solitary creature. I imagine that she'd be able to show me around and introduce me to the people," Richard said with a shrug. By the way that

Hayes' mouth twitched, he was not convinced in the slightest.

"I imagine that she will," was all that Hayes could muster. "I shall let her know and inform the hostler to have your horse ready for tomorrow morning. Ten o'clock?"

"Yes, and a horse for Eleana. I'm sure there's a calm mare or something that she could ride."

"I doubt she would want a horse," Hayes said flatly. Richard turned to look at the butler, his eyebrows raised until they nearly vanished under the wave of dark hair across his forehead. Hayes looked stiffly at the opposite wall, avoiding his gaze.

"Why not? She cannot run alongside all that way," Richard exclaimed in disbelief. Why was it that people seemed disinclined to give Eleana a horse? First that letter from Mr. Vaughn, then Hayes. Of course, when he had asked Eleana, she had been too busy to answer him, her hands full with the dog she had been bathing.

"Eleana has a distinct, ah, dislike for horses, m'lord," Hayes said, his tone telling Richard that he was going to stay no more on the matter. If Richard wanted to know more, he would just have to ask Eleana.

HAYES BOWED SLIGHTLY to Lord Byrns and left, obviously dismissed-though, he also did not bother to ask if there was anything else his lordship required. He went directly to his small office and found a young lad to run messages to Eleana and the hostler. Then, as was customary at the end of the night, Hayes pulled out a small glass and a bottle of fine wine, filling the glass and putting the bottle away. He sipped slowly and rested in his chair, thinking.

Mrs. Graham knocked on the door a moment later, a ledger in her hands. "I have a list of kitchen supplies and costs to put away."

"Of course," Hayes said, gesturing to the shelf behind him. He watched as she put it away. "I had a most interesting conversation with his lordship a short while ago. It seems that he is taking an interest in the running of the estate."

"Oh?" Mrs. Graham arched a brow.

"Indeed. I am inclined to think that this is a good sign. One that might indicate Belleview is to prosper."

Mrs. Graham shook her head, chortling. "Belleview will always prosper," she said. "so long as it has people like *us* to run it. But it is good that Lord Byrns is beginning to show interest. He's too young to have had such grief to carry. Belleview will do him good."

Hayes nodded, taking another sip of his wine. "I also noted a distinct interest in one Houndskeeper beyond what I would have expected."

At this, Hayes was surprised to note, Mrs. Graham blushed. "Well, that *is* something, isn't it?" she preened.

"My dear Mrs. Graham, is there something you would care to share with me?" Hayes asked, using his most imperious tone. Mrs. Graham was not fooled. She just smiled at him knowingly.

"Perhaps," Mrs. Graham said, nodding. "Time will tell. In this instance, I don't think it his lordship that is the problem. It is Eleana."

Hayes finished off his wine. He was inclined to agree.

CHAPTER 7

At exactly fifteen minutes before ten the next morning, Eleana found herself on the lawn near the front drive pointedly looking away from the horse that stood there. He was a tall, black creature, proud and strong, and he gave her the shivers. Eleana sat on one of the large rocks that bordered the drive and folded her arms, glaring at the ground. She did not want to be anywhere near the horse, let alone leading its rider around the country to visit towns under the care of Belleview. Despite her father's cajoling the day before, Eleana found herself in a particularly disfavourable mood towards Lord Byrns, and she was not afraid to let that fact remain clear.

The hostler finished going over the tack on Lord Byrns' horse and walked over to Eleana. Despite her dislike of the creatures under his charge, she did like the hostler. He was a small man with a lean frame, yet he had a way with the massive animals in his care. He went by the name Malachi, though many got away with calling him Mal.

"So, you're off to go show the master around?" he asked Eleana, sitting on a rock beside her and petting Hunter, who wagged his tail. Eleana nodded, rolling her eyes. Mal laughed. "Surely he cannot be *that* bad! I haven't had a chance to talk with him personally, but his horse is well taken care of and good natured, so he must be a generally good sort," he said, looking at Eleana through eyes surrounded by wrinkles that came from smiling. "I've a mind to approach him and ask about giving my nephew a position here. He's working as a footman over at Haverford, but he'd rather be with horses."

Eleana shrugged, not wanting to disillusion Mal about Lord Byrns. He was one of those types that saw the good in everyone no matter the circumstances, and Eleana wasn't sure she could define her dislike for Lord Byrns in any case. At least, not to anyone but her father and the ever-loyal Hunter. She took a deep breath and looked at the sky, wondering if she would have to wait forever to get this tour over with. She wondered if she would constantly be waiting for Lord Byrns, or if he would wait for her, every once in a while.

She had just finished these thoughts when Lord Byrns walked out the front doors with Smoke at his side, wearing a nicer set of buckskins and wool coat than Eleana could ever hope to own. It was likely a ploy to be presentable to the people he would meet. Though, to his credit, he did look slightly nervous. Mal stood from where he had been sitting and jogged over to the black horse, holding his head so Richard could mount. Eleana exchanged a look with Hunter and Smoke and rose as well, now walking over to the general vicinity of Lord Byrns but steering well clear of his horse.

"Well, Eleana," Lord Byrns cleared his throat, situating himself in the saddle and nodding his thanks to Mal. "I think everything is in order. Mrs. Graham assures me that we can have lunch in the towns and that, should we not be back in time for supper, we should just eat out as well. Shall we go?"

Eleana frowned, annoyed at the waste of a day of work. Her father's words played in her mind and she sighed. Lord Byrns *was* trying, at least, to become more involved in the goings-on of Belleview. He hadn't shown any interest in the matter before. Eleana wondered whether it was Hayes or Mrs. Graham that had prodded him into this. She would never have thought it to be herself.

Eleana took a deep breath and let it out slowly. Then, she signalled the two dogs to follow along while she ran slowly down the drive. Lord Byrns blinked, startled, then urged his horse after her, keeping pace at a slow trot. Eleana ran in fits and spurts for a bit until she settled into her stride, keeping a safe distance between her and the horse.

"Will you be alright running the whole way?" Lord Byrns asked, looking concerned. Eleana huffed from the exertion of her steps. "I can put you up here with me, if that would be easier," he suggested, sounding tentative.

Eleana widened her eyes and looked at him incredulously. She shook her head vigorously, somehow keeping her pace steady. She would not ride for all the hounds in the world if she could help it.

"Very well, then. You can just let me know if you need to stop," Lord Byrns replied quietly, his deep voice almost a whisper, his dark hair waving with the movement of his horse. Eleana wondered for a moment at his not wearing a horsehair wig, as was often common among his set, but she did not dwell on the thought for long. Truth was that she did not dislike his hair.

They travelled to Hartwell in silence but for the steady pounding of Eleana's boots on the dirt and the steps of the horse. Eleana kept her eyes fixed straight ahead, but it was difficult not to feel Lord Byrns watching her. Was he looking for a sign that he should slow? Or was he just curious?

They reached town fairly quickly, given their steady pace. The people on the streets stared, watching Eleana run past with two dogs at her heels, a man in fashionable and well-made clothes following behind on a grand horse. As they neared the centre of town, Eleana slowed her pace to a walk. Lord Byrns dismounted, which at least made it less awkward to walk beside him. The gesture also made him less intimidating to some of the others around them.

"Eleana, darling," a woman exclaimed, walking along with three children at her heels and a basket on her arms. The children were barefoot and their clothes dusty, and her dress was two years out of fashion, but the smile on her face showed that she did not care. Eleana smiled widely, recognising Mrs. Gardener. Hunter wagged his tail, too, in greeting. "I thought yesterday was your day off. What are you doing back here?"

"I am afraid that is my fault, Madam," Lord Byrns said as Eleana turned her head to look at him in explanation. "I asked Eleana to show me the towns nearby."

"Oh, you must be Lord Byrns, the new owner of Belleview!" Mrs. Gardener dropped into a curtsey while he looked on uncomfortably. The children huddled behind their mother's skirts and peered at the noble with curiosity and a bit of fear.

"Please, you needn't do that, Madam," Lord Byrns let loose a nervous chuckle, drawing the woman out of her curtsey and granting a friendly smile to the children watching with solemn eyes. "I just wished to be introduced around and all that deference is awkward for me."

"Oh, well, my apologies, m'lord," Mrs. Gardener murmured. She threw a look to Eleana, who had watched the proceedings without moving or attempting to break in and clear things up. She furrowed her brows. Had Lord Byrns always disliked such formality? Or perhaps it was being in the country that had changed him. Certainly, he did not seem to be so distempered as he had been.

The bravest of the three children, a young boy dressed in clothing too small, crept forwards towards Hunter, hand held out tentatively. The dog looked up at Eleana who gave her assent, then went forwards to press his head against the boy's hand, making him giggle. Smoke approached as well, tail wagging. It did not take long for the other children to appear from behind their mother's skirts, reaching out to pet the silky-haired dogs and run around, playing.

"You have fine children, Madam," Lord Byrns said, a wistful smile on his face. Eleana knew that he had lost his wife; it was common knowledge and often discussed. Had he wanted children, too? Had that been lost to him, as well?

"It's Mistress Gardener, if you please. And they are good sorts," she replied, smiling at the playful bunch. "I've one more, at twelve. He'll be needing to find an apprenticeship soon, but I've no notion where to send him. I can't seem to bear to have him far from home. Perhaps his father will take him on, though he already has an apprentice."

Lord Byrns nodded in understanding. "What does your husband work at, Mistress Gardener?"

Eleana raised her brows, surprised at the note of

sincerity in his voice. He wasn't just acting the interested landlord; he actually cared.

"He's a joiner, m'lord. Builds houses more than anything small, but occasionally he'll get a commission for furniture. Made my own house and everything in it," Mrs. Gardener preened, blushing in pride for her husband. Lord Byrns smiled at her pleasure, then glanced over at Eleana. She saw some strange emotion in his eyes but could not discern it. So, she turned her attention back to the children, grinning as Hunter lay on the ground, his belly up and ready for scratching and his tail whipping through the air. Smoke was already dominating the attentions of the two youngest, making them giggle and shriek every time he managed to lick them.

"What of schooling?" Lord Byrns asked. Eleana lowered her eyes at Mrs. Gardener's shock and embarrassment.

"Oh, no. That's far too dear. The nearest boy's school is two towns away and not under Belleview. Old Mr. Northwood once talked about building a school, but he never did," she said, averting her eyes. Eleana stepped forwards, prepared to comfort Mrs. Gardener or move Lord Byrns away should he say anything more tactless.

"A school is just what Belleview needs," Lord Byrns said. He grinned at Eleana and nodded firmly, despite her gaping jaw. "I shall have a school built halfway between here and Belleview Manor. And your husband will oversee the building. He could have it done by next spring, do you think?"

"M'lord!" Mrs. Gardener gasped, both in shock and by way of thanks. She faltered with her basket for a moment, wide-eyed and amazed at the benevolence of this new lord. "But a whole new building, a school! Oh, could you not just repurpose something? A school, a new building, is far too generous."

"I do not know of any place big enough apart from Belleview Manor, and if you do not mind, I think I should rather like to keep it," Lord Byrns chuckled. He looked at Eleana, confusion plain. She took a deep breath and drew a hand over her head as if painting something in the sky, then drew a house in the air.

"Do we have a summer house?" Lord Byrns asked, surprised. Eleana wanted to applaud him for understanding her at once instead of their usual song and dance routine. "Would that be too small for a boy's school?"

Eleana shook her head and held her hands far apart: it was big. Mrs. Gardener nodded vigorously, seemingly relieved. "Oh, yes. The summer house is quite large and with a few renovations, it would make a lovely school."

"Then it will be done. I will go over the details tomorrow and contact your husband regarding the building work. And when the school is complete, your son shall attend at no charge," Lord Byrns said, nodding his head in finality. Mrs. Gardener smiled and petted, though it was plain that she did not believe a word that Lord Byrns had said. She called her children to attention, and Hunter and Smoke returned to Eleana's side.

Eleana waved her hands in farewell to Mrs. Gardener, and Lord Byrns nodded his head formally. The group separated, the mother and her children to go and talk over the way the new lord simply said he would build a school from the Belleview summer house, and wish it would be so, though she would not make plans to that effect. Eleana and Lord Byrns walked towards the centre of town, Eleana watching him carefully.

Who was this person standing beside her? Everything she had experienced of him before this moment spoke of a self-absorbed grief and an outstanding anger, sometimes even arrogance. But occasionally, as when he had given her the dress, he showed glimmers of benevolence and kindness. Never once had she suspected him to do or say anything quite so drastic and so... wondrous. A school for children of the tenants? What nobleman would even consider such a thing? Eleana was amazed and completely thrown off balance. Suddenly, she did not know where she stood with this person. When Lord Byrns reached into his jacket pocket and pulled out his flask and taking a hasty drink, the world became right again.

He was nothing more than a man drunk on self-pity and alcohol and to hide his true nature, he would happily talk about building a school that would benefit Belleview, and never make good on his promise. With this fact in mind, Eleana led her master to the town centre, stopping in the small square and indicating the shops and pub and homes around her as if to say, 'This is Belleview. This is what you own but will never be a part of.'

RICHARD SAW Eleana's gesture and understood its meaning. The thought pained him, but he also knew that he *wanted* to be a part of Belleview and its people. His grief for Christina had lessened. He knew that he would never forget her. Now, though, he had a purpose in life. He would devote himself to it as he had to Christina. Belleview and its people. Eleana. That was his purpose.

"Well I'll be," a man said, catching the attention of both Eleana and Richard. Eleana turned and grinned, immediately rushing forwards to wrap her arms around this newcomer. Richard fought back a flare of jealously, though the man's age seemed to make such a liaison unlikely. The man chuckled, "What a treat, you coming to visit your da two days in a row."

"You are Eleana's father?" Richard asked, startled. The man looked up, an arm slung around Eleana's shoulders, laughter in his eyes. He was dressed simply in working trousers and a worn knit sweater, his hair mussed. But the way he carried himself—straight and tall—he could have passed for nobility.

"When she doesn't cause too much trouble, aye," the

man said with a nod, extending his hand. "You must be the new lord up at Belleview. Lord Richard Byrns, isn't it, m'lord?"

"Yes," Richard replied, dumbfounded. "Ah, just Richard, if you please." He hadn't even realised that Eleana's father was alive, much less within walking distance of Belleview. "I coerced your daughter into taking me on a tour of the towns under Belleview and I've just been talking about building a school at the summer house."

"Really? You should talk to Gardener. He's the best joiner and carpenter around for miles. My name's Joseph, by the way. Joseph Tarell, though if you call Mr. Tarell, I'll set Hunter on you. Or perhaps this black lad. Very handsome." Joseph knelt and patted Hunter's head, reaching out to let Smoke sniff him before stroking his fur.

"That's Smoke. He came with me from the city and Eleana's been, ah, fixing his training. I wasn't aware that you were a Houndskeeper, as well," Richard said, probing a bit to try and discern as much of Eleana's life as he could. Joseph looked up, his intelligent eyes seeing right through Richard's ploy.

"Not anymore. I used to be Houndskeeper up at Belleview Manor, but Eleana is far better at the job than I ever was, so I moved here to let her have the position. I've only got one dog, now. Old Colonel. He's not much use except as a companion. Nowadays, I do odd jobs around town, helping out where I can," Joseph said, straightening and ignoring the protests of the hounds. Eleana ordered them to sit and they sat at her feet, Hunter leaning against her leg.

"Ah," Richard said, trying to think of something else to say to the father of the woman he loved, though *she* did not know that. "Where is the best place to eat luncheon here? Mrs. Graham said we would be able to eat in Hartwell, though she did not say where."

"Mrs. Graham, eh? How is she? I haven't seen her for quite some time," Joseph said, putting his hands in his pockets and standing comfortably where Richard was awkward and afraid.

"I believe she is well. I doubt that she would tell me if she weren't," Richard replied. "Most of the Belleview staff seem to be of that vein, I'm afraid. It must be that I'm the lord."

"For most of them, yes. Though, Eleana here wouldn't tell you if something were wrong even if she were bleeding on the ground," Joseph said, chuckling at Eleana's indignant look. She made a series of rapid hand motions, too quickly for Richard to follow. Joseph laughed louder, patting his daughter on the shoulder in comfort. "There's no need to be like that. You know you're independent. You rely on yourself and occasionally on Hunter," Joseph teased. She pouted, folding her arms and glaring at the ground.

Richard wished that he could be comfortable enough with Eleana to tease her without expecting serious retributions. But he still stood far apart from her. In fact, he wasn't even sure she thought of him as anything but a drunken lord that she was to obey.

He desperately searched for another line of conversation in order to try and befriend Joseph but could think of nothing to do but pat the chin of his horse desperately. He could think of a hundred things he wanted to ask, but no way to present the topics or even muster the courage to simply state what was on his mind. This was nothing like making mindless conversation with other well-off people at parties where he was not expected to be marvellous at conversation and it was far too easy to let other people talk and for him to simply listen.

"Well, if you're looking to have luncheon," Joseph said, looking around. "then I'd try that little place in there. Barley and Maple. It's got good enough food and the drink is cheap. But, of course, you're welcome to come to my house. I have a nice bit of lamb I set to cooking this morning. It should be near done by now and I think I can rustle up a few potatoes and carrots."

Eleana stared at her father in alarm and Richard was afraid he shared her sentiments. He spluttered something unintelligible, his hand resting against his horse for comfort. "I, ah, wouldn't want to impose," Richard said hurriedly, covering up his gibberish, "and I was rather hoping to partake of the local businesses. Perhaps you would join us?"

Joseph smiled and nodded just as Richard realised his mistake. Eating at the public house or at Joseph's cottage, either way he was still having a luncheon with Eleana's father.

"Then Barley and Maple it is," Joseph said. "If you want, they'll feed and water your horse as well."

Richard nodded absently, wincing when Eleana threw him a look that plainly said this situation was his fault. It was and he knew it. The trio walked across the square to the Barley and Maple where Richard handed the reins of his horse over to a young stable boy, a coin promising that the stallion would be well taken care of.

They were well served, owing to Richard's status as the master of Belleview and whatever rumours had spread about his wealth. Eleana's presence only made things more rumour prone, which made the deferential treatment more than awkward. The three of them took a seat near the window so as to look out on the town square. Richard was offered the best food and drink in the establishment, which he accepted with a smile that didn't quite illuminate his features.

Eleana kept looking out the window to where Smoke and Hunter waited by the horse trough until Joseph finally said, "They'll be fine. You've been without Hunter for days at a time and you can do without him for an hour or two."

Eleana glared then held her hand above the floor at waist height. "Yes, of course that was many years ago, but surely you haven't grown so dependent on the dog," Joseph said. She threw up her hands in surrender and sulked, ignoring the serving girl who came to deliver the drinks. Scotch for Richard, a watered wine for Joseph, and tea with some lemon for Eleana.

"If you want something stronger, I have no problem

with your drinking," Richard said as he moved the cup closer to Eleana. She frowned and shook her head slightly, crossing her hands in front of her. "You do not drink? I'm sorry, I-" Richard broke off awkwardly. He lifted his own glass to his lips and sipped at it, for the first time in a long time not finding the taste to his liking. He still revelled in the feeling of the alcohol burning down his throat and preparing his bones for that blessed numbness. He closed his eyes for a moment as his constant pain dissipated, the action almost involuntary.

How disgusting he must be to Eleana, a fiery and beautiful girl who didn't drink, who was so kind to people and yet somehow managed to be on her own, standing apart, a spirit more kindred with nature than humanity. And here he was, a drunken man, a fool who couldn't seem to get over the fact that his wife had died, who buried his sorrow in alcohol and in projects, who left his previous life because he was not strong enough to face it.

Joseph said nothing, watching these emotions play across Richard's face though he tried to hide it. Eleana —ignorant, beautiful Eleana—stared out the window, obviously worried about her hounds. "For goodness sakes, Eleana, call for some chopped liver and go out to them. Our luncheon won't be here for another while yet and if you keep staring like that, Hunter will come in here of his own accord just to cheer you."

Eleana blushed and smiled sheepishly, pushing her chair back and making an apology to Richard and her father with her eyes. She found the serving girl and detailed what she wanted for her hounds, following her to the back to fetch some food for them. Left alone with Eleana's father, Richard tried not to reach desperately for his drink and empty it in a single tilt of his head, though the impulse was quite strong. Joseph simply took a small sip of his watered-down wine and fixed Richard in his gaze, eyes warm and intelligent yet dangerously sharp.

"Tell me about her," Joseph said simply. Richard started, confused.

"I do not know who you mean," he replied softly, eyes following Eleana while she walked out the door with a bowl of meat scraps, grinning happily. He saw Hunter and Smoke leap to their feet, waiting until Eleana gave the signal before moving towards the food.

"Your late wife," Joseph replied. "I don't have to listen to the gossip around town to know that you lost someone you loved. It's written in your eyes and in the way you reach for a drink like you're going to burn up without it."

Richard averted his gaze. He knew that he was a lord, if only a second son, and that he could make things quite difficult for Joseph for saying such things, but there was no way he would ever consider such a thing against this man. "She was the loveliest creature I had ever met. She was everything I was not: outgoing, exuberant, constantly laughing, constantly in touch with everyone around her. She remembered the birthdays of all our staff and there was not a cruel bone in her body. I was terrified of her at first, truthfully. Gradually, though, she became all I could think about. So, I married her. But we were so different... I do not think it mattered how much I loved her sometimes, because we fought like cats and dogs. She was so loud when she was angry with me, shouting and ranting. She hated that I just sat there and took every abuse, knowing that she would lose her passion and then I would just end everything with a few words. I loved her... And then, just as quickly as blinking, she was gone."

Joseph reached out across the table and put his hand over Richard's, his kind eyes meeting the desperate blue ones of this desperate lord. Richard took a breath and realised, not without some slight guilt and a small pang of joy, that he was not going to cry over Christina as he had so many times before.

"If you hadn't loved your late wife with every bone in your body, there would be little chance that I would say what I shall say to you now," Joseph said, his voice gone quiet, watching Eleana carefully out of the window. He drew his hand back and licked his lips as if nervous. "I used to think that no one would be good enough for my daughter. Yet, as these things often go, I have little choice in the matter. You... you have changed my mind. I know you love Eleana, though she can't see it yet. Maybe it's just that I'm her father and I have a sense of these things, but I know it's true. Knowing that, I give you my permission to love my daughter. But if she does not love you back—if she never loves you—promise me that you won't force her into anything. Promise me you that won't hurt her. Because she's been hurt in the past and I won't see it happen again."

Richard said nothing, completely taken aback. Then, with so many questions and pleas on the tip of his tongue, he swallowed them back and nodded.

CHAPTER 8

Richard was fairly certain he had shocked everyone when he actually started work on the renovations to the summer house for a school. He made a trip to the summer house with the joiner, Gardener, and found that it was more than adequate for the job. He was also certain that many other masters would have kept the summer house for their own use, but Richard could barely keep track of Belleview Manor. Nor did the summer house have kennels.

The perhaps more surprising thing to Richard, though, was that he and Eleana seemed to be actually getting along. Before going to the summer house each day, Richard would always stop by to fetch and end up talking for a few minutes with Eleana, or simply watching her train the dogs and hounds. When she came to collect Smoke each morning for his training, she would finally agree to his requests that she have a cup of tea. It seemed to Richard that they were becoming friends.

All of these happenings, pleasant though they were, distracted Richard from the fact that the hunting trip he had agreed to had arrived until the night before when his young valet began asking about what to pack. Richard was sitting at the small desk in his room, checking some figures in a small moleskin notebook. He started at the voice of a young Morris.

Morris was perhaps a little young for the position of a valet and dresser, but he was capable and did not make a fuss over things, which suited Richard just fine. He had a sneaking suspicion that the lad was Hayes's nephew or some such but did not mind.

"M'lord, do you want warmer things for the evenings or is your jacket acceptable?"

"I'm sorry, what?" Richard asked, putting the notebook away and thinking absently that he should talk with some of the individuals of import in the towns the next day to see about advertising for teachers and school masters.

"The hunting trip, m'lord. It is supposed to last two nights and two full days, with you returning on the third day. Mr. Vaughn has made arrangements for tents and cots, food and the sort, but you are to bring your own guns and weapons, hounds, and clothing. Eleana has been packed for two days, m'lord," Morris said. Richard stared blankly at his young servant, appalled at his own forgetfulness.

"Right. The hunting trip. I, ah… I shouldn't imagine

it would get cold in the evenings?" Richard asked, looking at Morris in plea. Morris returned a pitying smile and moved to the wardrobe.

"Shall I pack what you might need, m'lord?" he asked. Richard nodded, thinking that he hadn't been on a hunting trip in years. He hoped he still knew how to use a gun. And Eleana was going. Richard readily acknowledged her skill as a Houndskeeper, but why would she need to accompany the hounds on a hunting trip? He remembered, vaguely, that Mr. Vaughn had also made a special request for Eleana's presence.

Richard watched, frowning, as Morris packed the necessary supplies into a bag, which would be carried with packhorses or wagons supplied by Mr. Vaughn and delivered to a maid passing in the hall. "What time am I leaving tomorrow?" Richard asked, dreading the answer. That was one benefit of being a gentleman and of the nobility: he did not have to rise with the sun.

"Shortly before luncheon, m'lord. I expect you'll eat at Welton House then start the trip. Sir James doesn't particularly like early starts, and Eleana always complains, saying that the hounds get excitable by waiting, seeing as they know what's coming," Morris said. Richard nodded and put his writing supplies away, closing his desk until he could think freely on the project.

"Does Eleana always go on these hunting trips?" Richard asked, stretching and indicating to Smoke that he could climb on the bed, something of which he was sure Eleana would disapprove.

"More often than not. She keeps the hounds in line, but she's not really there for that. El's the best huntsman around and everyone here knows it. She heads the hunt," Morris said, smiling proudly. Richard started in surprise. Eleana *led* the hunt? Would there ever be anything about that woman that did not surprise him? He expected not. "Will you be needing me anymore tonight, m'lord?"

"No, no, that's fine. Goodnight, Morris." Richard said absently, his thoughts across the yard and with the mysterious Houndskeeper.

"Goodnight, m'lord," Morris offered, closing the door behind him. Richard nodded, but he did not hear. His thoughts were otherwise occupied.

Morning came too quickly. Richard was soon pulled away from his work on the school, mostly regarding drafting of advertisements, but there were now other matters to attend to. Specifically, that of playing the social circle. It would be good, perhaps, to see if he could convince some of the other landowners around to add their support to the school. That would open the school up for all the children of the tenant workers in the county.

Richard dressed swiftly in some well-worn trousers and a shirt for hunting, some small voice in the back of his mind telling him that the clothes were wrong. A thick wool coat to combat the fog seemed to quiet the voice. He called Smoke to his side and went out to find his horse already saddled and a cart with a large grey draft horse carrying his pack, Eleana's pack, and a resting Hunter. Eleana was nowhere to be seen, but the hostler Mal was standing nearby, checking the straps on the draft horse.

As soon as Richard approached with Smoke, Hunter lifted his head and wagged his tail. Eleana appeared from around the side of the house, three dogs at her heels. They were all fine hunters, with lean but powerful bodies and slightly rounded, drooping muzzles with wet black noses. Richard recognised the largest as Baron. He went over to pet the others and check the name badges on their collars. The one mottled with white and brown spots was Absalom; he held himself with the dignity of maturity. A younger, more energetic blue female by the name of Willow pranced around Eleana. She had grey stockings and darker, floppy ears. Her long whip-like tail was frantic while she exchanged scents with Smoke.

Eleana heaved a smaller pack into the back of the cart then furrowed her brows at Smoke. She looked up at Richard and shook her head, ordering the dog back to the house. Smoke whined.

"He cannot come?" Richard asked, suddenly disappointed. Eleana shook her head again and indicated the other four dogs. She would have her hands full with the hunting dogs from Belleview, not to mention those from the other riders. "Alright, boy, go on," Richard said. Smoke looked at his master in dejection and strolled back to the house with head and tail drooping. The pitiful sight was enough to make him chuckle.

"M'lord," Mal greeted, handing over the reins to

Richard, his small frame obscured by a large sweater. Richard wondered how such a small man could manage the horses so well, but then again, nothing at Belleview seemed to be the usual way of things. "I was wondering if I might ask you something."

"Of course," Richard said, checking his saddle once before mounting. His eyes tracked Eleana as she ordered the three hunters into the back of the cart, seating herself on the driver's bench and looking at the draft horse with distaste.

"My nephew, Theo, he's looking for a position with horses and I was wondering if he might come to work here. I know that he wouldn't be getting full hostler pay, but he wants nothing more than to work with horses and isn't happy as a footman. And, well, I thought, perhaps…" Mal trailed off, licking his lips. He did not meet Richard's gaze, obviously afraid at overstepping some boundary.

"He is very welcome," Richard said, nodding firmly. "I really should ride more and pay more attention to the horses. Another hand would be quite useful. Are we all set, Eleana?" Richard ignored the broad grin that Mal gave him, as well as his effusive thanks. He had meant it to be a kindness, but he was also serious in his desire to pay more attention to the horses. The overwhelming gratitude, though, Richard could do without. Eleana watched him, a slight furrow in her brow though she did not look unhappy. He smiled at her and she, instead, flicked the straps over the draft's back and set the journey into motion.

It was Eleana's fault that Richard grew to care more about the well-being of Belleview and its inhabitants. She fit in so well, here. It was obviously her home and one she loved. Richard tried to get to know that home. He had even stopped resisting the attempts of the household to serve him, accepting the help rather than arguing against it. It was also entirely her fault that Richard had stopped rubbing Eleana the wrong way on purpose, but he still managed to do so by accident. Perhaps most importantly, though, was that it was Eleana's fault that Richard could now think through his grief and focus on the world around him with a focused, if not entirely clear, mind. He still felt the pain that he had carried with him for so long. That, he convinced himself, was the reason he still felt relief at the flask in his jacket pocket.

The ride to Welton House was meant to take little more than an hour. Eleana glared at the horse she was driving the entire way, sitting as far back as the small seat would allow, looking thoroughly unhappy.

"I did not know you could drive a horse," Richard said, riding alongside and trying to think of something to break the awkward silence that had settled between them.

Eleana shook her head and pointed at the horse before her, then shivered as if in fear. Richard blinked. "You're afraid of horses?" The revelation was startling, and he nearly pulled his own stallion up short. That did explain why no one bothered to saddle a horse for Eleana. She nodded, the frown gracing her lips telling him that she did not like this particular weakness. "Then why are you driving? Hold a moment, stop the cart."

Eleana did as she was told, stopping the great beast in front of her and dropping the reins in obvious relief. Richard dismounted and tied the reins of his stallion to a bar along the side of the card, making sure they were tight, before climbing up and taking Eleana's spot at driving. "Better?" Richard asked, clicking his tongue to get the draft horse moving again.

Eleana nodded, staring at him with wide eyes. She held out her hands and shrugged her shoulders, as if to ask why he would choose to help her when it would be far easier to simply ride his horse. By leading the stallion, they would have to ride slower, likely making them late for luncheon at Welton House. "Because I do not want my Houndskeeper rattled when we get to Welton. And besides, I enjoy driving."

Eleana furrowed her brow but did not press the issue. Instead, she happily climbed into the back of the cart with her hounds, letting them climb over her. When Richard glanced back, he saw that Hunter had lain his head in Eleana's lap. He smiled then turned his attention back to the road. The remainder of the ride was quiet and though they were indeed late for luncheon by a few minutes, neither Richard nor Eleana seemed to care.

Upon reaching Welton House, which was pleasantly sized and made of grey stone peeking through vines, the horses and cart were taken by one of Mr. Vaughn's huntsmen. He was a big man with broad shoulders and keen eyes who nodded deferentially to Eleana. Richard tried not to stiffen at that. She signalled for the hounds to go lay near the house and followed the housekeeper of Welton House inside.

Eleana and Richard were led directly to the dining room where Sir James, Mr. Vaughn, Mr. Darlington, and a fourth man, presumably some bored noble come down from the city, were seated and eating heartily. Mr. Darlington was younger than both Sir James and Mr. Vaughn, though slightly older than Richard. The fourth man was slim and well groomed, with blonde hair and bright blue eyes; he was the youngest by at least a couple of years. All the men, not including Richard, wore bright red jackets and pristine buckskins. Richard swallowed and turned to look at the wall decor until his blush of embarrassment faded.

The only other woman in the room was Miss Martin, her eyes alight with excitement with the company she kept. Mrs. Vaughn was nowhere to be seen.

"Lord Richard Byrns and Eleana Tarell," the housekeeper announced, surveying the scene before her with cold civility. She turned and left abruptly, Richard and Eleana standing awkwardly in her wake.

"Well, there you are at last! We were wondering what had happened to you," Mr. Vaughn chuckled. He gestured to a pair of chairs and the two sat, gladly. "I see you have not bothered with these ridiculous red jackets. Smart of you, very smart! Always wondered that the critters didn't see us coming, myself."

"Oh," Richard said blandly. "I, ah, did not have the forethought to have a set made up. Never owned such a thing in the city, you know."

"We'll excuse your clothes, but not your tardiness," Sir James scolded, a twinkle in his eye and a grin wide on his face. He was, by the looks of things, on his way to being drunk.

"We had a late start is all," Richard replied, serving himself a plate of food only after he saw Eleana do the same.

"Lord Byrns, you know Mr. Darlington, but I do not believe you have met Lord Alistair? He has come down from the city for the shooting," Sir James said. The young lord inclined his head, and Richard nodded vaguely, trying to remember if the name were familiar to him.

"I am surprised that you do not know each other," Miss Martin said, taking a sip of her wine while she watched Richard pour his own glass. "Surely you were at some of the same parties in the city."

Her question was simply enough, but Richard saw through It. She wanted to know which of the two titled men in the room—even if one was only a second son— was a better candidate for marriage, which was wealthier or had more influence, though he was certain she would not object to either man.

To Richard's relief, Lord Alistair spoke, watching Richard with something like smug admiration. "I am not surprised that we have never met. Of course, I have *heard* of Lord Byrns, but we run different circles. He has far more influence than do I. His knowledge of financial markets is unparalleled."

"You flatter me," Richard said politely, trying to ignore the way that Eleana hid her chuckling behind her napkin. He reached for his wine and took a sip, thankful for the flavour and the effect of the drink.

"You had better drink up here, Lord Byrns," Sir James ordered with a smile, taking a large gulp of his own wine, his skin now growing flushed. "When we're out on the trip, there's not a drop of spirits allowed. Hunt Master's orders."

Richard swallowed. He set the glass down, feeling pale. He turned to Eleana, raising his brows in question, desperately hoping that what Sir James said was not true. She nodded in confirmation and indicated the wine then made as if she were shooting before shaking her head. Guns and alcohol did not mix. Richard leaned back in his seat, a quiet dread filling his stomach.

He was saved from having to explain the sudden pallor that appeared on his skin when Lord Alistair stared at Eleana in shock. "You're the Hunt Master?" he asked, the corners of his mouth twitching in unmistakeable amusement. Eleana nodded, her face set stoically. "Don't you speak?" Lord Alistair said, this time openly incredulous at the fact that no one seemed to contradict Eleana.

She shook her head slowly, her eyes slightly

narrowed and never once leaving those of the outspoken man. Lord Alistair did not seem to care about Eleana's gaze; he laughed openly, the sound rich and sharp.

"How does that work? A *mute* Hunt Master? And a *woman* at that," Lord Alistair sneered. "Did she never learn her place as a child? Or is she brought along for other purposes."

Mr. Vaughn and Sir James chuckled, shaking their heads. Sir James' wig was slightly askew and he looked practically ecstatic at Lord Alistair's words. Miss Martin focused her gaze on Richard, lids lowered in what was meant to be a seductive glance. Richard, though, was too focused on the trials that were to come to notice the undercurrents behind Lord Alistair's insolence or Miss Martin's smiles. Richard finished off his glass of wine, pouring another. Eleana made no move to defend herself.

"Eleana is the Houndskeeper at Belleview," Mr. Darlington said after a moment, glancing between the other gentlemen. "She is the best Houndskeeper I've ever known, and she is invaluable on a hunt. Whenever we have a hunting trip that lasts more than an afternoon, she is Hunt Master. I've tried to steal her away for my household, but Belleview has never given her up."

The words floated uselessly over Richard. Lord Alistair, though, said nothing further on the subject. He would occasionally glance over at Eleana and chuckle quietly to himself, but that was all. Miss Martin copied this new lord, giving Eleana suspicious looks then returning her attentions to the young men around her. Richard simply sat in solemn silence, trying to quell the dread building in the pit of his stomach. He drank two small glasses of wine over the course of the luncheon and then, far too soon, the meal was over and the party wandered outside just as Mrs. Vaughn and Lady Martin wandered out of the gardens, presumably to join Miss Martin in Welton House now that the men were going on their hunt.

ELEANA LOOKED over the two other huntsmen that would be joining them, one of which was the broad shouldered man who had taken the horses—by the name of Harry—and the other being of average size and bearing but with an intelligent look about him—George. The horses for each of the hunters was prepared, as well as one for each of the huntsmen but for Eleana. The three hunting hounds from Belleview, as well as her own dog, Hunter, sat where they had been left, watching while three other hounds came to greet Eleana, tails wagging eagerly at the sight of the mistress and alpha that had trained them all.

Eleana organised the hunt, watching as each rider went over the guns he had with him. She signalled the hounds to arrange themselves between the horses. The two huntsmen watched her instructions carefully, and Harry translated Eleana's motions to the riders.

Eleana paced as she relayed her instructions, making Harry turn his head to keep track of her. "On this hunt," he said, adding the necessary information where Eleana's motions did not place them, "there are four hunters and three huntsmen, including Eleana who will also oversee the hounds. Each hunter is to stay within sight of a huntsmen and if a shot is fired and prey killed or injured, the inspection will be left to Eleana, George, or myself. There will be no alcohol on this hunt and food eaten in the saddle must be eaten while in motion. Any rest stops will require the entire party to stop or for one of the huntsmen to stop with the hunter. Luncheon will be served each day from the cart with the supplies, which will travel alone and stop at the campsite for each night. Breakfast and supper will be eaten at the camp. If one of the huntsmen says to stop, stop. Eleana's word is law on this hunt, sirs, and if you do not wish to get hurt, lost or even killed, follow her instructions. This is not one of your afternoon jaunts, gentlemen."

The last bit was added only after Eleana had stopped her motions. Eleana nodded curtly before going over the hounds and gear one last time, leaving the horses to be checked by George and Harry. The two huntsmen mounted and Eleana signalled the hunt to leave, walking at pace with the horses while the women being left behind called out farewells.

The hunters, excluding Lord Byrns—Richard, she remembered he wanted to be called, though it still felt strange—who remained quiet, chatted cheerfully, knowing that the instructions at the beginning of each hunt were meant to scare them and that they were perfectly safe and in for a pleasant sport. This was not always the case; Eleana had seen more than one man get shot or injured by other means, faint from dehydration or ingest some poisonous plant. An afternoon hunt left you exposed to the wild for a few hours. Two days was usually more than most cared to venture. Only Richard seemed to be taking this seriously, as he rode with his hands tight on the reins of his horse. Eleana sighed softly and signalled to her hounds.

The group reached the forest before long and their chatter quieted to let the sounds of the forest take over, the loudest noise made by the steps of the horses. Eleana moved swiftly, easily keeping pace with the group. She watched the people and horses as they ranged about, searching for something to shoot. Hunter trotted along at her side, alert for any instructions Eleana might have.

Eleana froze at movement off to Richard's right. He was at the far end of the group, so it could not be another hunter or hound. He pulled out his gun and fired at a flash of light grey. The group halted, smiling broadly at Richard. Eleana held up her hands to be sure of everyone's position, then walked forwards to kneel by the rabbit. It was a clean shot, one that would not have caused it suffering. Eleana nodded in confirmation. George called out, "First kill to Lord Byrns!"

Eleana picked up the rabbit and carried it over to Richard to examine. He smiled weakly and tugged at his shirt collar. Eleana took the rabbit back and handed it to Harry, who would oversee the kills. Richard then pulled off his jacket, licking his lips as he tied the piece of clothing to the saddle behind him. He took a drink of water from the skin that had been provided.

Eleana looked at him, curious and not a little worried. He had taken the first shot, made the first kill. By all rights, he should be triumphant and cheerful, talking with the others while they waited for the forest to return to life after the sound of a shot. Yet he looked uncomfortable and slightly afraid. Eleana walked over to his horse and put a hand on his leg, making him jump. Eleana touched her head then moved her hand away, trying to relay her concern. Richard put his hand on Eleana's with a half-smile. "I'm alright. Do not worry about me. I just… I have not done this in quite a while, is all."

Eleana nodded, accepting the reasonable explanation, and signalled the hunt onwards once more. The rest of that first day was fairly successful, with Mr. Darlington bagging two pheasants—out of season, even—and Lord Alistair bringing in another rabbit. Mr. Vaughn and Sir James were too distracted with laughing and talking to do much shooting. Eleana could not say she was disappointed by that; they were difficult enough to manage on the ground and Sir James had a poor grip on his gun. Richard, meanwhile, kept quiet, his eyes more often than not focused on the saddle in front of him. Once, he seemed to waver in his seat, but he straightened before Eleana could fully catch a glimpse.

By the time the group reached the first campsite, they were all pleased to see that the tents—ridiculous, grand things with blankets and pillows and luxurious nonsense—had been erected. Richard claimed exhaustion and a headache and went directly to bed, ignoring Eleana's obvious concern. She did not have more than a minute to worry, though, because her attention was immediately demanded by the hunters wanting to discuss the day and the plans for tomorrow's venture. Sir James even vowed to bring down a deer.

Eleana tended to her hounds, making certain they were watered, fed, and resting. Then, she ate her supper. As Hunt Master, she was required to stay up and be certain that the people under her care did not do anything stupid, like try and go on a night hunt. But once the men crawled off to bed, spirits still high, Eleana staggered to her own small tent and bedroll. Her tent was set away from the main camp by a bit, as she was the only woman, and was smaller than the hunters' and the one that Harry and George shared. It was just large enough for the bedroll and herself and for Hunter to sleep beside her. Invariably, though, the other Belleview hounds managed to climb in and arrange themselves on and around her. Eleana always slept well like this, her head on Hunter's shoulder.

It was long past midnight and well into the dark hours of the morning when Eleana woke with a start, the sound of pained groans reaching her ears. She sat up and the hounds stirred around her. Hunter was immediately alert, his ears pricked and his tail held straight. But he was not afraid or even wary; there was no danger outside. Then where was the noise coming from? Eleana swept her hand through the air in the 'seek' command and Hunter crawled out of the tent, waiting while Eleana ordered the other hounds to stay.

Eleana followed Hunter, the black and white dog immediately going to the tent that belonged to Richard. She did not even bother to have Hunter make noise to announce herself but lit a lantern from the dying embers of the fire before opening the flap to Richard's tent. He lay entangled in the covers of his cot, wearing only his trousers, his shirt discarded and thrown to one side, soaked in sweat. His forehead and chest glistened with that selfsame sweat. Eleana knelt down next to her master, recoiling as he began to writhe around in pain, his hands shaking and his eyes wide, connecting with her own eyes as if they were a lifeline.

Eleana touched Richard's shoulders and pulled back her hand; he was clammy and cold, though he sweat still. She stared at him in shock and fear before wetting a spare shirt and wiping Richard's brow while she tried to think of what to do. She could treat a dog with ease, no matter what the problem was, but people were an entirely different matter. Eleana knew only that he was not well, his body twisting as he tried to get comfortable or lessen the pain.

Eleana stared into his eyes, frightened, and touched

his forehead in question, hoping that he was lucid enough to answer her question and tell her what was the matter. Richard opened his mouth but only a groan escaped it. Eleana grabbed his hand, squeezing it and trying to give as much comfort as she could. With her other hand, she sent Hunter to fetch help.

Harry entered the tent a few moments later, his shirt barely tucked into his breeches, his hair mussed with sleep. He took one look at Richard and became immediately awake and alert. His examinations were far more thorough than what Eleana would have known to do and when he had finished, he sat back on his heels and looked pityingly at Richard. "He's going through what doctors call withdrawal. I do not know from what—it does not look like morphia or laudanum addiction—but I doubt there's much we can do out here. This is quite severe and if he doesn't get proper medical attention, he could be in serious trouble."

Eleana knew what the substance was, and it was nothing so dangerous as morphia or some other drug. But that did not make the situation any better. She understood, now, why he had been so quiet and worried during the luncheon and throughout the hunt. He needed a drink and he needed a doctor and Eleana had neither to offer. She would be damned, though, if she would let him die. He was her master—if not a very good one—and he was her friend. His desperate blue eyes begged her for her help. So, no matter what had stood between them in the past, she would give it.

Eleana flew into action. Her hands whipped through the air as she gave orders. She needed to take Richard back to Welton House, or better yet, to Belleview. Harry and George would stay with the others since dealing with those fools was more than Eleana could handle at that moment. Harry and George could explain that Richard had not felt well and was taken home.

"That's fine," Harry said, already shoving Richard's belongings into his pack, "but how are you going to get him there? You don't ride."

Eleana worried her lip for a bit as she considered. Then, she pointed to the cart that had delivered the tents and supplies to the campsite. The horse that had pulled it was an old one, obviously used to leisurely walks, but it would have to do. She needed to move *now*.

"We'll send for another cart tomorrow," Harry said.

"And if these people don't like it, they can take it up with me. George, harness that horse. Eleana, help me get his lordship into the cart."

Eleana did as she was told, grabbing Richard under his shoulders while Harry took his legs. They half-carried, half dragged him to the cart and set him inside. He twisted and turned, resisting their efforts with all the strength of one who did not know what is going on around him. Eleana wrapped as many blankets underneath and around him as she could. Then, their packs tucked at his feet and the horse harnessed, she closed her eyes in a silent prayer and whipped the horse into motion.

They had travelled about ten miles in far from a straight line that day. Eleana was familiar with most of the forest in the county, but they were far from a path that was wide enough for the cart and that led to Belleview. Even Welton House was a good deal farther along than she would have liked. That meant she would have to cut through the woods themselves, trying not to get them lost in the dark.

Eleana signalled to Hunter, drawing a house in the air. Immediately, the dog cast about for a scent. He gave a soft whoof and set off into the night. Willow and Absalom followed close behind Hunter, looking back every so often to make sure that Eleana was following.

Driving an old cart horse during the day was one thing. This beast was obviously slow and preferred easy travelling. Treading through the forest in the dark, without a proper road, was another matter entirely.

The horse shied at every sound, nearly rearing up and twisting the harness twice. It stubbornly tried to refuse to go through the unfamiliar ground, prancing as it picked its way through the undergrowth with deliberate slowness. Eleana slapped the long leather reins along its back several times, but to no avail.

They travelled the first mile in this manner, Eleana's teeth grinding together. Behind her, she could hear the desperate groans that Richard produced. She had looked back at him once and saw that he had already thrown off the blankets and was tossing and turning, body glistening in sweat. His eyes found her occasionally, wide and terrified. And then there was that name, whispered with a desperate hope.

"Christina."

Eleana did not know whether he had just mistaken her for his late wife or if he were hallucinating. Either way, he was getting rapidly worse and they were not moving fast enough to make it back to Belleview before midmorning. Eleana slapped the reins again, silently pleading with the horse. Its ears flicked back, grey in the moonlight, but it moved no faster.

Finally, Eleana knew she had to do something. She lifted her hands for the dogs to see and made several motions. They whined in confusion, knowing the orders but never asked to do such a thing before. Eleana pointed at the horse and repeated the movements, her hands firm and precise. After a pause, Absalom did as he was told, Willow and Baron obeying a moment later. The three hunters lowered their heads and started growling low in their throats. They advanced on the horse from both sides.

The horse shied, trying to rear up and strike with its hooves. Eleana kept a firm grip on the reins, her arms struggling with effort. Baron let out a sharp bark. With that, the horse did the only thing it possibly could. It surged forwards with as much speed as its old bones could manage, the cart bumping after it.

Eleana refused to look anywhere but ahead, knowing that if she did so, she would feel that familiar terror that came with horses. The world would be moving too quickly. Everything was out of her control. Her heart beat faster, her vision narrowing until all she saw was the path ahead. Though her hands trembled on the reins, she held them. Over and over she told herself that she had to get Richard home. Home.

The horse stumbled, tripping over a root in a patch of forest not illuminated by the moon. With a great rending, the horse fell, letting out a scream. The harness broke, the wagon lurching as it slammed into the prone body of the horse and then stopped. Eleana was thrown from the driver's bench. She fell to the dirt, a rock scraping her brow. Immediately, her precious hounds were around her, licking her and whining. She pushed herself up, aching but not seriously injured, and pushed the hounds away. A trickle of blood ran down her face; she wiped it away and stood. There were more important things to tend to at the moment.

Eleana staggered over to Richard. He had remained in the back of the wagon, now too weak to do anything but stare up at the sky as he took in shallow breaths. His body still trembled. She then went to check next on the horse.

If she could have screamed in frustration, she would have. The horse's front left leg was broken, the limb stretched out unnaturally. The horse's head lay stretched back, bleeding from where it, too, had hit a rock. Its eyes fixed on Eleana and it let out another scream. She cursed behind silent lips, slamming her fist into her thigh. There was nothing to be done but to put the creature out of its misery.

Eleana dug her pack out of the wreck of the wagon and pulled out her hunting knife. She applied it to the horse without further delay, hating to do it and knowing that the creature was suffering. But when it was done, she wanted to scream even more. By her estimation, they were still some two miles from Belleview. Welton House, from the direction they had taken, was even farther. How would she get Richard to help?

Hunter whined at her side, his tail wagging slowly. Eleana patted his head gently, wincing at the horse blood still there. She took a deep breath, tears pricking her eyes. Richard let out a groan from the wagon, and Eleana hiccoughed a sob. She shook her head. No. This was not the end.

She marched to the wagon and pulled out some rope from her pack. With it, she tied the blankets around Richard, securing him safely inside. Then, she undid some of the tack from the horse and tied it as best she could around herself and Richard. Eleana pulled him from the wagon. She signalled once more for Hunter to find home, and she started off.

Eleana was strong and fit from her years as Houndskeeper. She could run for hours. She could carry a dog that weighed as much as she did with little problem. But Richard was taller and more muscular than she was, outweighing her by a good five stone. So, she was able to pull him through the woods for a while, using her anger and strength to move them along. But both of those quickly faded and all Eleana could do was put one foot before the other, the weight of her master dragging along behind her.

She kept her eyes on Hunter, fixated on him and little else. She could feel her legs trembling beneath her, the muscles in her chest and back straining. She wanted nothing more than to stop, but knew that if she were to do so, she would not get up again. Not in time for Richard, at least. So, step by step, Eleana kept moving. Occasionally, Baron or Absalom would press against Eleana as if trying to lend her their strength, but they could do little more than offer their comfort.

Eleana wasn't sure how long she had been walking when the sun began to shine between the trees. Dawn had come and she was still not home. Eleana looked at Hunter just as the dog's ears pricked. He looked back at Eleana and danced; they were nearly there.

The pain in her legs was suddenly more acute and her whole body felt like it was trembling. She knew that her shirt was soaked through with sweat and she would have severe marks where the leather tack and rope had cut into her and likely left her raw. Her breath came in short wheezing gasps and yet she walked on. There was no choice.

It was barely five minutes later that Belleview came into sight. Eleana moved as quickly as possible but she could stand no more. She stumbled and fell, too weak to bring up her hands to protect her face. Hunter turned and raced to Eleana, sniffing at her and whining. She looked up to the dog and gave a weak command: fetch help. Hunter whined again but raced off across the lawn, his long stride and quick pace showing his racer blood.

Eleana watched her faithful dog as long as she could before closing her eyes and drifting into an exhausted darkness. She became vaguely aware of Hunter's return, Hayes and Mrs. Graham and a young footman running behind the hound. She knew, barely, that she was being picked up by the butler, carried like a babe, while the footman lifted Richard, his youth's strength making little effort of the lord. Then, Eleana drifted into sleep and knew no more.

She woke in one of the beds of Belleview Manor, a light duvet tucked around her, pain lancing through her body. Her legs felt like leaden weights and her chest felt restricted. She lifted an arm to touch her chest and nearly gasped at the pain of moving. Still, she managed it and felt bandages wrapped around her. Her muscles—especially her legs and her back—felt as though they had been flayed open. She took a few deep breaths until the pain settled. The world about her resolved into definite detail.

Eleana looked about as much as she could without turning or moving too much and was slightly surprised to see that she was in a room papered with light green and blue stripes. The curtains were drawn, but there was enough light to see that they were dark green. The bed upon which she lay was plush and comfortable. This room, if she was not mistaken, was the Mistress' room, where the lady of the house was meant to reside. It was just down the hall from the Master's room. Was it a coincidence that she had been placed so close? Was it for the doctor to be able to check on them both?

The growling of her stomach distracted Eleana from these strange thoughts. She blinked, surprised at how famished she was. She must have been asleep for days for her hunger to be so acute. And where was everyone? There was no one in the room with her, not even Hunter. That was the part that worried her most. If Hunter wasn't with her, had something happened to him?

The door opened, making Eleana flinch. She immediately regretted that movement and winced accordingly as Fey and Mrs. Graham entered the room, Hunter between them. He saw that Eleana was awake and leaped onto the bed, bathing her with his tongue, tail thumping dramatically. Eleana laughed, though she could not muster the strength to push him away.

"Hunter, down," Mrs. Graham ordered sternly. The

dog regarded her before sighing and curling up at the end of Eleana's bed, an obvious compromise.

"You're awake," Fey said, walking forwards to help Eleana sit up, placing pillows behind her head. "I'm surprised that you awoke so soon, considering the state we found you in. Though, we were assured by the doctor that most of the blood came from the horse and not you." Eleana moved her hand into Fey's view and held her fingers apart, trying not to wince at the pain that action produced. "How long? One full day and night. You were cut badly from those straps. We had to cut them and your shirt from you. You look as though you overdid yourself quite badly, El, so I can only imagine that you dragged his lordship from that place where the wagon was found. Alone."

Eleana nodded slightly, her eyes drooping sleepily. The feat, now that it was over, seemed incredibly foolish and gargantuan. Still, she had done it and she now faced the consequences. Her stomach rumbled again, and Mrs. Graham clucked her tongue. "Now, Fey, stop that. She needs to eat and get some rest. You can interrogate her after she's well enough to start moving about on her own. Come, dear, put your arms around me and I'll take you to the necessary. Then we can get you something to eat."

Eleana did not resist Mrs. Graham's hold, though every bit of pressure she put on her legs and muscles was agony. Stubbornly, Eleana ground her teeth and made her way to the necessary, embarrassed to have to have Mrs. Graham there to help her sit. She finished and tottered back to the bed where Fey waited to help before sinking thankfully back into the pillows and dozing while food was brought.

She was dismayed by the simple bowl of soup and pieces of bread that was provided, her body claiming she needed more than that, but she had barely finished her first few bites before feeling nauseous. Eleana turned to the side of the bed and found a wide bowl already there. She rid herself of the food and wondered how often she had done that in the last day.

"Don't you worry, my dear," Mrs. Graham said, rubbing Eleana's shoulder while she coughed. "You just let us know when you're hungry again and we'll bring you something. There's water on the bedside table and we'll leave the bed. Now get some rest."

Eleana blinked, her mind moving sluggishly, but she finally managed to point to the door that led into the hall, a questioning look in her eyes.

Mrs. Graham looked to see where Eleana was pointing. She smiled. "He's alright, my dear. Doing much better than you, frankly. When we got him to the house and fetched the doctor, he said that his lordship was going through something called acute withdrawal syndrome or some such nonsense. His body was so used to alcohol that it was shutting down without it. We gave him a drink and some medicine to help the fever and the shakes and he slept off the rest. You, on the other hand, dragged a man taller and heavier than you through the forest in the middle of the night, nearly two miles. Your muscles, if not torn, were severely strained and you burned up every ounce of energy that you had, which is why you're so hungry and cannot keep anything down. And those cuts across your chest, from where the straps cut into you-" Mrs. Graham broke off, her voice shaking. She glared fiercely at Eleana. "I don't know what you were thinking but you must *never* do anything so *stupid* again!"

Fey nodded in agreement. Eleana tried to smile apologetically, but she could not feel guilty for helping Richard. Though, she did now wonder why she had bothered to drag him back if he turned out to be just fine. Even as Fey spoke to answer the unasked question, Eleana knew the answer. "If you hadn't brought his lordship back here, things would have turned out quite differently. He would be the one dead and you would be bringing home a corpse in the cart. If he's up and walking around in a while, I'll have him come in. He needs to thank you."

Eleana only nodded and closed her eyes, desperately tired. She didn't see Mrs. Graham or Fey leave and only stirred when Hunter wriggled closer to her, lending her his warmth and putting his head in her lap.

Eleana slept in fits and spurts, waking sometimes when Hunter would shift or leave with Fey, sometimes sleeping through everything. She nibbled on her bread and managed to keep that down, so the next morning she ploughed ravenously through eggs, sausage and toast. Still, when she tried to stand, her body felt shaky and she knew it would be a few more days before she was of any use. That fact annoyed her quite a lot.

She took to pressing Fey about the hounds and the doings of the house until finally, the maid snapped. "They're being taken care of by your father! He came in from town two days ago and is doing just fine. Now stop bothering me and relax. The doctor says you're to stay off your feet for another three days at least."

Eleana pouted and slumped her shoulders, an expression Fey knew to mean "I'm bored."

"Well, that's too bad," Fey sniffed and bustled out of the room, the breakfast tray gone with her. Eleana glared at the door. She tried to get out of bed, focusing her vision on a spot on the wall by the windows so she wouldn't see the floor and stumble. If she could prove that she was perfectly fine, they would let her go back to work. She had her feet on the ground and was half-way standing without support when her right leg buckled and she fell to the floor. Eleana swallowed back an angry sniffle and crossed her arms, sulking.

"Eleana?"

She recognised that voice. Eleana raised her hand above the bed, and a moment later, Richard appeared looking tired and worn. He was wearing loose trousers that had been well-worn and patched, and a shirt that was untucked and loose. There were faint bruises on his face from where Eleana had pulled him over rough ground. Richard leaned down and helped Eleana onto the bed, breathing with the effort after he had finished. Eleana leaned back against the pillows and set her legs straight while Richard leaned against the headboard.

"What a sad pair we are. You cannot walk and I cannot seem to do anything without feeling exhausted."

Eleana scoffed weakly, dismayed at the thought of being unable to move. She knew that she would improve, but the meantime was not something she cared for. She was always able to rely on herself—and Hunter. But here she was, unable to even cross to the vanity without help. Eleana suppressed a sigh, then turned to Richard. She put a hand to her head and then touched his shoulder in query.

"Yes," Richard said softly, his voice somehow still musical and soothing even though he was slightly hoarse. "I am well. Thanks to you. They told me you took me through the forest without a road by horse and cart until the horse broke its leg, then you *dragged* me from there to here. You must have torn every muscle in your body from the effort." Eleana nodded shyly, and he dipped his head. "Thank you, then, for saving my life. Though if you think about it, it was *your* doing that I was ill in the first place."

Eleana turned her head sharply and stared, ignoring the stab of pain that coursed through her body.

Richard chuckled weakly, showing he was kidding. "You were the one that said no alcohol on the hunt." Eleana rolled her eyes. She yawned, suddenly tired from her exertions. Richard blinked slowly and glared at the door, looking drowsy as well. "I suppose I had better return to my room, but this bed is really quite comfortable. And walking from my room to yours was quite the effort…" he trailed off. Eleana leaned back against the pillows and closed her eyes, breathing slow and deep. A moment later she was asleep.

Sometime during her rest, Eleana had shifted so that her head sat against something warm and comfortable. She blinked her eyes open, expecting to find Hunter beneath her head. Instead, she looked into the sleeping face of Richard Byrns. His mouth hung slightly open and he looked as weary as she felt.

Eleana sat up and moved away from him slightly. They had not touched in their sleep; there were several inches between them. Only her head had fallen to his shoulder. But what was he doing here? Had he fallen asleep before he could go back to his room? The impropriety was normally something Eleana would never have considered. She was a Houndskeeper on a country estate. She lived in a world of men, wearing men's clothes, and performing their labours. But this? Falling asleep in a bed with a man beside her? Even if they had been innocent of any wrongs, this was something startling.

Still, she found that she was not overly angry. Both of them had been through quite an ordeal, and she suspected that Richard wanted nothing of *that* sort from her. He was simply grateful. Trying to be friendly. And if he'd had the energy to return to his chambers, he would have done so.

Right?

The door opened, letting Mrs. Graham in. Hunter

ran after her and leaped on to the bed. She opened her mouth to scold the dog then froze in shock at the sight of Richard asleep on Eleana's bed. The housekeeper flicked her eyes to Eleana, who shrugged. Richard stirred at Hunter's nosing his hand. He stretched languidly, even going so far to smile at Mrs. Graham.

"Is it luncheon already? Thank goodness; I'm starved," he said.

Mrs. Graham sighed. She handed the tray to Eleana, shaking her head at the two. "I'll be back with your food, m'lord," she said, bustling out. Richard grinned sheepishly and leaned back into the pillows as he watched Eleana eat, his own stomach rumbling in protest. Eleana looked at him curiously and took another bite of her roll.

"I hope you do not mind my falling asleep here," Richard said. "The walk to my room just seemed so long and I was so tired."

Eleana shrugged and continued eating, giving Hunter a steely look when the dog inched forwards between Eleana and Richard, his nose questing for food. She huffed and Hunter stopped immediately, his head resting on his paws.

As promised, Mrs. Graham returned with Richard's food, Smoke not far behind. She waited until both Eleana and Richard were done eating then took the trays. "Do you want anything else? Books? A chess set? Your business papers and a writing desk?"

Richard frowned at the last option even as Eleana made a face of dislike. "I'll not see to my business until

I'm quite well again," Richard assured her. Mrs. Graham raised her brows but said nothing. She just left, leaving the door closed behind her.

Eleana stretched experimentally and winced a bit at the pain. Richard watched with interest, though he frowned. "Does… does it hurt?"

She shrugged and shook her head, holding her fingers slightly apart.

"I'm sorry, you know. Thankful that you did drag me back here, but it was my own fault. If I hadn't been so into the bottle, drunk most every minute of the day, then this would not have happened." He pressed a hand to his head, as if warding off a headache.

Eleana watched him for a moment, noting the sheen of sweat and the paleness of his skin. She tilted her head back, holding her hand as if she had a drink. Richard frowned, displeasure written cleanly over his face.

"The doctor says that if I do not stop drinking, I will die. Clearly, stopping on the spot is not going to work. So, they are controlling my intake and are slowly weaning me off the alcohol. Frankly, it's rotten. I have a headache most of the time and my body feels like water whenever I try to do anything."

He fell silent, his fingers picking at the fabric of the duvet. Eleana did not press the matter, instead stroking Hunter and watching while Smoke stretched out at the end of the bed.

"I started drinking to dull the pain," Richard breathed. "It was the only outlet I had after Christina died. I still lived in the city and had to deal with things, and everything reminded me of her. Except the drink. So that became where I lived. At first, it was enough to have two glasses of scotch a day, but soon it took more and more and more to get the same result. But the thing is, the pain never really went away. I still grieved for Christina every time I drew in a breath and all the alcohol did was cloud everything else, make it less… overwhelming. Then, I could not deal with pain any longer. I simply rented out my house in the city, sold all of Christina's belongings and bought Belleview. I had hoped that a change of scenery would not remind me so much of her."

Eleana listened carefully, surprised that he was telling her all of this. Perhaps it was because she had saved him. They had grown more friendly since that day in town, but this was something else entirely. She gave a questioning shrug of her shoulders, holding her hands out, palms facing the ceiling.

Richard sighed. "What next? Well, I figured out that I could do nothing about the fact that Christina was dead and that by pining over her, I was essentially dead as well. I had to start living my own life again, find interest in something other than my grief. Truthfully, you started that whole process."

Eleana straightened. She turned slightly to look at him, though he stared resolutely at the wall papers.

"You… you scolded me for being stupid about Smoke. You did not care that I was a widower or your new master or anything of the sort. You just saw a fool and did something about it. I suppose it made me realise that not everything revolves around my grief." Eleana snorted and swooned melodramatically. Richard frowned and folded his arms. "Oh, like you're one to claim I'm being dramatic. You attacked my dog for being exuberant, remember?"

Eleana rolled her eyes and held her hands up in surrender. Richard grinned. He watched her for a moment as she sank back into the bed, her posture stiffened with pain. He was silent for a few heartbeats. Then, "Eleana? We're friends, are we not?"

Eleana nodded. She reached out and touched her wrist to his, their fingers touching at the tips but not entwining.

Friends.

CHAPTER 10

Richard wandered the grounds some days later, Smoke at his side. He spotted Eleana, sitting calmly in the grass with her hounds running about her, and smiled. Then, he frowned. She was still weak, despite her resting and all the efforts of Mrs. Graham. But her father had returned to Hartwell the day before and she seemed to manage her duties well enough. Still, Richard saw the thinness in her and the way she winced when she overexerted herself.

He shook his head, moving forwards and intent on his errand. This would give him a chance to spend more time with her, and he was not unaware of the fact that Mrs. Graham's scheming was behind this particular outing. Nor was he unappreciative.

Hunter sat up at Richard's approach, trading sniffs and wagging tails with Smoke. Eleana waved her hand at the hounds running around and they settled. She looked up at her master with a lazy smile.

"I have been clearly informed by Mrs. Graham that if I do not go see Sir James and Mr. Vaughn, then they will come here seeking after my health. So, I thought I might see if you would go with me and make this chore a little more bearable." Richard tried not to show how much he really did not want to go, nor how much he wanted her to agree.

Eleana made a face at his proposal. With a heave of her shoulders, she sighed. And nodded.

Richard straightened his shoulders, grinning. "Thank goodness. I'm not certain that I could face Miss Martin alone."

Eleana laughed. She pushed herself to her feet, despite Richard's offered hand, and brushed off the dirt. Then, she narrowed her eyes at him and pointed to the drive, then off into the distance. Richard shrugged.

"I, ah, though we could take the cart. I will drive, of course," he said hurriedly. Eleana made another face but walked towards the drive where Mal had already gotten the cart ready. Smoke trotted eagerly along beside her, Hunter following at a more leisurely pace. Eleana hopped into the back of the cart, gesturing the two hounds up. Richard took the driver's bench and, with a knowing look from Mal, they were off.

The pair visited the Haverford estate first, a stroke of luck since everyone besides Mrs. Vaughn was present. Lord Alistair was staying to finish out the season and it seemed that Mr. Vaughn spent as much time there as he did at home. Richard drew the cart to a stop, the jolt waking a lightly dozing Eleana. Hunter and Smoke jumped down and went to inspect their new surroundings, though Richard noted that neither went far.

A footman appeared wearing the ridiculous livery of the Haverford estate. He looked at Eleana with distaste and at the dogs with unabashed annoyance.

"The dogs will stay outside," he said. Then, with a sniff, he turned and led Eleana and Richard into the house. She made a face at the footman's back but dutifully signalled Smoke and Hunter to remain with the cart. Richard had to pretend to cough quite severely to keep himself from laughing. The footman did not turn back but stiffened his shoulders and walked into the drawing room.

"Lord Byrns and Eleana," he announced. Richard led the way into the room. The footman gave another sniff, then vanished.

Sir James looked at the two of them in shock for a moment before smiling widely. "Come in, come in! I had thought about sending up a servant to inquire about your health, but I'm pleased that you came down yourself. You look much better than the last time I saw you, Lord Byrns, if a bit drawn. And Eleana, my goodness! You look as though you've dropped a stone you could not well afford to lose. What did you do, my dear, drag Lord Byrns all the way to Belleview?"

Sir James flapped a hand at the two to sit before adjusting his horsehair wig. Eleana waited until

Richard had done so before joining him on the corner of a chaise lounge.

"Not the entire distance, no, but more than a mile and three quarters, yes," Richard said calmly. "My, ah, illness was quite pressing."

Lord Alistair chuckled derisively. "Come, now, you must be joking. Surely, she cannot be that strong. I very much doubt that she just grabbed you by the ankles and pulled you to Belleview," he said, leaning back in the chair he was occupying and looking past Eleana as if she were not there.

"She used the horse's tack and fashioned a right to pull me the distance," Richard said. He didn't want to talk any further about this, especially since he saw the spark of interest in Lord Alistair's eyes, as well as those of Sir James. Mr. Vaughn, to his credit, looked disinterested. But Miss Martin, who was sitting quietly in a corner with a book, was watching with extreme interest.

"How astonishing," Sir James said. "I've never known a woman to be so strong. But, then, Eleana has always been controversial, given her position and the attire she insists on wearing."

Richard frowned at Sir James' words and noticed how Eleana bristled at the thinly veiled insult. He straightened his posture and looked at the other people in the room.

"Only her unmatched skill at training hounds is unusual, and I do not take issue with such skill. Perhaps if we were to stop underestimating women, it would not be such an unusual thing to have such strength."

Lord Alistair gave an acknowledging nod of his head, looking bored. Miss Martin looked away to hide her shock.

"Perhaps you're right," Mr. Vaughn allowed. "Tell me, are you truly building a school in the summer house of Belleview estate? I've heard such rumours."

Richard nearly smiled in relief at the tactfulness of Mr. Vaughn. He felt more than saw Eleana relax beside him and it was perfectly obvious that the topic of her daring—or scandalous—rescue would not be brought up again. Happy to oblige Mr. Vaughn, Richard explained the nuances of getting a school arranged and was soon caught up in a discussion of where to find professors and whom to hire as cooks and maids, matron, headmaster and the like. Unfortunately, he had timed this conversation ill and when the invitation was made for he and Eleana to stay for tea, Richard could hardly refuse.

He glanced at Eleana. She had made no move to communicate through the earlier conversation, but she hadn't looked unhappy or bored. He couldn't help but worry, though. After all, she had come of her own accord on the basis that they were friends.

The small group moved to the parlour for tea. Two maids walked in, carrying trays of tea and food, their gazes directed downwards. Eleana grew pale and stayed away from the two, watching them carefully. Richard looked between her and the maids and raised his brows. Eleana shook her head subtly and made no motions to explain. She did not have to.

The maids finished setting out tea and had turned to curtsey to Sir James. Footmen were taking their place, ready to serve the guests. As they were leaving, the maids caught sight of Eleana standing near Richard. The taller of the two smirked viciously. The second, who seemed to take her cues from the woman beside her, had to smother a giggle. Eleana touched her throat and turned her head away. Richard had caught the glances the two maids threw, but unfortunately, so had Sir James.

"Do you know Eleana?" he asked, seemingly more curious that the maids had become visible to his guests than the fact that they obviously held Eleana in contempt.

"Yes, sir," the first said, her blonde hair pulled neatly back on the top of her head, making her face seem sharper and crueller. "We met at the servant's celebration you so graciously threw the night of the Haverford ball not more than a month ago."

"Oh, of course," Sir James said, dismissing them with a wave of his hand and turning to the tea. Everyone else did the same, uncaring about a connection between servants. All but Richard. Eleana stared after the departing forms of the two maids. She recoiled in shock as the first turned and shot a significant glance between Eleana and Richard then cupped a hand behind her ear.

Richard tightened his lips, realising suddenly why

she had seemed so distressed the night of the Haver-ford ball. He understood why she had been so pale, why she did not communicate with him on the return journey, not even to accuse him of something in order to glare at him. Her actions that night and the days that followed became all too clear. Guilt struck Richard like a knife. He had made Eleana attend that ridiculous event simply because he hadn't wanted to attend. And, at the time, he had hated her for his own feelings. So many things had changed since then; Richard hadn't thought about that night since.

He thought about it now, though.

The group sat to tea and Lord Alistair took a sip before looking between Richard and Eleana. "Would not your Houndskeeper be more comfortable having tea in the servant's hall?"

"She came as my guest," Richard said drily, cursed be the consequences. What must everyone think of him and Eleana? They thought he had taken her as mistress, or something like it. Perhaps they thought him bound by gratitude to her for saving him. He hoped it was the latter. Because while they would not judge him for such a relationship, they *would* judge her. And Richard would not want that for anything. "I would not presume to make the mistake of sending a guest to have tea with the servants."

Miss Martin manoeuvred herself to sit between Lord Alistair and Richard, her smile meant to be endearing. "Oh, do stop teasing the poor girl," she preened. Richard was uncertain to whom that comment was directed. "I imagine that this is awkward enough for her as it is."

Eleana frowned and clutched her teacup, the slight line caused by her furrowed brows proving Miss Martin right. Richard knew that she was out of sorts, out of place. Frankly, he didn't blame her. He hated these social affairs and their subtle insinuations. He would much rather have been out riding the grounds of Belleview, or better yet, talking with Eleana.

Richard said very little for the remainder of the tea. This was, thankfully, not seen as out of character for him, so he was able to remain quiet without much speculation or mishap. He ignored the attempts of Miss Martin to draw him into conversation or make herself more appealing to him—though, thankfully, she seemed to have set her sights firmly on Lord Alistair. He listened politely to his host and nodded occasionally at a comment Mr. Vaughn made. Eleana made no motions or attempts to communicate at all, finishing her tea as quickly as was polite and then waiting patiently, hands folded in her lap, for Richard to find a moment to excuse them.

He finally finished his tea and set the cup down. "We must be returning to Belleview. Eleana has her duties to attend to and I must see to a few matters of business."

"Matters of business," Miss Martin purred, her statement almost a question.

"Indeed," Richard replied, then bowed to the group and took his leave amongst invitations to return soon.

Eleana followed, eyes ahead while she ignored the chuckles that she received from Miss Martin and Lord Alistair. Once they were safely outside, climbing into the cart with Hunter dancing around Eleana's legs, Richard let out a breath he didn't know he had been holding.

He wished strongly for a drink.

Richard closed his eyes as he pushed the need down. He gripped the horse's reins tightly in his hands, turning his knuckles white. After a moment, he relaxed and opened his eyes, giving Eleana an apologetic glance.

"I'm sorry," Richard said gruffly. "I only wanted to make sure that they knew I was well. I did not... I did not expect them to be so harsh. And the Haverford ball... I'm sorry about that, too. I had not realised people would be so cruel to you because of what I had done."

Eleana shook her head as the cart began to move under Richard's direction, placing her hand on his arm and giving a slight squeeze. She did not blame him. Or, she didn't think it was his fault. Richard wasn't sure which one it was, and he wasn't sure he wanted to know. The simple fact that Eleana forgave him was enough, though he was still angry at the others' behaviour.

"Let's go home."

Eleana smiled and closed her eyes, laying in the sunlight in the back of the cart. Richard sighed, trying to coax more speed out of the dray pulling the cart.

They neared the drive to Belleview when another ride came up the road. The driver was young—no more than a year or two older than Eleana—and wearing simple clothes. His light brown hair matched the colour of his horse, an old creature that looked to be well tended, if slow. The man was obviously not from the gentry but had done his best with what he had. None of that seemed to matter, for he was well-built and wore a bright smile. Richard imagined that he did quite well with the womenfolk about.

"Hullo there," he said, bringing his horse to a slow walk as he came up beside the cart. He was closest to Eleana and Richard frowned when he saw Hunter come to attention, immediately pricking his ears, though his body remained relaxed. Eleana watched the horse with obvious wariness, though she eyed the rider with curiosity. She made it clear that he was not known to her. "I was wondering if you could tell me the way to Belleview?"

"Belleview," Richard said, his mouth twitching in a smile at the coincidence. The man nodded brightly and patted the neck of his horse.

"I'm to meet my uncle and take up a post as an extra hand with the horses," he said. Richard nodded knowingly. He nearly laughed with amusement when Eleana shied away from the proximity of the horse, the rider drawing closer as he tried to match the cart's speed.

"You must be Theo, then," Richard said, turning the cart up the drive to Belleview. The man furrowed his brows at Richard and examined him closely.

"I'm sorry, do I know you?" he asked, moving the horse away as he turned. Eleana relaxed slightly.

"I doubt it," Richard said. "I am Lord Richard Byrns, and Belleview is mine. Mal told me he is expecting you, though I hadn't thought you would arrive for another week."

Theo sat up in shock and tried to bow as much as being horseback would allow. "I'm sorry, m'lord, I didn't realise. I hadn't thought to meet with such a great honour riding to Belleview."

Richard waved his hand in dismissal and Eleana rolled her eyes quite obviously at the flattering defer-ence. "Do not bother with the formalities. I came from the city so that I could avoid such things. Welcome to Belleview."

Theo nodded, obviously unsure of what to say to this unconventional lord. Instead, he turned his atten-tion to Eleana, bowing his head. "And is this the lady of Belleview?"

Eleana laughed, the silent mirth startling Theo and making Richard uncomfortable. Was being the lady of Belleview really so amusing to her? Such a joke? Because he would give everything he had for it to be true, for her to be his. Even after all he had done to fight it. Richard pushed aside those thoughts, knowing that for the moment, he must be content with being her friend. Instead, Richard forced an amused smile to his lips and shook his head. "This is Eleana Tarell. She is Houndskeeper at Belleview. And this is Hunter. That black mongrel is Smoke."

Theo relaxed slightly and smiled at Eleana. "It's nice to meet you, Eleana. Do you have many handsome hounds like Hunter here?"

Eleana smiled and nodded. She glanced at Richard, obviously hoping he would explain. Richard got the hint and answered in specifics that he had made himself learn properly, just to get close to Eleana's interests. "Belleview sports thirty some odd hounds, fighters, racers, two ladies' dogs and even a team of tricksters."

Theo blinked. "Don't you talk?" he asked Eleana blatantly. Eleana shook her head, a slight rose tingeing her cheeks. She tapped her throat twice and crossed her hands in the air before her, an obvious no. Theo smiled, a look meant to endear and charm, even perhaps to seduce. "Well, I'll just have to learn to speak your language."

Eleana nodded, turning her attention forwards. Richard did, too, and felt a measure of relief when the Belleview manor came into view. Mal appeared from around the house as they pulled to a stop. He spotted Theo and grinned.

"Welcome back, m'lord. Theo! How are you? It's so good to see you. I hadn't thought you would be coming until later, so your room's not ready yet. You can make do, I imagine," Mal greeted, taking the dray's head and grinning proudly at his nephew.

Theo dismounted his horse and shook hands firmly with his uncle. "It's good to see you, too."

Richard climbed off the cart and walked around to

help Eleana. Theo, though, got there first. He caught hold of her hand and helped her out of the cart. The dogs leaped to the ground with ease, eager to smell this new person. Meanwhile, Eleana ducked her head in thanks and walked off towards the kennels, waving to Richard as she did so.

He waved back weakly in reply, then turned towards the two men before him, forcing himself to smile pleasantly. "Well, I'm glad for Mal's sake that you could come. I hope you'll enjoy Belleview. I had planned a small celebration for the servants for your arrival, but I'm afraid you'll have caught Mrs. Graham by surprise. Tomorrow, then, we can see about the celebration."

He didn't wait for his words to be politely refuted, as he knew they would be, but instead turned and walked up to Belleview manor, desperately wishing that he had a drink. He couldn't help but be jealous of Theo for having the foresight and the gallantry to help Eleana out of the cart. He could see that the new hand was interested in Eleana. While Richard didn't know where her feelings stood, he was certain that she would not dislike Theo. And to enjoy the company of someone closer to her own station... So, he was jealous. There had to be something he could do that would prove his love to Eleana.

Still, even Richard could not dislike Theo. He had such a happy manner about him, had such charm and ease. Nor did he seem to be cruel or false.

Richard stormed into the library and grumbled to

himself as he sat at his desk, staring blankly at the letters to be answered before him. Someone knocked on his door and Hayes came in with a tray and a single, small glass of amber liquid in the centre.

"Is that all?" Richard breathed as Hayes handed over the glass.

"Yes, m'lord," Hayes said. Richard put the drink to his lips and threw back his head, empty the glass with practised ease. He knew that this was the only option, that he had to stop his drinking or he would end up drowning his sorrows permanently. It was a good thing that he was lessening his dose of alcohol until he could go one day, then two, then a week, without that drink. And yet, as he set his shaking hands on the desk, he wanted more.

Hayes spared a sympathetic look to his master and took the empty glass, leaving the room and Richard in solitude.

Richard curled his fingers to a fist and slammed it down on the table, wanting to scream or to cry or anything. Instead, he took three deep breaths and forced himself to relax, turning instead to his letters of business and reading through the first one to be answered. He threw himself into his work because he could not throw himself into the drink, or Eleana. Though, he had a feeling that she was the only one who really understood what he was going through.

THEO ADAPTED QUICKLY to his work, Eleana noted. It took less than a day for him to be well known amongst the household. Many of the women and girls in the household also took to making eyes at him when he passed and giggling together when he was gone. Eleana had only seen this twice, during breakfast and luncheon, but she couldn't help but be amused.

That night, though, there was a true reason to be grateful for Theo's appearance: the celebration. It was really little more than a small feast for the household staff, but it was still an excuse to dress up and to eat good food. Only, Eleana forgot about the banquet until her growling stomach told her she'd been working too hard. She'd not been able to do everything that she would have liked, thanks to her still weakened state. She was trying to build her strength again, but she hadn't been eating as much.

This banquet could be a good thing.

Eleana slunk into the servant's hall a few minutes late. Everyone was already assembled and watched her as she took her normal seat. Fey suppressed a smile and shook her head at Eleana's shrug of apology. She hadn't even changed from her patched breeches and shirt, unlike the rest of the staff.

Theo had been placed in the seat beside hers. Eleana was handed a plate of food and tried to ignore the questing look of Theo beside her, annoyed and embarrassed to feel her cheeks grow warm. Hayes stood.

"We are pleased to hold this banquet in honour of

the newest member of the household, Theo. We hope that you will get along well here at Belleview."

Theo nodded and smiled, making a few of the other servants grin and blush with pleasure. Hayes shook his head and sat. Everyone did the same, immediately taking part of the comparative feast.

Theo had barely taken two bites of his dinner when his attention diverted to Eleana, eating with well-mannered gusto. "Does Hunter always go where you are?"

Eleana looked up from her meal and met the warm brown eyes of Theo, surprised at the question. She glanced at Hunter who lay at her feet, his head resting on his paws while he watched her. At her attention, he lifted his head hopefully. Eleana petted him then nodded to Theo, smiling more at her dog than at him.

But that was, apparently, enough for Theo. "He is quite the hound. And very well trained."

Eleana gave a modest, half-shrug of her shoulders and tried to return her attention to her food. She was unsuccessful. Theo managed another couple of mouthfuls before launching once again into conversation with her, seemingly unintimidated by the fact that she had to signal her words to him, the gestures grandiose because he did not yet understand her nuances.

Hayes stood sometime later, signalling the end of the meal. Eleana blinked and was surprised to realise that it felt like very little time had passed at all. Perhaps Theo would be a pleasant dinner companion after all. Still, Eleana stood as well, getting out of the way of the kitchen maids and walking towards the door. Theo followed.

The night air was crisp and cool. Eleana stretched happily, wincing slightly as her shoulder muscles strained, not completely healed yet.

"Are you alright?" Theo asked, having seen the discomfort on her face. Eleana flapped a hand dismissively and started across the yard to the kennels and her own cottage, Hunter at her heels. Theo looked towards the stables then back to Eleana. "Wait," he called.

Eleana turned, confused, though not unhappy.

Theo caught up with her and smiled rakishly at her. "May I walk you to your cottage?"

Eleana narrowed her eyes playfully and shrugged. It was nothing to her whether he did or didn't. Besides, he was pleasant enough company. Maybe he wanted to inspect the hounds. She set off for her cottage, Theo beside her. Hunter raced ahead and then back to his mistress' side, tongue lolling. Eleana laughed when Theo tried to chase the dog.

They reached the door to Eleana's cottage soon enough and she opened the door, letting Hunter race inside before turning to bid goodnight to Theo.

"Goodnight," he said, suddenly much closer than Eleana had thought. Unconsciously, she took a step backwards, bumping into the doorframe, glad for the support of the cottage. Theo watched her movements for a second before slowly stepping forwards until their two bodies were brushing.

"Eleana," Theo said, "please don't think me forward, but I am going to kiss you now."

And he did just that. The touch of his lips against hers was light and gentle and yet sent a tingling sensation coursing through Eleana's body. She couldn't help it; she kissed him back. Theo pulled away a moment later, smiling contentedly. He dipped his head respectfully to her then turned and walked away, hands swinging at his side.

Eleana remained against the wall of her cottage, her hand brushing her lips, staring after Theo. She wasn't quite certain what she felt about this newcomer, but this sort of diversion was most assuredly a pleasant one.

CHAPTER 11

Eleana couldn't help but think about the kiss. It had felt good, if a little strange. Part of her wanted him to do it again. Part of her, though, knew that the guilt was too much. She hadn't done anything like, hadn't had anyone interested in her like that, for so long. Not since that day, nearly six years ago... Eleana shook her head to clear her mind, but the knowledge of what she'd done, no matter how good it felt, hung over her like a cloud.

Thankfully, the next few weeks passed without a repeat of the kiss, though Eleana was happy to talk with Theo at mealtimes. During the day, they were both too busy to spend much time together, for which Eleana was quietly grateful. She liked Theo. She didn't want to hurt him, and she was certain that they would be good friends. But she wanted no more than that.

Grateful for any distraction, Eleana trained her hounds as always, giving them baths on a weekly basis.

Her efforts did not go unnoticed. Richard, his now pristinely trained Smoke at his side, would wander out to the kennels nearly every day. His simple friendship granted Eleana the chance to be open and free, unguarded, unlike how she had to be around Theo.

"You're working with the tricksters quite a bit," Richard noted as he looked up at Eleana from where he lounged on the grass, a portable writing desk propped at his side, letters waiting to be read and attended to sitting in a pile beside him. Eleana nodded, releasing the hounds from that set so they could flop on the ground and enjoy the sun.

She sat on the ground beside Richard, warm and tired, the sun beating down on her mercilessly now that summer was full upon them. Eleana considered for a moment, then put her fingers to the corner of her mouth and grinned widely, then frowned, her face screwed up in melodramatic sadness. She stood and pretended to balance as she took a few steps forwards and started a strange, gypsy dance.

Finally, the shock dissipated from Richard's features as understanding took hold. "A fair?" he asked, flushing slightly from the heat of the day. Eleana nodded and sat down again with a huff. She gestured to the tricksters. "You compete? Or do you just show them?" Richard asked, now closing his writing desk. Eleana indicated the first option. She stretched and lay back, staring up at the sky, her braid splayed on the ground beneath her head. "Does it come every year?" Richard pressed, sporting a boyish grin.

Eleana nodded, quirking her brows.

"I haven't been to a fair since I was a child," Richard said. "My father used to take me every year. We would go to a small village just outside of town and stay at an inn for a couple of nights, going to the fair during the day. I remember watching the dancers and eating food with my fingers. It was… magical."

She smiled, nodding.

"Of course," Richard continued wryly, "my mother did not approve of such common and frivolous activity."

Eleana scoffed. She propped her head up in a hand and rolled her eyes.

"It is unbecoming for the son of a Marquess and the heir to a fortune. He should be studying literature or politics, preparing for a life in parliament or law," Richard mocked, pitching his voice an octave higher. Eleana laughed, trying to cover her mouth in politeness. Richard's face, though, was bright and happy and a bit ridiculous, making all her efforts in vain. She shook her head at him and lay back on the ground. She would have been happy to do nothing but rest there a while, warmed by the sun and kept company by a friend.

Work beckoned, though. Eleana sighed and sat up, climbing to her feet. She called her dozing dogs to attention and they began the set again. Absently, Eleana noted that Richard was frowning when he stared down at his writing desk, but she did not stop to question. It was not her place.

RICHARD ENJOYED these afternoon tete-a-tetes with Eleana more than he could express. He had become so accustomed to them that he no longer bothered with waiting until Eleana had begun training the dogs. He would just meet her outside, waiting with a book or papers to sort through or simply a stalk of grass between his fingers. Until, that is, one afternoon when he went out to meet her as usual. Richard passed the stables and Theo, the new hand, greeted him with a cheerful smile. Smoke walked at Richard's heel, sniffing around eagerly. He made it all the way to the kennels before realising that there was no sign of Eleana.

He poked his head into the kennels and saw all the hounds in their cages, sitting or pacing, sleeping, or just watching the world. But there was no Eleana. The connecting door to the cottage was ajar, though. Curious, not yet worried, Richard knocked before opening the door and walking inside.

He had never been inside Eleana's cottage before and was amazed at how simple it was. The furnishings were all old and worn and there were very few decorations or homely touches at all. The actual living space was small and yet seemed perfectly suited to Eleana. A slight clicking sound caught his attention and Richard saw Hunter walking out of the bedroom, his claws scraping against the wood.

"Hello," he said, crouching to greet the dog. He

looked around, expecting Eleana to appear directly after her faithful hound. She did not. Smoke touched noses with Hunter and Richard stood, a slight knot of worry building in his chest. He knocked on the door to the bedroom before looking inside. Eleana was nowhere to be seen. "Eleana?" Richard called, moving out of the bedroom and searching the rest of the cottage. Panic rose within him. He searched the buildings thrice before accepting the fact that she was not there.

He looked at Hunter and wondered, with steadily growing alarm, where Eleana would have gone without her dog. He left the cottage by way of the kennel, ordering Smoke and Hunter to follow him, and jogged back to the house. He passed the stables on the way and saw Theo, hauling a bale of hay, sweat dripping down his brow.

"Have you seen Eleana?" Richard asked. Theo looked up in surprise. He frowned at the sight of Hunter at Richard's heel, but shook his head. Richard nodded, trying to remain calm. "Right, thank you." He turned and walked swiftly up to the house, ducking into the servants' entrance and looking around wildly. The cook stared in shock before dropping into a curtsey.

Mrs. Graham walked in, a ledger in her hands, and caught sight of Richard. She smiled. "M'lord, what are you doing down—ah. I see." She had spotted Hunter and her expression went from cheerful to flat almost instantaneously. She closed the ledger with a snap. "I think you had better come with me."

Mrs. Graham led Richard to the small room that Hayes used as an office to manage everything and closed the door behind her, gesturing to the small wooden chair that stood against the wall. "Sit."

Richard sat.

Smoke leaned against his legs, and Hunter sat a few inches away, calm and collected, as if he went without Eleana every day.

"I went out to the kennels and she was not there. I thought perhaps she was in her cottage. Hunter was there, but she was not. I've never seen her without him, what else could I do? I panicked." Richard rubbed his palms on his legs.

Mrs. Graham looked solemnly at Richard and leaned against the simple desk that dominated the room. She folded her hands primly in front of her. "I'm going to tell you this because I very much doubt that Eleana will do so and because it is high time you knew. Truthfully, I doubt Eleana has ever discussed this with anyone. Very few who are around now remember it or even knew about it, truth be told."

Richard swallowed in terror, imagining all sorts of catastrophes involving Eleana's lack of speech or perhaps her death mother. He never could have guessed the truth.

"When Eleana was ten and learning the ropes of training, as well as putting her own stamp on things, considering her silence, a boy came to Belleview. He was fourteen and was an orphan, sent from the workhouse to be an apprentice to the head groundsman. His name was William Renaulds. From the beginning, he and Eleana were friends. Being the only children on the estate, it was only natural that Eleana adored William. She hung on his every word and when she wasn't with her father or the hounds and dogs, she was trailing him. It got to be so that you would never see one without the other."

Mrs. Graham smiled, caught up in the memory. Richard felt a stab of jealousy deep in his chest. He knew it was futile—or he hoped so—but there it remained all the same.

"When Eleana turned sixteen, beautiful and silent, William asked her to marry him. They would live in the little cottage next to the kennels and work at Belleview. They would raise their children here. By this time, of course, Eleana's father had bequeathed his position to her and, expecting that she would live happily with William, had moved to Hartwell. Everything was joy for those two. They were so perfectly suited to one another. Oh, they fought sometimes. Wild, raging fights which left one or the other sleeping in the servants' quarters at the main house, but the next day they forgave one another, and it was as if nothing had ever come between them."

Richard wasn't certain he liked this story, not for any particular reason but that he knew it was going to end badly. Eleana's happiness would be ruined and tragedy would set in. Had William beaten her? Had he run off with someone else? But what did that have to do with Hunter? And why was Eleana alone, nowhere to be found?

Mrs. Graham took in a deep breath, her gaze now focused on the wall over Richard's shoulder. "It was after one of these fights, worse than the others, that William decided to buy Eleana a gift to make up for his behaviour. Now, neither of them had much money, so what he wanted to do was that much more dramatic. He went to town and bought Eleana her very own pup. This dog would not be owned by Belleview; he would be hers. The dog was a little less than a year old at the time, untrained, a bit wild. William was bringing the dog back to Eleana, half-soaked from a storm that had broken out. She… she walked out to greet him, all forgiven. Then thunder broke. The dog was startled and frightened out of his wits."

"No," Richard whispered. Mrs. Graham nodded.

"He turned on William, savaging his arm and his leg. William… he died two days later," Mrs. Graham said, her voice no longer full of emotion but clinical and distant, as if she were discussing the news from the former colonies rather than remembering someone she had known. "Eleana was devastated. She communicated with no one, not even her father, for months. She spent all her time training that last gift William had given her because she couldn't bear to abandon something he had bought especially for her. She came away from those training sessions bruised and heartbroken."

"Hunter," Richard said, looking at the beautiful

black and white dog before him. He tried to imagine the loyal, quiet, well-trained and loving hound killing a man. He was horrified. Mrs. Graham nodded again.

"That is the best dog she's ever trained, and I think it is the only thing she's allowed herself to love after losing William. Frankly, I'm not sure she ever quite healed from that. She wouldn't communicate with anyone about it, and she still won't. She never opened herself up to another man since. Maybe that's why she's such a good Houndskeeper, setting aside the fact that she's been training her whole life. Because she has nothing else," Mrs. Graham said with a shrug. Richard pulled his lips tight.

"But where is she?" he finally asked. "And why isn't Hunter with her?"

Mrs Graham looked startled, as if she thought that she had answered his questions already. "Today is the anniversary of his death. She always puts Hunter in her cottage and spends the day at his grave. She visits often enough, but she only lets herself truly remember him on this day every year. She opens those old wounds and comes back more broken than before. It's a terrifying thing to watch."

Richard baulked. The anxiety that had been building in him was now justifiably acute. He couldn't let her go out there and ruin herself over a lover six years dead, no matter what scars had been opened or unhealed. It was precisely what he had been doing over his Christina and look what that had made him: drunk, angry, destructive, and alone. He did not know where the gravesite was, and he very much doubted that Mrs. Graham would tell him.

"Thank you," Richard murmured. Mrs. Graham wrung her hands together before taking a deep breath and straightening. She then shuffled towards the door.

"You needed to know," she said. "And if you were wise, you wouldn't mention it to her." Richard returned her advice with a grim smile. Mrs. Graham frowned. "You wouldn't."

"I have to," he replied. "I love her."

With that, Richard called the dogs to him and strode from the house. He crouched before Hunter, unable to suppress the slight distress when he now looked at the dog. Smoke wagged his tail and bounded in circles, but Hunter just sat, calm and solemn and quiet. Richard looked into the dog's eyes and whispered a command that he desperately hoped would work. "Find Eleana."

Hunter pricked his ears and started off immediately, his tail held in the air like a banner. Hunter kept looking back, as if silently chastising Richard for being so slow. The dog moved to the forest, breaking out into a trot as he reached the main path. Richard ran behind, wondering when he had gotten to be so old that he couldn't run without feeling his lungs weighing him down. Or perhaps that was his worry.

It seemed ages before Hunter veered off from the path, darting down a sparsely travelled trail that was nearly covered by undergrowth. Richard grumbled as he was forced to slow, the nettles tugging at his breeches and boots. Soon, though, the undergrowth cleared, and the gravesite opened before him.

Hunter halted at the edge of the clearing, a single whine revealing his desire to go to his mistress. Smoke, too, stayed away, seeming to sense that something was not right. Only Richard walked forwards into the heart wrenching scene before him. Eleana knelt on the ground before a stone marker. She wore a simple frock that was wrinkled and twisted from clenching her hands in the fabric. Her hair looked as though it had been pulled at more than once. Her arms were wrapped around her middle, fingers clenching tightly. Her face was twisted in a picture of agony; she was trying to scream, but no matter how much she strained, she could make no noise.

Richard's heart nearly cracked at the sight of Eleana in such pain. He stepped forwards and carefully, softly, knelt down next to her and put his hand on her shoulder. "It's going to be alright."

To his surprise, Eleana did not start at his presence or seem to resent his words. Instead, she turned and moved into his arms, burying her tear-streaked face into his chest. Richard wrapped his arms around her and rocked her gently from side to side, murmuring to her over and over again, "It's going to be alright."

He let Eleana cry herself out, only feeling a twinge of guilt at feeling pleased to have her in his arms, to have her need him. And when her despair turned to anger, he let her beat against his shoulders until she subsided into tears again. Finally, she had calmed and was simply laying in Richard's arms, safe from reality. He murmured to her stories of his own pain, trying to take her mind off of things.

"...I mean, I loved her. Everything about her. And when she was gone, it was like my whole life was ripped away. That was not true, though. I came here and I started over. I'm starting a school. I get to talk with you. I'm well on my way to becoming sober, though that was not intended. And I find that I'm not quite so sad anymore. Yes, I loved her. I lost her. But that does not mean I have to stop loving her or that I cannot be happy. I can love more than one person. Life moves on. She would not have wanted me to linger over her memory, desperate and in pain, hating the world around me because it was making me happy and I felt I did not deserve such a thing when she was not here. So, here I am. And I think I'm doing alright, wouldn't you say?"

Eleana turned in his arms so that she could look up at him, her eyes red and blotchy, a sad smile now flickering across her lips.

Richard smiled in return. "There. Is that better?"

Eleana nodded, taking a deep breath. Richard let out a small sigh, knowing that he would lose the strength that was keeping him from kissing Eleana if he sat like that for much longer. He stood, helping Eleana to her feet. She kept hold of him as she did so, her arm twining with his.

They walked back through the forest like that, side by side, the dogs following a pace behind. "Do you still love him?" Richard asked, unable to prevent himself. Eleana considered for a moment then shook her head. She touched her temple as if thinking then touched her heart. "You love the memory," Richard said. He understood; it was much the same with him. He loved the memory of his wife, but she was not there. His heart was free to be given to Eleana.

Richard said nothing further on that topic, content for the moment to simply walk with Eleana on his arm, under his protection.

She looked up at him and touched her lips, bowing her head. The gesture surprised Richard for a moment and he thought she wanted him to kiss her. He realised, before he did just that, that the gesture was one of profound thanks. The question in Eleana's eyes when she looked up again confirmed it. "You're welcome," Richard said, choosing to acknowledge the thanks before the question. "As to why… I did it because you needed me."

Eleana furrowed her brows, confused by his answer. Richard searching his mind to try and find an explanation that would work without having to say the fateful word that seemed continuously on his tongue around Eleana. "Because that's what friends do. And we are friends, are we not?"

Eleana nodded and touched her wrist with his, their fingers barely touching. Friends. The gesture nearly broke Richard's heart.

ONCE THEY REACHED the edge of the forest, Richard and Eleana moved apart, both feeling regret at the motion. They walked out into the yard together, close but not touching. He smiled at her and then walked slowly back towards the main house, Smoke at his side.

Eleana went into the cottage and drew a bath, her mind working furiously while she tried to come to terms with everything. She cleaned herself and pulled on her most comfortable pair of trousers and a shirt, deciding to take the rest of the day off. She tidied up around the cottage and fed her hounds before walking across the lawn to the servant's entrance at the dinner bell. She did not particularly want to be in company, but it would be better than being alone.

Theo was already sitting in the seat beside Eleana's, talking with one of the groundsmen at his left. Eleana slipped onto the bench beside him and Hayes gave the signal for food to be served and eaten. Eleana ate slowly, content to just listen the conversations around her.

Theo, though, was already trying to draw her into conversation. "My uncle says that once the brood mare drops her foal, I'll be the one to train it. For now, though, I'm stuck hauling hay and mucking out the stables. You know the horse his lordship rides? Well, I've been looking it over and I've never seen such a well-built horse. It's certainly not a racer or a draft horse, but it's got good blood. I wonder who the sire and dam were."

Eleana tried to make her smile more than polite. It

was good to hear about Theo's passions and interests, especially when they reflected her own so well. But she was worn out from her day. Even as their conversation moved from horses to the upcoming fair, the memories of William that Eleana had been carrying around for so many years didn't seem so painful. By the time she was detailing her plans for the tricksters, the pain of her memories was completely forgotten.

"I thought you had to be in the fair to compete," Theo said, brows pushed together in confusion. "I'm sure your dogs will do well, but isn't it a bit unusual?"

Eleana shrugged and shook her head, a wide sweep of her hands and a few twists of her fingers telling Theo that anyone could compete so long as they had dogs. "I wonder if Uncle would let me try out some of the horses. I doubt it, though. He doesn't keep any jumpers or show horses around. Just his lordship's stallion, the two for the coach, a brood mare, and an old hunter ready for pasture. There are the horses that the tenant farmers use, but they're all draft horses, useful for labour. Oh, well. I suppose it doesn't matter. I'll just have to watch you compete and then we can wander about."

Eleana blinked and tilted her head in question at Theo, remaining seated even as a kitchen maid took the empty plate from before her. Even as Fey waved to Eleana in an invitation to talk.

Theo smiled sheepishly. "If that is alright with you, of course."

Eleana's half-shrug spoke her confusion.

"Well, I was rather hoping that we could go to the fair… together."

Eleana blushed. She neatly scolded herself for her folly. But Theo looked so earnest, so bright and cheerful. And, thanks to Richard, her heart no longer ached as it once had. Eleana rubbed her breastbone, easing the ache there, and she nodded.

CHAPTER 12

The fair arrived in Hartwell with a flurry of activity and excitement. Children dashed in from the fields or their lessons, yelling and playing as the fair folk set everything up. The news of its arrival, and of all the wonderful things it contained, spread like wildfire through the county. The boy that ran the message up to Belleview received a large sweet cake for his troubles. From there, every person in Belleview knew of the fair before luncheon.

"The fair's here," Fey said to Eleana while the Houndskeeper trouped in for her own luncheon. Eleana straightened and grinned widely, excitement coursing through her. "Are you going to go down early to register your tricksters or go down with Theo later?" Eleana furrowed her brows. "Oh, don't even try to play that game with me. I know you're going to the fair with Theo. Do you want me to help you with your hair or clothes?"

Eleana chuckled and shook her head, waving to Fey. It wasn't like *that*, she tried to impress. Fey just smirked and shook her head, earning a sigh from Eleana. She held out her hands in supplication.

"Don't look at me! You got yourself into this mess, you get yourself out of it," Fey laughed. "You can be the one to tell Theo that you're *just* friends."

Eleana huffed and shook her head. Fey opened her mouth to say more when Theo walked in, sliding into the chair beside Eleana and giving Hunter an absent pat on the head.

He looked at Eleana, a sly smile dancing at the corners of his mouth. "What would you say about having dinner in town? I know that we were planning on going after dinner here, but I've heard of this nice place that I thought you might like. And then we can go straight on to the fair," Theo said, eyes sparkling.

Eleana threw Fey a desperate glance but the other woman just shook her head, still smiling. She shrugged to Theo before pointing to Hunter and holding up three fingers, twirling them through the air.

Theo frowned. "Oh, right. I forgot you have to register the tricksters. I… I suppose we'll go down after dinner." Eleana covered Theo's hand with her own, eyes apologetic. Theo blinked away his disappointment and squeezed Eleana's hand. "Don't be sorry. You're going to win a great prize for Belleview, proving to everyone that you're the best Houndskeeper around. We can have dinner another time."

That hadn't been quite what she meant, but the

result was close enough. Eleana stared at her place setting, trying to pay attention to the small talk that Theo was producing while they waited for everyone else to filter into the hall for luncheon. Hayes was just walking in when a footman, who was on duty should something happen during their meal, burst in, an alarmed look on his face.

"There's someone coming up the drive to Belleview. A coach and two is pulling and I'd say that the coach is of fine quality. There are trunks on the back and a servant riding," the footman huffed to Hayes, catching the attention of everyone in the hall.

"That's unusual. His lordship doesn't have visitors, especially not for the long term. And if he were expecting someone, he would have told either Mrs Graham or myself," Hayes muttered. He looked at the expectant group of people and sighed in annoyance. "We will have luncheon once I've cleared this matter up. I shall want you, Mrs Graham, and two footmen. Theo, you see to the horses. If they're hired, just give them water and a bit of feed. If not, then see to them. Step lively, everyone."

Eleana made a face at Hunter. The dog was already on his feet, watching the activity with interest. She gestured towards the door. Hunter preceded her and she spared one longing look for the luncheon before trudging back to the kennels.

RICHARD EXAMINED an original sketch of Belleview manor as it was being built, wondering if there were something that he should be doing to improve the house. All the work on the summer house revealed very few problems that needed fixing, but it was twenty years more modern than Belleview manor. Mrs. Graham burst into the room, startling Richard. She looked flustered and a little alarmed. His heart leapt into his throat. Had something happened to Eleana?

"M'lord," Mrs. Graham said, trying to sound calm. She failed. "There's someone coming up the drive. It looks as though they mean to stay for a while."

"What?" Richard asked, simultaneously relieved and alarmed. Who would be coming to stay *here*? "I shall see to it," he said, following Mrs. Graham to the main hall where Hayes was already waiting, wringing his hands. The butler opened the door for Richard and he went outside just as the coach was pulling up to the entrance, the driver looking relieved to be at the end of his journey. Richard spotted a man seated at the back of the coach and frowned. He seemed familiar.

The moment the coach stopped, the door flew open. Richard knew then precisely why the man in the back of the coach looked familiar, and why the occupant of the coach was here. He was mildly pleased, completely shocked, and slightly annoyed at this unexpected intrusion from a time he had thought long past. Richard took a deep breath before marching down the steps as his past stepped out to greet him, a look of wonderment on his face.

He was tall and lean, his features finely sculpted and his blonde hair tied back with a simple ribbon. None of the ridiculous wigs and fashions for him, Richard knew, just whatever looked best to his advantage. His appearance was one designed to impress, to seem both cavalier and precise. Richard smiled at the memories, earning a grin from his guest. "You old dog! This is a magnificent place you have here."

"Henry Marduke," Richard said, smiling almost as broadly. "I have to say, I never thought I'd see you here at Belleview."

At this Henry frowned, his expression serious. "That's only because you dashed away from town with no good-bye, no forwarding address, nothing," Richard winced. He directed his friend into the house while Theo took care of the horses. Hayes greeted Henry's driver and then Richard and his guest were left alone.

"I'm sorry for that," Richard admitted, sitting on one of the couches in the drawing room. Smoke nudged his hand. "It's just…"

"Richard, I know just what it was," Henry sighed. "And I understand. I place no blame on you. That's all in the past, though I wish that you would have at least sent a letter telling me that you were alright. I had to track down someone who was a friend of someone else who worked with your solicitor to find out where you were."

"And then you decided to show up unannounced

and stay?" Richard asked, a little surprised at the teasing tone in his voice. Henry nodded. He flicked out the skirt of his coat and sat on a chair beside Richard, looking as rakish as Richard remembered.

"If I had written ahead, would you have let me stay?" Henry asked, giving him a knowing glance. Richard smiled and laughed.

"I know full well the consequences if I had refused. You are always welcome at Belleview, Henry," he said. "How long have you been travelling? You must be hungry. Mrs. Graham? Oh, just when you want her— There you are! Mrs. Graham, would it be possible to get luncheon early today? Or perhaps some tea, if that interferes too much with your schedule."

Mrs. Graham blinked, looking between the two men. She nodded, somewhere between confused and deferential. "Of course we can have an early luncheon made up, m'lord. I shall see to it immediately." With that, she bustled off.

Henry watched her go, then settled into the chair, looking at the drawing room with a pleased expression. "I must say, old boy, this is quite the pile. And it looks as though the country's done you some good. There's none of that drooping grief about you. I'm astonished." Richard gave a vague mumble of an answer and patted Smoke's head, the dog looking at Henry with a sloppy grin. "And surely that's not the same Smoke that you had in the city," Henry said, pointing at the dog. He leaned closer to peer at him.

"Of course it is," Richard scoffed.

Henry shook his head. "That is not the same Smoke. The dog that I knew wouldn't hesitate to run forwards and slather me with his tongue, getting dirt and who knows what else on my trousers. This dog is well-behaved and hasn't even run forwards once. He's sitting quietly. I never knew Smoke to sit quietly," Henry chuckled. Richard was about to tell his friend about the wonders of Eleana when he froze. Did he want his friend from a life that seemed to belong to someone else to know about his love? Not that he could ever reveal it to Eleana. Not yet, at least. He scolded himself; he was being silly. What harm could Henry possibly do?

"The Houndskeeper here is exceptional," Richard said. "Best trained dogs I've ever seen. In fact, three tricksters of the Belleview estate are going to be entered in competition at the fair, today."

"A fair? Well, I came at just the right time, then," Henry said with a mischievous grin. "Tricksters, eh? I thought they were the hardest to train, what with all the special commands for certain executions and such. After luncheon, you really must show me around. I want to see the estate."

"The entirety of Belleview would take quite a while to see," Richard said. Henry raised his brows in question and Richard suddenly felt a little foolish. "There's near twenty thousand acres."

"My, my. When you buy a country estate, you really buy a country estate, old boy," Henry laughed outright. Richard smiled, knowing that he was right. He had bought Belleview almost without thinking, without realising the enormity of the place and certainly without worrying about the price. He didn't regret it in the slightest.

Though he hadn't seen Henry in many months, Richard had no trouble talking with his friend. The two discussed everything that had happened in the last few months over luncheon and then Richard led a tour of the house and grounds. He told Henry everything except for the one thing that mattered: Eleana. There was something holding him back and even though he took Henry near the kennels, they didn't get much closer than a vague distance.

Eleana learned of Henry Marduke through Theo, who had spoken to Fey who had spoken with Mrs. Graham who had heard near everything that Richard had said with the newcomer. Not that she was eaves-dropping, of course.

"He's a friend of his lordship from the city," Theo said, bringing Eleana her portion of the late and hurried servant's luncheon. She had missed it, as she was working with one of the fighters who had recently had pups. She was refining the dog's training and introducing the pups to human contact, sitting on the ground and playing with them while listening to Theo.

He sat next to her and took Eleana's pup, letting her eat. "Apparently, his lordship left the city without a good-bye or saying where he was going. He sold his belongings and left, and this friend of his had to ask around to figure out where he had gone. So, now he's staying for a while," Theo explained, yelping as the pup closed his jaws on his finger. Eleana laughed as he pried the dog's jaws open and pulled out his finger. He grumbled and Eleana reached for the pup, drawing his lips up and showing Theo. "Just because the dog doesn't have teeth doesn't mean that didn't hurt," he muttered.

Eleana laughed all the harder, her features lit up with mirth and her silent laughter infectious. Theo tried to keep a straight face, tried to pout and draw sympathy from Eleana, but she would have none of it. Finally, she saw the carefully concealed hurt in Theo's eyes and knew that behind his smile, he was feeling wounded, either because she had laughed at him or because she hadn't cared that he had been bitten. Eleana stopped laughing, though she continued to smile, and reached out for Theo's 'hurt' hand.

The hostler held out his hand, watching carefully as she held up his finger and inspected it. Eleana knew there was no true injury to his hand but held it gingerly in any case, lifting it to her eyes and examining it from every angle. Then, she kissed her finger and touched it to his. She nodded firmly and released Theo's hand. He sighed and rolled his eyes. "Yes, that's much better."

She nodded and let go of Theo's hand to lunge for the pup as he reached her food. The mother huffed when Eleana deposited the pup near her paws. Eleana looked distastefully at her luncheon, now ruined. She sighed and set it aside.

"I'll see if I can beg something from the kitchens, if you like," Theo suggested. Eleana considered this for a moment before shaking her head. She climbed to her feet and stretched before rounding up mother and puppies and taking them all back into the kennel. Theo was up when Eleana returned, holding the remains of what looked to have been a tasty lunch, before the pup got in the way, that is.

"I have to go get ready for the fair, what with the early dinner and the walk and everything," Theo said, stepping closer to Eleana. "I'll see you in a few hours, alright?" He reached for her hand. Eleana quickly nodded, smiling, while sticking her hands in her pockets. She ignored the look Theo gave her. But he said nothing further, just walked away across the yard, his gait light and his posture easy.

The fair, for being a travelling event and in a small, country town, was full of entertainment. There were fire dancers and lively musicians, games for children to play and games for adults. There were booths of wares to be sold, pens of exotic animals, rings for competitions, various food and drink, and enough to keep everyone enthralled for the entirety of the fair's duration. It drew in people from all over the county, even beyond, and was one of the most anticipated events of the year.

The first night of the fair, though, was something special.

Those from Belleview who were inclined to go straggled down to the fair at various points in the evening, with Eleana and Theo going first to register the tricksters, Richard and Henry going after their dinner, and various others coming down at different points in the evening. Even Mrs Graham made her way to the fair, leaving a fussy Hayes behind to watch over the remaining staff.

"Come on, El," Theo urged, pulling Eleana away from the kennel where she had registered the three dogs, Hunter staying to guard them, though Eleana doubted anything would happen. "I hear music and where there's music, there's dancing."

Eleana allowed herself to be pulled through the crowds of people, marvelling at the sights of the fair and wondering if it got more elaborate each year or if it were just her own thoughts. Theo was right, of course, about the music and he barely asked her permission before swinging her into the ring of dancers, grinning as she threw back her head and laughed, silent as always.

The wonderful thing about the fair was that it brought people from all walks of life. The wealthy danced with the tenant farmer's wife. The lowly labourer could talk freely with those high above his station. Eleana was twirled from hostler to solicitor to doctor and back to Theo, not one of them minding her strange attire or her silence. Fey passed her, wearing colourful skirts and a smile wide enough to rival Theo's.

After three dances, Eleana finally managed to stumble out of the myriad of dancers and to a bench where she could rest. Theo found her a moment later, holding two glasses of what looked to be spiced wine. She eagerly drank one, smiling her gratitude.

A gong, followed by some eager shouts, sounded from across the fairgrounds, catching her attention. Eleana put the spiced wine down on the bench and jumped to her feet, grinning. She started off, her legs carrying her towards the sound. Theo called out in alarm and followed close behind. They ran through the throngs of people, Eleana trying her best to be polite in her excitement. She stopped at the edge of a large circuit ringed with the temporary kennels holding the various teams of tricksters. Eleana bounced on the balls of her feet, her entire body thrumming with excitement, and she moved towards her own kennel, signalling Hunter through the swarms of patrons.

"Eleana, wait!" Theo called, trying to keep up with her.

Eleana stopped before the kennel, kneeling down and exchanging grins with her dogs. They knew what was coming and they were just as excited as their mistress, their entire bodies wriggling with energy. Hunter nudged Eleana and she pressed her head to his, starting in surprise when Theo touched her arm. She turned and Theo looked on her with wide eyes.

"Don't do that. I was worried that something was wrong."

Eleana shook her head and stood, pointing towards

the circuit, smile wide. Theo sighed and ran a hand over his hair. "Yes, I realise that now but when you just took off, I thought something had gone wrong." Eleana pouted dramatically and he chuckled, though he still seemed upset. "Yes, alright. You're forgiven."

A hush fell over those around as an older man with sly eyes and gaudy, mismatched clothing stepped into the centre of the circuit, addressing those around him. "Welcome, my lovely ladies and magnificent gentle-men. We thank you for coming out this evening to witness this competition of talents. The first event of the night is the competition of tricksters, hounds trained to dance and twirl, to jump and spin. They are beautiful and perhaps some of the most difficult hounds to train properly. Tonight, for your pleasure, we have teams of tricksters from all over entered in this contest. We even have a team of our own and we are pleased to present, for your entertainment, Gerald and his two hounds, Juniper and Pine."

The man stepped back, letting a younger man take his place. He was slim and wiry, with dark hair and brown skin. He was dressed in a fiery red shirt and dark breeches with tall, black boots. His hounds were sleek and black, with longer legs than the red and white tricksters of Belleview. The spectators murmured amongst themselves, in awe at the costume and the beautiful hounds.

"Thank you, lovely people, for coming. This is Juniper and that is Pine, and I hope you enjoy this performance of shadow and fire."

He moved, whispering out commands as he began to dance, music suddenly springing to life from a group of performers at the edge of the ring. The tall hounds responded to his commands and he was just as much part of the performance as they were, with the hounds jumping and leaping over him, around him, their moves coordinated only by his commands. He bent nearly in half and one of the black hounds jumped onto his back, making him bend just a little further, his knees bending to shorten him. He whispered one final command and the remaining hound leaped over the pair, twisting mid-air. The music stopped and the audience applauded. "Bow," the gypsy ordered his hounds and they did so, much to the pleasure of the audience.

There were five more teams, each muttering or speaking commands to their dogs, each part of the performance, each with music improvised by the performers with their drums and fiddle. After the fifth team had finished, one of the dogs slipping on the grass, to the disappointed comments from the audience, the older man stepped into the ring once more, turning once to look everyone in the eye. "And now, our final team. Three dogs, one trainer, locked in silence. Ladies and gentlemen, I give you the hounds of Belleview, Eleana and her red dogs, Caesar, Nero, Justinian."

Eleana opened the door to the kennel and walked into the ring, a flick of her wrist ordering Hunter to remain with Theo, the russet tricksters to follow her. There was silence from those watching. The locals knew of Eleana. Those who had travelled from afar to win prizes or marvel at the fair were shocked at her gender, at the clothes she was wearing. Murmurs broke out, along with snickers and shocked gasps. Eleana ignored them all. Then, she halted in the middle of the circuit, a devious smile on her face.

Eleana indicated each of her three dogs and held a finger to her lips to incite silence. The tension in the air increased. With a flurry of motion between her hands and fingers, Eleana stepped away from her dogs and let them dance. They began in silence and only after a startled moment did the fiddler strike up a slow, mournful tune, the three dogs adjusting their timing with a flutter of Eleana's fingers. She did not participate in the dance as the other teams had, nor did she mutter her commands. She only had to start the hounds off and let them do the routine on their own.

And they were magnificent.

When the hounds executed one final, elaborate manoeuvre and landed in a line, their front paws forwards, their chests touching the ground, tails in the air in a bow and the musicians stopped, there was silence. The audience was stunned for a few moments, then there was applause. It was neither tentative nor polite; it was enthusiastic and astonished. Eleana gestured to her hounds again and took a bow before signalling her hounds and returning to the crowd of people around the circuit, kneeling down to praise each of the tricksters, her hands entwined in their silky fur, her nose touching theirs or pressing her head against a furry one.

"Eleana, you were magnificent," Theo murmered in awe, helping Eleana to her feet. She blushed with pleasure and shook her head, indicating the happy dogs at her feet. Theo smiled, "Somehow, I don't think they did all the work." Eleana rolled her eyes and pushed her way through the crowd, her dogs following at her heels, ignoring the final speech from the old gypsy. She knew she had done well.

RICHARD HAD WATCHED each of the teams of tricksters with Henry at his side, standing amongst the people, though there was a slight gap between him and everyone; no one seemed to want to get too close to this obviously powerful and wealthy man. Truth be told, he didn't notice. His focus was entirely on Eleana and her tricksters. At every jump and every twist of the hounds, his heart soared and at the elation on Eleana's face, he felt just as elated. He would have sworn that he held his breath through the entire routine, though he knew that to be impossible.

"Richard," Henry said, watching Eleana disappear through the crowd, "that's your Houndskeeper, isn't it?"

"Yes," Richard breathed, still in awe after the performance, not really looking at anything and not moving with the crowd of people, either. "That's Eleana."

"She's amazing," Henry said. "I've never seen hounds

respond to a trainer like that. And a woman at that! She never said anything to them, just wiggled her fingers and off they went."

"Oh," Richard said, his friend's words bringing him back to reality, "that's because she can't speak. Her hounds respond to spoken commands, too, but she trains them with gestures only."

"So, she can do that with all of her hounds?" Henry asked. Richard nodded. "Well, I'm impressed. She seems nice, too. Very pretty."

"Indeed," Richard said, his voice dazed, his thoughts obviously elsewhere. Henry looked at his dark-haired friend and frowned, narrowing his eyes while he inspected Richard's features. Then, he straightened and pulled Richard away from those around them, through the pathways that were between the booths and tents, until they were outside the fair, in an open field, the fading light barely illuminating the world around them.

"Richard," Henry said, "I've known you twenty years and I can tell when something's on your mind. I could tell when you married my sister and I can tell now. There's something about this Eleana, isn't there?"

"You know I loved Christina…" Richard said slowly. "I loved her with everything I had. But Christina… she's gone. I must face that. I can't spend my entire life pining away after her. Then I came here, and I met Eleana… I loved her immediately. And she's done so much for me."

"Done what?" Henry asked, his features twisted in

grief. Richard had to remember that Henry, too, had lost a beloved sister. It was different for Richard though, and he knew that he was causing Henry pain at this. It needed to be said. It all needed to be said.

"She saved my life," Richard said simply. He told Henry everything, from the first moment he met Eleana—fiery and furious—to their declaration of friendship, when Richard desperately wanted more. Henry staggered away a few feet in shock.

"Rich," Henry said, a note of urgency in his voice.

"I *know,*" Richard replied, glaring at the horizon. "I know I should say nothing. I have been married once already and she has her whole life ahead of her. She is my Houndskeeper and I love her."

He turned to look at Henry and staggered backwards in horror. Standing not three feet from Henry was Eleana, Hunter, and the three tricksters at her heels, her expression unreadable. Richard tried to summon the courage to speak or to move or to *breathe* but he could not. Instead, he watched, frozen, as Eleana turned and ran.

CHAPTER 13

*R*ichard was not quite sure how he managed to get back to Belleview, but he became aware that he was pacing the length of the library. Mrs. Graham set a tray of tea on a table and Henry sat in a club chair nearby, looking grim. Richard was dazed, his mind locked on that unreadable look on Eleana's face, right before she ran.

Ran from *him*.

A cup of tea was pushed into his hands and he drained it, revelling in the scalding pain to his mouth and realising that, more than anything, he wanted a drink. A proper drink.

He forced himself to set the teacup down instead of hurling it against the wall and rounded on Henry, a snarl on his lips. "This is all your fault," he growled, furious. Henry, to his credit, said nothing. Richard jabbed his finger at his friend, the brother of his dead wife, wanting to cause as much pain as had been caused to him, "You wanted to know everything and I, the stupid fool that I am, told you. And you didn't warn me that Eleana was standing there, listening to every word that I said. You did *nothing*."

"Richard," Henry said, remaining calm as he gently pushed Richard's hand away, "I tried to say something. You did not listen."

"Rich," he snapped. "You said 'Rich'. That's all. Is that supposed to mean something to me? Damn it, Henry, she wasn't supposed to find out about it like that."

"How was she going to find out?" Henry asked softly. He looked up at Richard and saw the pain in the blue depths then nodded slowly. "You weren't planning on telling her, were you?"

"No!" Richard yelled, reaching for his empty tea cup and giving in to the desire to throw it. The porcelain shattered against the wall, scattering on the carpet and Richard felt a mild sense of guilt but no relief. "No, Eleana was not supposed to know! What was I supposed to say to her? Oh, yes, I happen to be your employer, your master, a man completely above you in station and wealth and by the way, I'm desperately in love with you. What do you think she would do? She would have no choice but to do as I wanted because I own her! She has nowhere else to go and she cannot refuse me. I would never do that to her."

"How do you know she would *want* to refuse you? How do you know she would be unable to say no? Do you think such an unconventional woman as Eleana—who trains hounds and wears men's clothes unabashedly—would be cowed by something so… so… *trivial* as station? As wealth?" Henry asked quietly, steepling his fingers before his mouth while his friend paced like a caged wolf.

"Look at me," Richard snarled. Henry did so. He saw a man who had once been torn by grief, who had turned to drink and somehow, some way, found a way to move on and love again. But beyond that, or perhaps before that, he saw a man who was dishevelled, wide-eyed, and terrified. "How could you possibly think that Eleana would want me? I'm broken."

"You managed to piece yourself together," Henry pointed out. Richard laughed, the sound sarcastic and derisive.

"I managed to stop grieving for a woman I loved. I was forced out of drinking. I'm not pieced together, Henry. I forced myself from society and into seclusion because I could not stand the way that people would look at me," Richard said, his voice cracking with pain. "Pity," he spat the word, jabbing himself in the chest. "They looked at me with pity and that, above all else, is the one thing I did not want. They didn't understand. And if it was not pity, it was desire. For my title, for my money, for a whisper in someone's ear on the behalf of people I barely knew. I was an object to be used and taken advantage of and pitied. So, I put myself into self-imposed exile and I found the one thing I never expected to find again. But I'm not worthy of her. I'm broken and while I might be able to pick up the pieces, I'll never be whole again."

"And why would you think that Eleana would scoff at your state? She has not given you pity. She has not coveted your wealth or title or power. She was your friend, just for the sake of being your friend," Henry said, his calm tone fuelling Richard's anger. "So why is loving you any different?"

"Because she deserves so much better," Richard screamed, his rage driving him to the edge. He sounded a wordless cry and fell to his knees, prostrated and in pain. He cried out again, this time quieter, the sound one of a wounded animal rather than one of fury. "I'm nothing close to being deserving of her. I'm used, I'm broken, I've lived once already. She has her whole life ahead of her and I won't be the one to take that away from her," he said, his words no longer loud and angry, but soft and full of pain.

Henry stood from where he had been sitting, his movements sure. He walked over to where Richard knelt and crouched down, his hand on Richard's shoulder. "That sentiment alone proves you love her more than anything and that you deserve her. You may not think so, and others may not think so, but it's the truth. Now come, my brother, and rest. Things will be better in the morning," Henry said, hauling Richard to his feet.

The two walked to Richard's room, and Henry helped his friend to his bed, looking back once at the despondency that filled Richard's entire mien. Then, he blew out the candles and left.

Eleana allowed herself to light candles in her own cottage only after putting the tricksters to kennel and shakily drawing water for each of her hounds for the night. She hadn't even stayed long enough at the fair to hear the pronouncement of who won the contest. She hadn't cared. She had simply fled directly from that field, from *him*, her hounds behind her. Hunter sensed her distress and when she finally stopped moving to collapse into a chair at her table, walked up to her and put his paw on her lap, his sad brown eyes watching her carefully.

Eleana was shocked, to say the least. She wasn't sure what to think of Richard's unintended admission. She only knew that there was uneasiness brewing in her stomach and that she couldn't wrap her mind around it. She tried to convince herself that there had been no basis for his admission, but she knew she was wrong. There were so many little things that, when taken cumulatively, pointed exactly to Richard's feelings. Only she had been too blind to see it.

Friends, he had said. They were *friends*. Could it be that she had taken everything he had given her and offered under the simple flag of friendship? That was the only possible explanation for her sheer stupidity. She had let Richard get far closer to her than she had any other man since William. She knew, without a doubt, that she was very careful, that she kept anyone who might proclaim interest in her at arm's length. But

Richard, he had slipped past that and she had let him. They were *friends*.

Eleana ground her teeth and slammed her fist on the table. How could she be so foolish? And now that she knew, what was she going to do about it? He was her master, second son of a Marquess, for goodness sakes. No, she shook her head. That didn't matter. She was just picking up excuses, now. The real question was whether she wanted to continue being friends with Richard or if she wanted to step further, just far enough to try a relationship.

But there was a third option, one that even she was reluctant to admit, but one which she knew was likely the best choice. She could put an end to any friendship or relationship and banish Richard from her thoughts, like she had done many times before.

Hunter whined and Eleana looked at her hound, her loyal friend. She wrapped her arms around him and let herself fall into tears. She didn't want to make that choice. Not yet. She didn't know what to choose. She needed time. Vacillating between numbness and fury, Eleana dressed in her nightclothes and went to bed, staring at the flickering flame of her candle before blowing it out in a huff of anger and resentment.

She slept very little, and what sleep she did receive was interrupted by her wild thoughts. An hour or so before dawn, Eleana gave up on sleeping and dressed in the first set of work clothes she could find, huffing her way out to the kennels to take care of her hounds, Hunter yawning as he walked alongside her. Eleana clanged and snarled her way through her morning chores, which involved letting each of the hounds have at least ten minutes exercise, cleaning the kennels, feeding and watering each dog, and seriously considering giving each one a bath, just to keep her busy.

She worked almost non-stop from dawn until near eleven and she put her mind fully into her work so she wouldn't have to think about what had happened the night before, what Richard had said that shouldn't have mattered but that changed everything.

She dipped her brush into a bucket at her side and resumed scrubbing the kennel floors, something she never did but for once a year.

Sluice the general dirt off with water, sure. Keep the kennels clean and safe for her dogs, absolutely. Scrub the floor with the aim of removing every single mote of dirt she could get at? It did not seem to be helping her anger at all.

"Eleana?" The voice made Eleana jump, her brush flying out of her hand when she turned to face the intruder. Theo ducked, the scrub brush narrowly missing his arm while he looked at her in confusion. "Did I do something wrong?" he asked, holding out a plate with some food on it, an apologetic smile trying to make up for whatever he had done.

Eleana hurriedly shook her head and Theo relaxed.

"Oh, thank goodness. I was so worried when you didn't come to breakfast that I had done something wrong. And last night, when you just vanished, I figured that I… that I had overstepped. And I wanted to apologise. So, I brought you something to eat since you hadn't been to the kitchens and I'm blabbering. I was really hoping that I wouldn't blabber, and I'll just stop now."

Eleana stared at Theo while he talked, taking in the sheepish look on his face and the way that he held out the food to her, like an offering of peace. She stood and, not caring about the dirt that was on her clothes or the fact that half of her was wet from kneeling on the floor and splashing water about, wrapped her arms around Theo's neck, pulling him down to her and kissing him. Theo started in surprise and dropped the plate of food, sinking into the kiss that was desperate and passionate and yet gentle at the same time. He deepened it, his hands roaming Eleana's body, finally resting on her hips as he pushed her against a wall, nipping her lip so that she let him roam further with his tongue. He groaned in pleasure when Eleana let her head back, exposing her long, graceful neck. Theo pressed his lips against her jaw, her neck, finally stopping where her shirt met her shoulder.

"Oh," a voice said and immediately, Eleana and Theo sprang apart, turning to face the intruder. Eleana saw Smoke first and then slowly, she lifted her eyes to take in the stricken expression Richard displayed. He stood there, hair dishevelled, clothes slightly askew, and Eleana couldn't but help the stab of guilt that coursed through her. Then she remembered her anger and her eyes flashed dangerously. Richard winced and Theo furrowed his brows, having missed the exchange of glances. "I came to apologise," Richard said quietly and cleared his throat before looking at the ground, "and to talk."

Eleana did not move, her face just as unreadable as the night before but for her eyes which were filled with fire.

RICHARD MADE a slight choking sound in his throat and turned, walking briskly back towards the main house, wanting to run but knowing that his pride and his fear of humiliation kept him from doing so. He ducked into the house, passing Henry on the way.

"I take it that did not go well," Henry sighed when Richard brushed by him and the lord let out a strangled cry. Henry said nothing, knowing that this time, Richard needed to be left alone to wallow in his grief and self-pity.

Richard went immediately to the library, closing the door behind him and moving towards a cabinet near the back of the room. The key was missing but that did not stop Richard. He simply took a hold of the handles and broke the lock in pure desperation, throwing the doors open to reveal what was inside. The alcohol of the house sat there, locked away for Richard's well-being. He supposed that Hayes and Mrs. Graham hadn't counted on his own stupidity.

He didn't even bother with the glass that was set out on a silver tray, half full of water, but simply took the mostly-full bottle of scotch and pressed it to his lips, relief tingling through his veins at the feel of the alcohol, the dulling of his pain. The sensation was wondrous, burning, and Richard sank against a shelf of books after the first swallow, eyes closed with dubious pleasure. He hadn't realised how much he had wanted a drink until the taste of it flooded his mouth.

Perhaps it was because he had been sober for a while or perhaps it was because he had so desired the taste of alcohol, but Richard got very drunk. More than he had been in many, many months. It was not the pain-numbing drunkenness that he had lived with nearly every day for so long, but the loss of common sense, blurring of the edges, getting rid of inhibitions drunk. And when Eleana walked in the room, closing the door behind her so that they could talk in peace, Richard was glad for the feeling of alcohol.

"I wondered," he said, voice surprisingly clear, "how long it would take you to come up here and scold me. That is what you're going to do, isn't it? After all, I've been ill-mannered and inappropriate."

Eleana frowned and looked at the bottle, mostly empty in his fist, and another full one on the floor. She folded her arms and looked at Richard, gesturing with a hand to the bottle. He laughed, the sound deep and raucous. "Of course I'm drunk! Do you honestly think that I could have made it through this without being drunk? That's what I do, dear, lovely Eleana. I drown out the world with the drink and you know what? Right now, everything is just wonderful. Well, except for the fact that I'm an idiot. A complete idiot. By the way, you never actually did tell me what you think of this whole situation."

Eleana gaped openly then flew into her anger, giving up on trying to control herself. She gave her half-shrug of question and touched her head, drawing her hand away quickly, her lips curled at Richard in frustration.

"Why? Why do I love you or why did I not tell you or why did you have to find out that way? You know, since I do not really feel like trying to translate which of those you mean, I'm just going to answer every single one and you're going to listen to the answers whether you like it or not," he said, taking a step forwards and bringing the bottle to his lips. Eleana stepped back against the door, worry replacing her anger.

"Why did you have to find out like that? Because Henry is a fool for not warning me and because I have absolutely no tact. If it were up to me, you would have learned of it in a romantic setting, perhaps dinner with candles. No, no, that was how I proposed to Christina. No, you would be told while dancing, Hunter laying nearby, the stars overhead, imagining music in our heads. It would be a beautiful night and you would gently lean your head against my shoulder, and I would whisper it to you. And look what happened instead?"

Richard finished off the bottle and, looking at it, threw it to the ground in annoyance. Eleana winced.

"That's right, you get a stunning revelation in the

middle of a field because I'm a gutless coward and you're too damned quiet for your own good. Now, the second question. Why did I not tell you? Well, why do you think? I've lost my wife, came out here to get away from everything and then I meet you and it's love, instantly. I hated you for it and I hated me for hating you for it and I hated me just because. And then, to make matters worse, I'm Lord Byrns, peer of the realm. You are in my employ and must do as I say and so that just makes things unfair because what if you did not love me back? That, and I did not wish to ruin things for you because you have so much to live for. Of course, it turns out that you have had just as much pain as I have, perhaps more because it was sudden, and you still have William's killer walking next to you."

Richard stopped, his breath coming quickly as he tried to fight the pull of the alcohol and his anger and his desire. He stood five feet away from Eleana, staring at the worry and the slight bit of fear on her face. Richard snarled and turned, lunging for the cabinet to grab a wine of considerable age. He stabbed the corkscrew into it and ripped out the cork with a practised ease that showed he had done as much before, many times.

"Maybe," he continued, his voice quieter as he shuddered with pleasure at the taste of the wine, "that is why I love you. Because you have suffered through hell and yet you still manage to be cheerful. You still manage to be graceful and wonderful with dogs, the best trainer I've ever met. The kindest person. The most beautiful…You walk around with the killer of your lover at your heels and it's obvious you've forgiven him. How could you not? Hunter did not know any better. But so many people would simply kill the dog. Not you. You *saved* him. Just like you saved me, even though you would have been perfectly justified in handing me off to somebody else, or even sending one of the others to fetch help. But you could not do that, because it just goes against your beliefs. You had to help me, had to save me, and so you did, even though you nearly killed yourself in the process."

Richard took another mouthful of the wine and Eleana tried to intervene, hands out towards the bottle, shaking her head.

"Of course, it's a bad idea. But that doesn't mean I'm going to give up," Richard said, understanding not quite reaching him.

Eleana took a step forwards, trying to take the bottle from his hands and suddenly Richard drew himself up, looking at her with sparks in his eyes, his breath hitched and desire pounding through his veins, set free by his inebriation.

"Of course, I did not know any of that when I first laid eyes on you," Richard said. "No, I just thought that you were the most beautiful creature I had ever seen and you, so powerful and strong, asking for no one's help with Smoke and rounding on me just as soon as you'd won, it was marvellous. Maybe it's the fact that you look like a nymph, maybe it's the fact that you did not care who I was and all that mattered was that I was at fault. I do not know, but the fact is, Eleana, I'm in love with you."

Richard reached out and touched, ever so gently, Eleana on the lips, his tongue darting out to wet his own as thoughts of taking her sprang into his head. Then he remembered what had happened to put him into his state and he pulled back, watching as Eleana backed up again, green eyes wide. Richard scowled and drank of the wine again.

"Theo," he spat. "I saw you. You were kissing Theo. Or maybe he was kissing you. It does not matter. Because now I've ruined everything. I cannot fight that, because I'm a damned honourable person. I won't go near you without your assent because I'm too honourable for that. And you know what, Eleana? If you want Theo, have him!"

Richard stepped forwards, his anger with himself making him bear down on Eleana. He set the wine aside.

"I will not interfere," he said in disgust, watching as Eleana stepped back again, her body pressed against the door, eyes wide. "You probably came here to talk reasonably to me," he murmured. "To ask me to keep my distance and to explain what you were doing in the field last night. But here I've ruined everything, just like always." Richard held out his arms, opening himself up as a target and stepping forwards once more, narrowing the gap between him and Eleana so he could see her eyes in full detail. Then, he couldn't help but notice the curve of her cheek, the swell of her lips, open as if she were going to protest.

Richard closed that final gap and put his hands on Eleana's cheeks, angling her head as he did his own, pressing his lips to hers, unable to keep anything back.

His control was gone. He put every ounce of passion into that kiss, forcing Eleana back against the door of the library, his chest pressing against hers, his legs trapping hers, until there was no space between them, and she was unable to move. He kissed her and, to his immense pleasure, she sank into him and kissed him back. She lifted her hands to wrap around his neck, opening her mouth to admit him. Richard groaned and his hands slipped from Eleana's face to glide over her shoulders, her breasts, her hips.

He hooked one hand behind her leg and let the other brace against the door, pulling her up to wrap her thigh around him. Eleana gasped as she felt the pressure of him between her legs and suddenly, Richard sobered.

He threw himself backwards, tripping over the bottle of scotch to land on the floor, horrified at what he had just done. Eleana remained standing, though her legs wobbled beneath her and the door was holding her upright. She was breathing heavily, and her eyes were wide with shock. She did not move, only stared at Richard in complete disbelief.

"I'm sorry," Richard breathed, backing away from her. "I'm so sorry. I'll never come near you again, I swear it."

Eleana did not respond at first but put her fingers to her lips as if surprised to realise their presence. She blinked twice before taking a deep breath and looking at Richard. She circled one finger in the air between herself and Richard then touched the corner of her eye. Then, in an instant, she was gone, the library door thrown open and her long legs carrying her far away from Richard.

Richard, though, remained on the floor, not quite as horrified, a small smile playing on his lips. "We'll see," he translated belatedly.

He laughed to himself and lay back completely on the floor, just the memory of having kissed Eleana enough to awaken him. He felt his desire for her burning through his veins, stronger, if possible, than before. Richard laughed again, his joy overwhelming.

"We'll see," he said again. It was not an invitation, but nor was it a refusal. He had sworn, had intended to uphold his promise and stay far away from her. "We'll see," he murmured, longing to go and run after Eleana, to trap her beneath him and make her gasp with pleasure.

ELEANA, though she desperately tried to deny otherwise, she was wanting the same thing. She couldn't get rid of the memory of that moment, when Richard had pushed forwards just far enough, when she had felt him, hard and tempting, when that flame of longing had flooded her. She locked the doors to her cottage, not trusting that someone wouldn't come walking in to disturb her thoughts.

What was she doing? She did not love him. He was her master, and, at best, they were tentative friends. But that touch, that kiss, it set her skin to tingling. And what did it matter that he was already in love with her? No. She shook her head, trying to rid herself of such thoughts. She couldn't do that, would not get involved like that.

Theo. What about Theo? He had kissed her—well, she had kissed him first—and that had sent shivers up her spine. Yet the memory of that was nothing like what she had felt with Richard. Eleana paced back and forth in her cottage, Hunter watching her, his ears pricked, and his expression confused.

What had she done? She should have just run after what Richard had done. And he promised that he wouldn't go near her. Then she had ruined it all with a simple gesture.

"We'll see."

Unfortunately for her, that simple "we'll see" meant Eleana had to figure out what exactly she wanted, and she had no idea how to do so.

CHAPTER 14

Richard paced before Henry, wringing his hands. "Her saying 'we'll see' means that I can't approach her," he said. "Or can I? Do I have to let her come to me? Or is it the other way around?" He looked desperately at his friend, who was lounging on the terrace, a glass of lemonade nearby.

"If you wish to court Eleana," Henry admonished, slightly amused at the distress of his friend, "then you must do so. Of course, you have already stepped out of conventionality and propriety by spewing out your drunken feelings to her."

"Yes," Richard said with a wince. "Perhaps that was not the best set of circumstances in which to, ah, divulge my feelings for her. But I was not expecting her to come to me, and I was wallowing in despair after having witnessed..." he trailed off, waving his hand vaguely. Henry nodded, knowing the situation Richard meant, and took a sip of his lemonade.

"What's done is done," Henry said. "Now, she hasn't completely refused you and so you must tentatively stake your claim. I suggest you invite her to dine with you."

"To dine with me," Richard nodded then rounded on his blonde friend, fire in his eyes. "Are you insane? I cannot invite Eleana to dinner. It would be so awkward and strange and, and…And you're exactly right. But I would not want to invite the scrutiny of everyone here. She knows everyone and people would be bound to talk. Even though everyone at Belleview is fond of her, it does rather…we are so far apart."

"I very much doubt that matters to her, or to anyone here. Has your Mrs. Graham admonished you? Has Hayes? No. So invite Eleana to dine with you. Something unconventional, perhaps. Dinner on the floor of the drawing room, before the fire. Or maybe a night-time picnic. She would appreciate that, if I'm to understand her correctly," Henry replied. Richard nodded and frowned, continuing to pace as the details of such a matter wound through his thoughts. Henry grinned. "Good. Now go up there and invite her. I will speak with your staff and get something nice prepared and set everything up. I'd also like to know what her favourite dish is, for the matter. Then, I will simply make myself scarce this evening."

"Right. Good. Yes," Richard said. "But…I cannot go up there to invite her."

"Why not?" Henry asked, standing to glower at Richard. "You can't be that cowardly."

"No, of course not," Richard spat. "But if I go up there after what happened yesterday, then I will be assuming that she's agreed to my admission and desire for courtship. I do not want to assume anything. I know this is stupid, but I want her to come to me. I want her to want to come to me. Not to impose upon her because of those two words. I know! I shall write her a letter."

"A letter," Henry said drily. "Richard, you cannot be serious." He received only a sharp look in reply and followed as Richard walked into the house and up to his study. Richard took out a piece of fine stationary and wrote out a quick invitation and before he could second guess himself, signed it, then addressed it with her name and rang the bell for a servant. Mrs. Graham appeared a few moments later and looked at Richard in surprise.

"Please take this to Eleana," Richard said, pressing the letter into Mrs. Graham's hands. "Before I change my mind."

She raised her eyebrows. "Very well, m'lord," she said, a knowing look in her eyes. Then, she turned and walked out. Henry approached Richard and frowned, putting his hand on Richard's shoulder.

"You," he said, "are a fool."

Richard could do nothing but look at his friend in desperation and wish that he were following the letter he had scrawled out to Eleana. A letter. He let out a cry of anguish and dropped into a chair, his head in his hands. Henry simply sighed and returned to the terrace to drink his lemonade and watch the Houndskeeper upon the lawn.

MRS. GRAHAM personally carried the note out to Eleana, holding her skirts carefully while she crossed the yard and came upon the Houndskeeper. Eleana was putting her racers through their courses, running along behind and smiling at the exertion and the pleasure of the slim-bodied hounds. She stopped when she saw Mrs. Graham and walked over to the woman, panting for breath just as her animals panted beside her.

"I have a note for you, dear." Mrs. Graham held out the slip of paper, folded, with Eleana's name written on the top. Eleana took it tentatively and nodded, opening it slowly, brows furrowed. "I think his lordship is desperate, sending you letters as he is. I would ask what happened between the two of you, but I have no doubt that you would not tell me. Eleana, just know this: I like our Lord Byrns. He is a good man. However, I also think he's been through enough hardship in his life, so don't you go trifling with him. Either you agree to see where things go with him, and him alone, or you tell him now that you don't want this and let dear Theo court you. You cannot have both."

Eleana blushed brightly. She started waving her hands, desperately trying to communicate, but Mrs. Graham held up a hand and shook her head, then walked away, leaving her to her thoughts. Eleana huffed and sat on the grass. Not a moment later, Hunter walked up beside her from where he had been laying out in the sun. He settled next to her and Eleana absently stroked his head while staring at the letter, her fingers running over the patterns of ink. She bit her lip and sank backwards, laying out fully until she was staring up at the sky, the letter clutched in one hand, her thoughts desperate.

Did she want to pursue this, whatever *this* was, with Richard? Or did she want to remain safe with the occasional thought of Theo to distract her? No matter that she hadn't much thought of Theo in *that* way. Not before she impetuously—perhaps foolishly—kissed him. There was the memory of that kiss, though. The one that stirred her passion and touched her heart, all under the ministrations of Richard's gentle and yet desperate hands. It was more than what she had felt while kissing Theo and while she longed for it to happen again, she was also afraid.

Eleana touched the paper in her hands again and made up her mind. If she got hurt, then she would get hurt. She would get over it. Wouldn't she? She stood and, ordering her racers to stay at the cottage, marched across the yard, Hunter at her heels.

"Try the library," Henry Marduke said, waving at her from the terrace.

Eleana blushed, but she was also resolved. She ducked into the house and went to the library, walking as quietly as she knew how so as not to draw attention. It was silly, but her heart raced far less for it. The library seemed strangely quiet, almost as if it were empty. Haunted. But Richard was inside, tucked into a chair, his posture slouched and despondent. He must have heard Hunter's claws on the floor, though, because he looked up.

Richard sat up and stared at Eleana. She tried not to fidget with her rumpled work clothes or worry about having just been running around outside. Instead, she focused her attention on one dark wave of hair that dangled over his forehead. Carefully, she stepped forwards and thrust the letter at him.

Richard took the letter with trembling fingers and lowered his head. "I'm sorry. I did not mean to offend you or to press the issue or to cause you any discomfort and I realise that I have broken the promise I made to you—" He stopped when Eleana knelt before him so she could look into his eyes, her frustration apparent.

She shook her head and pointed to the note then to herself.

"You cannot come?" Richard asked, shoulders drooping.

Eleana threw up her hands before standing and picking up a book that lay on Richard's desk, thumbing through the pages. She gestured at the pages of the book and pointed to her eyes before shaking her head. Richard gaped at her in astonishment.

"You cannot *read*?" he asked and Eleana flushed even as she frowned and confirmed his question with a nod.

She put the book down and pointed to the note

before shrugging her shoulders in question. She did not want to acknowledge the tears that pricked in her eyes at his open-mouthed astonishment at her inability to read.

"I, um… I had asked if you wanted to dine with me tonight. A picnic, out on the terrace or the lawn or something," Richard said then looked closely at Eleana. "What do you mean you cannot read? I thought that when we were both invalided that you—"

Eleana shook her head and pointed to Richard, her mouth moving as if speaking. Richard sank back into his chair, looking thoughtful.

"Yes, that's right. I did read aloud. Did not your father teach you?" Eleana frowned and shook her head again. She touched her head and pointed to Hunter. "He taught you about being a Houndskeeper. And of course, you never went to school since you spent your time here, at Belleview."

Eleana nodded and turned away to stand before the window, her skin hot. Richard stood and walked up behind her, carefully reaching out to touch her arm.

"There's no need to be ashamed, Eleana. Many people do not know how to read. I can teach you, if you like, and no one has to know." Eleana rounded on Richard, her green eyes wide and hopeful. Her hands waved through the air. Richard did not even struggle with the translation. He just chuckled. "Truly, Eleana. I would be my pleasure to teach you."

She nodded eagerly and impulsively wrapped her arms around him in excitement. Richard stiffened, and she pulled back, brows furrowed. Richard licked his lips nervously and cleared his throat.

Eleana's eyes widened when she realised Richard's problem and pulled back, tucking an errant strand of hair behind her ear. Then, she looked behind him at the book on the table and beamed, the pleasure at soon being able to read warming her. It was something she had hidden for years. People always assumed that a mute girl would be able to read and to write in order to convey her meanings. The lack was a great shame.

Richard smiled as well. "That's the history of Belleview. I have been looking at it off and on for a few weeks, to try and familiarise myself with the estate."

Eleana looked at the spine of the book, peering at it closely before pointing to one of the gilded words written there. Richard blinked and stepped forwards to look at the title.

"That's 'region'." And when she pointed to another word, "Belleview." Richard put his hand on the book and pushed it gently to the desk. "Perhaps we should start these lessons tomorrow. I must think on how to go about this and I must see what Henry has gotten up to with the plans for dinner. You are able to come?"

She nodded briskly then flushed slightly, bending over to pat Hunter's ears so as to hide her embarrassment.

Richard relaxed. "Oh, thank goodness. I was so worried that you would say no and that you wouldn't want anything further to do with me and I'm going to be quiet now before I ruin everything." Eleana laughed and rolled her eyes before sighing. She pointed to herself then to the door and to Hunter. "I understand," Richard said with a nod. "I'm sure your hounds have great need of you."

He got out of her way so that Eleana had a clear path to the door and she hesitated a moment before moving. Had she not hesitated, waited that extra breath, Richard would not have let his will slip. Instead, he swiftly turned Eleana towards him and kissed her, his arms instinctively going around her waist, pulling her close to him.

Eleana could not think properly. All she knew was that any gentleness she had felt yesterday had vanished and she was faced with pure passion and need. Richard took from her and when her knees began to grow weak and she opened her mouth to take in a calming breath, he took more. He pressed in on her, his tongue exploring her even as his hands held her in place, unable to escape. Soon, it was only his arms supporting Eleana, and she gave into his questing whole-heartedly, kissing him back deeply and giving of herself what he needed.

When it finally seemed that Richard could go no further, he moved his hands to her hips and his fingers curled into her, his touch sensual and demanding. Eleana gasped, her muscles going taught with expectation before melting again. Richard pulled back, slowly, letting Eleana gather herself before she stepped away completely, pleasure emanating off of her in waves. She smiled and quickly left the study before Richard could do anything further. As she left, she passed Henry and her eyes widened at the unsurprised look Richard's friend bore. She ducked her head and marched away, sure she had never blushed so much in her entire life.

"WHAT DID YOU DO TO HER?" Henry asked, closing the door of the study behind him. "She looked golden from head to toe and I'm fairly sure that her silent gesturing didn't colour her lips that particular shade."

"I just gave her something to think about," Richard replied smugly, turning to touch the book Eleana had examined. He chuckled softly to himself and smiled. "Oh, yes, I think she'll be thinking about that for a while."

"I'm not quite sure what to say about that," Henry said, smirking. "You certainly aren't going about this in a conventional manner, are you?"

"I can't," Richard said softly. "Everything about Eleana is unconventional and she pushes the boundaries of everything I've ever known. So, I have no choice but to push back...What did you plan for dinner?"

"I managed to get some lovely things out of your dear Mrs. Graham," Henry grinned mischievously. "I think she has a soft spot for you, because she did not complain once. Everything will be magnificent."

And it was.

Richard had the terrace cleared and a blanket set on

the ground so that he and Eleana could oversee Belle-view's forest in the distance. Candles were arranged to give light when the sun set, and the meal was warm enough to fight away the slight evening chill. Cushions stollen from chairs and pillows from couches in unused rooms were laid about, and Richard even had some furs brought out should Eleana get cold. He left the lighting of candles to Henry under the direction of Mrs. Graham and dressed in dark breeches and a nice, white shirt, taking special care to look his best.

Then, he waited.

He sat fiddling with the blanket, searching the grounds for any sign of movement, just so he could be prepared when Eleana came up. He cursed himself for being stupid, not telling her that the meal would occur at his supper time rather than that of the servants' then cursed himself again for thinking she was not smart enough to figure that out. But if she did not realise that, then where was she? Had she changed her mind?

He was tempted to go out searching for her or to start pacing when Eleana walked up to him from the direction of the house. She was wearing the dress he had given her before the Haverford ball and, to his surprise, Hunter was nowhere to be seen. Her hair had been done up in an elaborate mass, leaving her graceful neck exposed, her cheeks flushed with pleasure. Eleana fidgeted with the skirt of her dress, biting her lip and Richard realised he was gawping.

"You look wondrous," he said quickly, standing to take her hand and kiss it. Eleana smiled nervously and indicated the picnic, smiling. "Do you like it? I thought this would be more fun than dinner at that enormous table I'm forced to use. Besides, this way we can see the stars come out," Richard internally breathed a sigh of relief as he regained the power of speech. Or at least, coherent, charming speech.

Eleana looked up at the sky when she sank down, guided by Richard's gentle touch. The sun was just setting and while they could see no stars, it promised to be a spectacular night. Richard sat across the blanket from Eleana and watched her as she looked at the sky. When her attention shifted, he suddenly realised that he had no idea what he was doing. Desperately, he reached for the supper that had been prepared.

"Henry, uh, thought that a good chicken stew would be our meal and since I really cannot argue with him, well, we have chicken stew and some fresh bread. I hope you do not mind," Richard said, setting out the ladle and bowls just so. Eleana grinned and nodded, putting a hand over her stomach and slumping her posture dramatically. Richard pretended to look affronted. "I do not work you that hard, so it's your own fault if you're starving."

Eleana laughed and folded her arms as if pouting. Richard simply looked at her, smirking slightly, and she gave up. She picked up her bowl and held it out, eyes wide and begging.

"Very well," Richard replied, carefully serving her the stew. He did the same for himself and the two spent a quiet moment simply enjoying the meal. After a few bites, Richard lowered his bowl, stirring the thick liquid with his spoon. "Frankly, I'm not sure what I'm doing. You already know how I feel, and I don't want to make you feel awkward or in any way obliged to me, but this is strange." Eleana tilted her head in question, reaching for a slice of bread. "Strange in that I feel as though I've taken two steps backwards from where I was with you, even though we've never done anything like this. Courting you—make no mistake, Eleana, I *am* courting you—is so much different than courting Christina."

Eleana blushed slightly at Richard's assertion of courting, but she did not respond to that. Instead, she tilted her head again, a strand of hair falling across her face. Richard longed to reach out and brush it back, feel it against his skin, and his hand was half-lifted when he stopped himself and forced himself to take a bite of stew. Then, he leaned back on his elbows and looked up at the swiftly darkening sky.

"With Christina, though I knew her through Henry, it was a slow and steady progression from affection to courting to love to marriage. I never felt this, ah, desperate, throbbing passion that I feel with you. I loved her, of that there was no doubt, but it was completely different. It was a love borne of affection and friendship, steady and simple. With you, I never know just what is going to happen. I've never been around someone like you and it's a completely new experience."

A shiver ran down Eleana's arms and almost

instantly, Richard was sitting up, reaching for the furs to wrap around her. She accepted them gratefully and turned her head once more to the stars. Then, she looked at Richard and gestured to the picnic and to the two of them, touching her head with both hands.

"I give you a headache?" Richard asked, teasing even as he feigned hurt. Eleana scowled. Richard laughed, "I take it William never courted you as I am." She pursed her lips and shook her head slowly. Eleana held out her hand and moved it through the air, like a wheeling eagle. "A slow love, then. That's right, you were only a child when you met him," Richard said. He gave a 'huh' of surprise, "I hadn't realised that it was so similar between Christina and William and ourselves. Maybe that's why we get along."

Eleana did not reply to that, only wrapped herself tighter in the furs and finished her stew before setting the bowl carefully to the side. She picked up one of the cushions and lay her head on it, stretching out beneath the open sky. Richard watched her movements, marvelling at her grace and simple pleasures.

"Eleana, am I acting like a fool?" he asked quietly, no teasing in his tones, no talk of love, no questions of his past, just simple curiosity. Eleana flickered her eyes to him in surprise and sat up on one elbow, showing the elegant curves of her body, the sleeve of the dress slipping slightly off her shoulder. She peered at Richard as if thinking then pointed to the stars. Her free arm waved broadly, indicating the sky. Then, gravely, she touched Richard's shoulder and then her own, a question in her eyes. Richard nodded and lay back, as well, propping his head up with two cushions, his fingers intwined and resting on his chest.

"Before the stars," he translated, "we are all fools."

Eleana nodded and lay down, stroking the furs absently. They said nothing for a few minutes, just basking in the glory of the night, listening to the sounds of the land, quietly revelling in the closeness of each other.

"I love you, Eleana, and I know you do not love me back. Not yet. Perhaps you never will. I admire you for taking this leap of faith with me, but I want you to know that I will not talk of love or of marriage or of anything of that sort if it makes you uncomfortable. I will just take things day by day. I will court you as subtly as you need."

Eleana turned her head towards Richard and touched her lips, bowing her head slightly. Thank you. Richard smiled and turned his head towards the stars.

He pointed to a constellation, "Do you see that group of stars there, the ones that look like a hawk?" Eleana nodded. "I was told, when I was a boy in school, that those stars were called Erowain, after a legendary bird. He belonged to a sorcerer of untold power and it was through Erowain that this sorcerer was able to use his magic. But when the sorcerer was young, still learning, and Erowain was a mere hatchling, the sorcerer was experimenting with magic. He accidentally turned Erowain into a starling and though he desperately tried to change his hawk back, he couldn't seem to get it right. So, he carried Erowain, now in the shape of a lizard, to the Mountain of Eagles, and begged the King of Eagles to turn his hawk back to normal. The Eagle took pity on Erowain and fed the lizard a magic worm. Erowain turned back into his normal self and, for eating the worm, became as powerful as an Eagle."

Eleana frowned and folded her arms, turning her head to look at Richard skeptically.

He laughed, "Alright, so there was no magic worm and the hawk never turned into a lizard. But he was a valiant bird, who sacrificed his own well-being in order to allow his master to work magic through him. I always felt bad for him and thought him a slave of a cruel sorcerer. Now, though, I think he loved his master and was willing to give himself up to allow the sorcerer to succeed."

Richard moved closer to Eleana so that their arms were almost touching. He tucked the furs around her and she sighed, pointing to the stars. Her eyes sparkled in the half-light of the candles and the eagerness there surprised Richard.

"Another one? What about Hagrung, the old hermit of the forest who stole from an angry baker and was sentenced to a lifetime of kneading bread?" Richard asked, finger drawing out the shape of a bent man. Eleana laughed and hit Richard's arm in jest, her nose wrinkled in her mirth.

She was so beautiful, Richard thought. He wanted to hold her there in his arms forever, but he knew that she would not be his unless she gave herself over to him willingly. It had to be her choice, her own will that gave him her heart. Without that, Richard knew that Eleana would never truly love him. And if she did not give him her heart, if she did not choose to love him, where would that leave him? He wasn't sure he could bear the answer.

He turned his attention towards the stars again, forcing a smile to his lips, "I'm serious! My father thought that Hagrung was a particularly good teaching tool for a young, reckless, and indignant boy. Of course, I thought it was funnier than anything and didn't see what Hagrung had to do with me. When I figured it out, I simply retorted with the story of Arreis and Therbe, the apprentice who got the better of her master. Those stars, there. The ones shaped like a cat." Eleana lifted her hand to point and Richard nodded, reaching out to take her hand and help her trace the stars. He pulled her fingers to his lips and kissed the tips gently, eyes locked with hers. "Those ones exactly," he said.

CHAPTER 15

"Can't you see that he's enthralling you?" Theo snarled, pacing before Eleana on the lawn while she stood, her arms folded. When Theo had come, looking to talk about the rumours he had heard regarding Eleana's relationship with Richard, she had explained that he was courting her and she was letting him, which meant she couldn't be involved with Theo. He hadn't seemed as upset about that as about her involvement with the lord of Belleview.

Hunter sat at Eleana's side, watching Theo's movements.

Eleana shook her head. Theo stopped and looked at her desperately, "Eleana, what reason could he possibly have for courting you except to take advantage?"

Eleana inhaled sharply and turned her head away, burning with anger. Theo groaned and rubbed the back of his neck.

"I don't mean to offend you, but you must see the

truth. He's an extremely wealthy man. He's titled, even if he is only a second son. But a son to a Marquess! He's also a widower. He's lonely and he doesn't want to marry into society, proved by his movement from town to Belleview. And here you are, innocent and beautiful and, frankly, open to friendship, and he sees his opportunity. He's taking advantage of you, Eleana."

Eleana rolled her eyes and shook her head. She pointed to the house and touched her eye, then her heart.

"You think you can see his true nature now, but I think you're being blinded by the light of his interest in you. It's flattering and you like it, so why should you doubt," Theo argued.

Eleana snorted in derision and gave Theo a look before tapping her head. She knew what Richard's intentions were. She wasn't in love with him, as he claimed to be with her, but she would give him time and perhaps she would come to love him. If not, she would simply walk away. As long as she believed him to be honest, then there was little room for hurt.

Theo said nothing but just searched Eleana's eyes for signs of giving in. She smiled at him and took his hand, touching her wrist with his. Then, she walked off towards the house, Hunter following along at her heels. Theo stared after her. "You're going to get hurt." he called, but Eleana did not hear him.

She walked through the house in search of Richard, seeing everything as if in a new light. She had lived at Belleview her entire life and knew the grounds and the house as well as she knew herself. She had grown up running in and around the house, but her association—relationship, whatever it was—with Richard put a gleam of magnificence on the house. Eleana found Richard in his library, pacing while he read a letter then lowered it, his eyes vacant, then lifted the letter again and read it through.

Softly, Eleana knocked against the door frame, making Richard jump as he turned to face her. He relaxed once he realised who was standing there, "Oh, you scared me. How do you do that?"

Eleana furrowed her brows and held her hands up as if claws, pretending to snarl like a monster.

"Ha, ha. I meant walking so quietly," Richard chuckled. Eleana walked into the room, tromping about like a great creature then walked normally, shrugging. "Fine. I get your point. Here for your reading lesson?" Richard asked, walking over to close the door behind Eleana. She nodded and reached for the book set on the table, looking at it eagerly.

These reading lessons had turned into the high points of her days. She enjoyed the challenge and Richard had said she had a natural aptitude for reading. He seemed to especially enjoy the pantomimes she did for the meanings of the words.

"Right," Richard said, sitting beside her. "Where were we?" Eleana flipped through the book until she came to the third chapter.

Without having to be instructed, Eleana put her finger on the page and started reading, slowly, painstakingly. She was methodical and went word by word, line by line, at a steady pace until she came to one which she did not know. Pausing, Eleana looked up at Richard hopefully.

"Let's go through it," he said patiently, revelling in the fact that her leg was touching his as they shared the book. "First letter?"

As Eleana pointed to each letter, Richard would say the sound until the word had been said. Then, Eleana would look at the word again and act it out. She curled her lips in a snarl and pretended to roar, then blew fire over everything, making Hunter lift up his head with interest.

Richard laughed. "Dragon. Exactly. If you keep going at this pace, you won't need me anymore."

Eleana touched the pages of the book gently and looked at Richard, who was watching her with a sad smile. She leaned against him, pointing at the page of the book again. This slow reading continued for another hour, with Eleana learning the rules of reading and grammar. At the end of the hour, Richard would take out some paper and a pen, letting Eleana practise her writing.

While she was writing, Hayes came in with the post on a silver platter. Richard took the letters and, casting two aside for later reading, opened the seal on the third. He read the letter through once, twice, then set his jaw in a grim line, picking up the letter he had been musing over before Eleana walked in. He sat in his chair before the desk and put the two letters side by side.

"Damn," he cursed. Eleana looked up and walked over to the desk, peering down at the letters.

"They're about the school," Richard said. "And the estate. Apparently, my solicitor in town is having a difficult time getting the permits finalised for the school. And there is the matter of appointing a board of trustees and hiring professors and a headmaster and various staff members. Then there is the matter of the estate. It has been doing fairly well under the current line of investment, but there are some assets which have recently come to light and which I must settle. Of course, all of this can only be dealt with in person."

Eleana looked at him in confusion. She didn't see the problem and that much was obvious to Richard.

"I have to go into town, probably for a month or so. I was hoping that I would not have to go back there for many years, but these matters cannot be settled by letter. I'm not overly fond of town," Richard grumbled, more to himself than to Eleana. Eleana gave a sympathetic look to Richard then tapped the letters twice before shrugging one shoulder. "When will I leave? Tomorrow, if I can manage it."

Eleana frowned and went over to the table where she had been practising writing. Richard followed her with his eyes and sighed.

"I would not go so soon if this weren't urgent. If the school is to open this year, then I must act swiftly. The sooner I get there, the faster this whole affair can be over with. I'll have to open the house and I'm sure that there will be parties and dinners that I will be obligated to attend. I hate them just as much as you do, and I won't have you there to share in my misery."

Eleana grimaced at the thought of attending such parties and Richard laughed even as he rang the bell for Hayes or Mrs. Graham.

He detailed the issue and the need to leave the next day. "And you might as well inform Henry. I'll take him with me, make things easier for the lot of us."

"And will Eleana be going with you?" Hayes asked, smiling kindly while he looked at Eleana. She blushed as the proposition and started to shake her head when Richard held up his hand out of curiosity.

"I hadn't considered that," Richard said, looking over at Eleana. "Do you want to come with me? I would be engaged on business during most days, but you could explore the city and such." Eleana blinked in surprise and immediately turned her attention to Hunter before looking back at Richard, her green eyes thoughtful. She gestured to Hunter then to the window. "Your father might be able to step in. Or perhaps one of the boys from the town you've been quietly training. It wouldn't be any trouble. Please, will you come?"

She bit her lip and fiddled with the pen, looking between Hayes and the pleading hope of Richard. After what seemed like ages, she nodded and Hayes bowed, grinning as he left the room. Richard relaxed in his chair, relieved.

"Thank you," he said. "I'm not sure what I would

have done had I been forced to go without seeing you for a month." Eleana replied with a nervous smile and took her leave, claiming she needed to prepare.

She practically ran to the cottage, Hunter bounding along beside her, whining at the distress of his mistress. Eleana closed the cottage door behind her and leaned against it, sinking to the ground in dismay at what she had just done. Hunter whined again and put his head on her knee, brown eyes wide and soulful. Eleana held her arms open and the dog stepped forwards, letting her bury her head in his fur.

What had she done? Was she insane?

She couldn't simply go to town for a *month* with Richard, not as things stood between them. Were she simply his Houndskeeper, it might have been better, but somehow, she doubted that very much. Only if she were his wife or his sister would rumours escape her. Now, just because he had asked and she hadn't had time to think properly, she was opening herself up to ridicule and gossip.

She didn't even have any proper dresses to wear but for the worn frock she used when visiting her father and the nicer blue one Richard had given her. She couldn't simply walk around the city in trousers and a shirt, no matter her relationship with Richard. It was simply not done. Yet here she was, with no other option. Eleana couldn't remove her promise to go; it had already been given and she was a woman of her word. She also didn't have enough money to buy a single appropriate frock in town, let alone enough to last the month.

She would be soundly ridiculed, abused, and become the subject of the gossip. Perhaps if she kept her head down, people would not know about her. Or they would not assume that she and Richard were…

She hugged Hunter deeper, breathing in his earthy scent and thinking that perhaps he was her only friend in such times as this. Richard wouldn't understand. He had never been the object of such ridicule and no one would dare cross him. But her situation was different. She had no money, no status, was simply a servant and as such could not stop people from talking. It was no help that she could not defend herself.

Not for the first time, Eleana wished with all her heart that she could talk. She remembered being a little girl and realising that she was unable to make any sort of noise. She had even driven herself to various hurts, trying to elicit a desperate howl from the shock of the pain. It had been her only goal for so long, until one day Eleana realised that no matter how hard she tried, she was locked into silence forever. Since then, she had accepted that fact and had even come to enjoy it, watching people try and understand her with pleasure. But every now and again, she felt like a little girl, shut off from those around her because of her lack of speech and she wished with every fibre of her being for a voice.

Hunter patiently let Eleana seek her comfort from him and when she finally took a deep breath, uncertain of what the future would hold but knowing she had to face it, he pressed his nose against her hand and licked the tips of her fingers gently. Eleana smiled at him and pet his silky fur before standing and grabbing a small trunk, throwing her clothing inside and, when that was done, wished it were more full.

THE NEXT MORNING, Eleana's pitifully small trunk was loaded onto the carriage while Richard was overseeing the loading of the others. Eleana paced beside Theo and Fey, who had come to see her off.

She paused beside Fey, touching her head with both hands then throwing them into the air.

"You weren't thinking," Fey agreed, not bothering to cower under the glare that Eleana threw her. "You didn't have a chance. This was all very last minute, and you were being pressed for an answer. I can't say I don't wish you had outright refused, but under those circumstances, it would have been difficult."

Eleana stopped pacing and looked at the carriage with apprehension. She touched her chest and shrugged her shoulders desperately.

"The only thing you can do," Theo said simply. "You hold your head high and spend all of your time at the various kennels so that no one can speculate on the purpose of your visit." Eleana slouched, taking a deep breath and letting it out swiftly before burying her head in her hands.

Theo took a step closer and tentatively put his hand on her shoulder, keeping a strict distance between them so that no one, not even Eleana, could get the wrong idea regarding his motives. Fey joined him. Eleana turned to her and pressed in close for a hug. She was trembling with nerves. She had never been away from Belleview before, and now to do so under *these* circumstances?

The world felt like it was crumbling beneath her feet.

Eleana looked up and bit her lip as she glanced at the carriage again.

Richard was checking the last of the straps on the trunks, despite the protest of Hayes and the dismay of the footmen charged with loading the luggage. Henry stood near the door, looking more dishevelled than usual.

Eleana turned to Theo, her hand held out in a gesture of farewell. He gripped her hand, their wrists touching, their fingers not quite entwined. They were friends, no matter the strangeness between them these last few days. "Maybe," Theo murmured softly enough so that only Eleana, Fey, and the sharp eared hounds could hear, "this trip will show you that Lord Byrns isn't all that you think him to be. I don't want you to get hurt, Eleana, but if this is the only way to make you see, then so be it. Belleview will be waiting here for you when you get back. We all will."

Eleana pulled her hand away, frowning at Theo. Her gaze softened and she flashed her friends an understanding smile before she called the hounds to attention and moved towards the door of the enclosed carriage. She gravely accepted Henry's hand to help her inside. The two gentlemen climbed in after her and the hounds followed suit, making all three of the party grateful for the large size of the carriage. The seating situation was fairly tight, but they were not cramped or terribly uncomfortable.

No one spoke much during the journey to the city; Henry was considerate enough not to chastise Richard in the presence of Eleana, Richard was too busy going over the matters of business and admiring Eleana, whereas the Houndskeeper kept herself occupied by watching the scenery move past outside the window, her leg pressed against Hunter's side. She had never been far from Belleview and, if the knowledge of what looks and words awaited her in the city were not enough, the thought of being so far from home terrified her. Now, more than ever, she was wishing that she hadn't agreed. Maybe Theo and Fey were right, and she should just leave Richard who, despite his protestations, belonged in a class completely separate from her own.

Then, though, there was that spark of adventure. She was going to be harassed, and was farther from home than she had ever been in her life, but she was also going to explore. To experience life. Everything would be new and, with Richard dealing with his solicitor during the days, she would be left on her own to see the city, to figure out things for herself. Part of

Eleana revelled in that fact and was looking forwards to the opportunity. She was not one to cower from hardship, despite the other part of her that was quivering in fear.

The city was two days' travel from Belleview at a leisurely pace, and with Richard pushing the driver as much as possible, they only had to stop and change horses once. The group made it to the city long into the night, sated by the basket of food that Mrs. Graham had seen fit to provide. The house at which the carriage stopped was grand and the finest in a neighbourhood of fine houses. A light was burning in the drawing room window and, as the three travellers and the two hounds alighted, the door was opened by a severe looking butler.

"Welcome, m'lord Byrns," the man said, taking in every detail of the people before him and raising his eyebrows a fraction as he took in Eleana's figure and the attire she wore. "I have dinner waiting, should you wish it."

"No, thank you," Richard said, stifling a yawn. "I would much rather just go straight to bed."

"Very good, m'lord. I have prepared the master suite for you and the main guest quarters for Mr. Marduke, the secondary quarters for, ahem, Miss Tarell," the butler said. Richard nodded, not noticing the slight hesitation, but Eleana immediately stiffened. She ordered the two hounds to follow along beside her and followed the butler up the grand marble staircase. Henry bid a good night to the pair and ducked off to his room, obviously familiar with the layout of Richard's city house. The butler vanished, leaving Richard and Eleana alone.

"Thank you," Richard said, reaching out to take Eleana's fingers, kissing the tips lightly. The touch sent tingles through Eleana, but she couldn't bring herself to smile more than a fraction.

No matter how he physically excited her, or that she knew him to have a good heart, it was by his hand that she was put into this situation. She couldn't lay the blame solely on him, for she knew it was her fault as well. But the fact that he didn't realise what he had done frustrated her. Was he really that oblivious? Or perhaps it was simple innocence. Maybe he just didn't realise the position he was placing Eleana in by bringing her along.

"I know you didn't want to leave the kennels, but I'm really glad you came," Richard murmured, stepping closer, a tired smile gracing his handsome features. "I would have missed you at Belleview. And now, you're here. It's like a dream," he whispered, placing a gentle hand under her chin to tilt her face up. Richard kissed her, lightly, gently, pleasantly, the act making Eleana relax slightly. He pulled away and pressed his lips to her forehead before breathing, "Goodnight." He left Eleana in the hallway, standing before her door.

A dream? She couldn't disagree; this entire affair was like a dream. Rich widower moves to country estate and falls in love, immediately, with the Houndskeeper. He begins courting her and whisks her away to the city. Eleana shook her head and ordered Hunter into the room before closing the door behind her. She changed into a nightshift and brushed out her hair before the vanity and studied her reflection. Something told her this dream might just turn out to be a nightmare.

Morning came all too quickly and Eleana, donning her old frock and wrinkling her nose at the reflection in the mirror, walked down the great stairs of the house, sniffing her way to the dining room where breakfast was already laid out. Henry was nowhere to be seen, but Richard was sitting at the head of the table, drinking his tea while he read over the morning newspaper. His plate was empty but for a few scraps and it looked as if he had been up for nearly an hour already.

Upon seeing Eleana enter, he smiled and stood, walking over to kiss her lightly on the cheek. "Good morning. I hope you slept well. I'm sorry I can't sit at breakfast with you, today, but I must get going. The affairs of the estate must be dealt with before I can even begin the matters of the school and I want to get everything sorted out as quickly as possible. Help yourself to breakfast and feel free to explore the city. As long as you have Hunter and Smoke with you, that is."

Eleana didn't have time to protest, about to say she could take care of herself, when Richard ordered Smoke to stay with her and darted out of the room, leaving her standing alone. She looked at the two dogs helplessly then huffed and sat down, not bothering to look around and see if the butler would be there to serve food or tea. She helped herself, as she had done her entire life, and ate quickly.

She was done with breakfast and nearly out the door, a woollen shawl over her shoulders, when Henry appeared at the top of the stairs, his clothes rumpled and his blonde hair sticking out in wayward directions. He looked as if he had just rolled out of bed and his yawn did not discourage the theory. He spotted Eleana and frowned. She did nothing, her hand on the doorknob, wondering if she would now be the object of pity or annoyance with Richard's greatest friend, the brother of his late wife.

"Be careful," Henry said simply, his normally cheerful and vibrant expression solemn. Eleana ducked her head in a nod and let herself out of the house, making careful note of the address before embarking on her exploration. She tried to analyse the meaning behind Henry's words, wondering if he meant them simply as a warning, that the city was dangerous to lone women. Then, his gaze wouldn't have been so serious and understanding.

He knew what Eleana had inadvertently walked into. He knew what Richard did not.

Shaking her head and wrapping the shawl closer around her shoulders, Eleana called Hunter and Smoke to heel and started off in an easterly direction, glad for the early hour. There were few people out on the street and those that were about gave Eleana little notice. They likely thought her a servant in one of the houses, setting out on an early morning errand for her mistress or master. The fact that two hounds were following her was strange, but not nearly enough so for any comment.

Eleana wandered along the street for a while, taking the largest street at every crossroads, and eventually she ran into one of the many shopping centres. There were shops all along the street, many catering to those looking for apparel, some jewellery, housing needs, specialty foods and the like. Eleana, her meagre sum of money in a purse at her sash, contented herself with walking from window to window, admiring the wares.

The hours passed and, around midday, Eleana bought herself a small luncheon in a tea shoppe that did not charge too much for a simple meal. She noted that more people were wandering about but still no one seemed to take any special attention to Eleana. Once, even, she exchanged a smile with a young woman wearing the starched uniform of a maid who was shopping with a basket on one arm.

Eleana's spirits grew as the day passed and she was loath to leave the little shopping centre, though she had been up and down the street twice. She could not reasonably linger without stepping inside one of the shoppes and her money was preciously guarded, meant for food alone. So, she instead crossed the street to where the beginnings of a park looked to be and wandered along a path there, feeling slightly over-whelmed by the number of people that were crowding around her.

The park rejuvenated her spirits and Eleana finally wandered back to the house feeling much better about her stay in the city, thinking that perhaps things wouldn't be as bad as she had predicted. She was wrong.

"I'm sorry," Richard said over breakfast, a newspaper folded as he looked at Eleana. "I know I said I would come with you today, but I have some urgent business at the solicitor's office. Can you manage on your own?"

Eleana, slightly disappointed, responded with an encouraging smile and nod. She hadn't seen much of Richard in the time she had spent in town, occasionally catching him for an hour or so just before dinner or before she turned in for the night. He would ask her about her day in the city and Eleana detailed her adventures, knowing full well that he wasn't really listening, but simply taking comfort in her presence. He was distracted, of that there was no doubt, but he was still considerate towards Eleana, seeing to her needs and occasionally kissing her fingertips or, if he were feeling more bold, her lips.

She was there in town with him, close to him, staying in his house, and yet she felt more apart and lonely than ever before. He was acting more like a distant brother than a lover or a friend and, but for the two dogs which followed Eleana everywhere, she was alone.

Wandering about the city after the first day had proven to be more troublesome than Eleana had hoped.

She had travelled in various directions and soon it was well known that she was staying as a guest at the house of Lord Byrns, though they were not married or related. The looks that people threw here were contemptuous and hardly did Eleana pass by a group of people before they were whispering about her, speculating on her station and her involvement with Richard. He was not at fault, of course, but was caught up in her feminine wiles.

Eleana ignored these comments as much as she could, knowing full well that she incited them. The constant barrage of insults against her was wearing and many times, she did not stay out much past luncheon, instead returning to the house to struggle valiantly through one of the books in the small library.

The city was so much louder and full of people and, truth be told, Eleana knew she was out of her depth. She had never left Belleview before and while she was used to coming and going from the village of Hartwell, used to people on the estate and the surrounding county, this was so much busier. People were every-where, walking, riding, and driving. It was fairly over-whelming. Still, she was determined to enjoy herself and so she explored, learning of the whereabouts of two of the city kennels. When Richard said he could not accompany her that day, Eleana smiled bravely and decided she would visit the kennels without him.

She was dressed in the blue dress Richard had given her, a woollen shawl wrapped around her shoulders to protect from the morning chill. Hunter walked faith-fully at her right and Smoke at her left when Eleana turned off of one of the main streets to head to a different part of the city.

"Do you see her? Look how brazen she is," a woman's shrill voice said, carrying over the sounds of the street. There were other replies, the words lost in the noise, then the woman spoke again, "I just feel so badly for poor Lord Byrns. If only he would marry again, things would be different. He could stop carrying on with a lowly servant."

Eleana stiffened and forced herself to keep walking, annoyance rising in her blood. She was away from the street in another minute and, upon finding herself on a street filled with people of middle-class orientation and cabs, coaches, even a carriage or cart, sighed in relief. These people were too busy to take much notice of her. Mothers were walking hand in hand with their children, young boys ran to and fro, shouting chal-lenges to one another. A group of men passed by, their pace brisk, their heads bent together as they discussed some matter or another.

Clutching the shawl closer, Eleana ducked and darted her way through the people, her dress marking her as one of them. No one took notice of the lone girl with two dogs, and when she turned on a street that would lead her to the closest kennels, no one cared. Smoke sniffed the air eagerly and moved faster, his steps taking him to the edge of the street where he pressed his nose to the ground. Eleana snapped her fingers and the dog apologetically moved back to her side.

The trip to the kennels was swift and Eleana felt herself relax when she stepped through the gate and into the yard which surrounded the building. There were two men with dogs in the yard, training them, and at the approach of Eleana, one hound—a hunter pup—raced towards them, tongue lolling eagerly.

"Grant, stop," the trainer snarled and immediately, the pup skidded to a stop, hunching his shoulders as if expecting a blow. Eleana frowned. "I'm sorry about that. I haven't been training him for long and he still gets excited." The trainer was short and still well-muscled, numerous cuts on his hand showing that he had been training a vicious dog more than once, some a long time ago and some recently.

Eleana gave a shrug and ordered Hunter and Smoke to sit before holding out her hand to the trainer. He smiled awkwardly before turning his attention to the hounds.

"Those are fine dogs you have. Though that black one looks similar to Smoke, Lord Byrns' hound." Eleana nodded and the trainer blinked in surprise. He peered closely at her as if waiting for an explanation and Eleana tapped her throat to signify her muteness. "Mute, eh? And with two dogs following you around, one of which belongs to Lord Byrns himself," the trainer said, looking at Hunter and Smoke as much as Eleana. He grinned. "You must be that Houndskeeper out at Belleview I've heard about. Eleana, right?"

She nodded, smiling modestly. He laughed and called out to the other man, a taller, thicker and older man working with a lady's dog, delicately boned with a pelt of pure white,

"Hey, Norman, come over here. We got ourselves the Houndskeeper from Belleview over here."

Eleana blushed slightly from the attention but happily shook hands with the other trainer and crouched down so she could examine and pet the two other dogs. The hunter pup wriggled with excitement, flopping to the ground and exposing his belly almost as soon as Eleana started petting him. The lady's dog was far more dignified, simply thrusting her nose into Eleana's hand as a sign of affection.

"Come on, we'll show you the kennels," Norman said, patting a willing Smoke on the head. "I must say, you've done a good job with this one. The trainer that handled him before Lord Byrns moved to the country wasn't nearly as skilled as one would like. But you got him sorted out. And the other, ah, Hunter it says on the collar. I've never seen a more well-behaved dog in my life."

Eleana ducked her head in embarrassment and waved away the praise, following the trainers into the kennels. She spent the good part of the morning there, examining dogs at the request of the two trainers and watching as they put some of the dogs through their paces. She coddled week old puppies and even ate luncheon with the two men, graciously accepting some fruit and a small sandwich from their supplies.

The distant chiming of the city clock sounded four times and Eleana jerked to attention, aghast at the time. She stood and, brushing as much fur as she could from her dress, waved to the two trainers who were working in tandem with a vicious fighter.

"It was nice meeting you," Norman called, his attention hardly wavering from the dog. Eleana smiled and walked towards the gate, Smoke and Hunter close at her heels, both dogs looking tired and happy from having played the whole day away.

Exhausted as the dogs were, Eleana only had to walk along and they would follow. She made it back to the street leading to Richard's house without mishap, impervious to the looks of the people she passed in her glow of happiness. She was startled to find that the street was far busier than she had previously seen, the way crowded with people and horses, coaches and cabs, carts and the like. She saw a few people out with their hounds or dogs on a late afternoon stroll and, knowing how tired her own dogs were, didn't bother to enforce her command of heel.

Hunter pressed closer to Eleana while people crowded around on the sidewalks, Smoke trailing only a few steps behind.

Because of that, it was almost too late when Eleana realised that Smoke was off, moving through the crowd of people swiftly and with a purpose, despite his exhaustion. She looked at Hunter, about to order him to fetch, when she stopped altogether. Hunter was too loyal to Eleana to dart away from her side, but the cause of Smoke's disappearance was apparent. Hunter's nose was in the air, his plumed tail held high, his legs spread wide. He whined. Eleana paled. There was a bitch somewhere nearby, and that bitch was in heat.

She ordered Hunter to bark, once, sharply, in an attempt to call Smoke back, but all that happened was the black dog stopped for a moment in the centre of the street. Eleana saw him and was off like a shot, darting as best she could through the throng of people, avoiding coaches and carts, until she was a mere metre away from Smoke. He was sniffing the air eagerly, his tail buffeting the air. Eleana's vision narrowed, focusing on the dog, and she lunged, not realising that a coach pulled by two great horses was bearing down on her.

Eleana grabbed the dog's collar just as the driver of the coach shouted in alarm, the horses letting out whinnies of fear as their reins were jerked. The one closest to Eleana rose up as much as the harness would allow, great hooves pawing the air. She turned and opened her mouth in a silent scream as the horse came down on top of her. The pain was immediate and blinding. Her shoulder felt like it was on fire and that fire was spreading down her side. She was barely aware of what happened next but for Hunter, standing over her, his lips drawn in a snarl at any who would dare approach her.

"Hunter, sit!" a firm voice said and Eleana's heart soared in hope. Hunter did as the voice said, obviously recognising the person and Eleana tried to focus her gaze on her saviour, her vision clouded with pain, barely holding onto consciousness. The only thing she noticed before she slipped into unconsciousness was that the person who lifted her into his arms had blonde hair, not black as she had expected. Then, it was dark.

Eleana awoke to agony, her left shoulder and side burning fiercely. She instinctively clenched her muscles, writhing on the bed where she lay, her teeth bared in a grimace of pain, her eyes squeezed shut against the pain. For a moment, the pain subsided then returned, stronger than ever. Eleana wished she could scream.

"Calm yourself," a male voice said. Eleana opened her eyes as much as she could and saw Henry Marduke sitting over her, his face concerned, a damp cloth in his hand.

He placed the free hand on Eleana's uninjured shoulder and dipped the cloth into a poultice, dabbing it into the open wound on her shoulder. She arched back, straining her neck against the pain. Henry pulled away and dipped the cloth into the poultice again, seeming to ignore the struggles she made. A few minutes passed and the pain slackened, the fire turning into a dull throbbing.

Eleana looked up at Henry, her breathing heavy, furrowing her brows in question, tears leaking from her eyes as she fought the pain. She had so many questions on her mind and she wanted an answer to all of them. She wanted Henry to talk and tell her what had happened and what was going on, to glean answers and to have something other than her pain upon which to focus. But mostly, she wanted to know why this man, with whom she had only a tentative connection, was sitting over her, tending her wounds, when Richard was nowhere to be seen.

"Relax, Eleana," Henry said, his voice soft and soothing. Eleana complied as best she could, though her hands still clenched with pain. Henry touched her tight fists and said again, "Relax." Eleana forced herself to do so and immediate relief flooded her. She took a deep breath and locked her gaze with Henry once more, her questioning eyes insistent.

Henry dabbed the cloth against her shoulder, whatever was in the mixture soothing and numbing her simultaneously.

"You went after Smoke in the street, do you remember? I had just arrived at the house in search of Richard when I heard the driver of the coach shout. I saw the horses panic and I saw them come down on you. I didn't know you, then, but once I saw Hunter running through the crowds of people, I realised what had happened. I went to pick you up out of the street and carried you to the house, half-expecting Richard to be there sending someone to summon a doctor. He was not, so I sent the butler to do so and brought you to your room.

"The doctor came quickly, having been on a house call nearby and he cleaned you up as best he could. I'm sorry, but the dress was ruined, and it had to be cut away," Henry admitted.

Eleana noticed for the first time that her shoulders were bare and that a sheet covered the parts of her which were unwounded. Her left shoulder and side were exposed, and she knew that she should have been embarrassed by her lack of modesty, but she couldn't bring herself to care.

Henry continued, careful to keep his face placid as he dabbed at Eleana's shoulder, slowly moving down her side. "The horse did a number on you, catching your arm at just the right angle to cut you up pretty badly. Your shoulder is relatively undamaged but for the fact that your muscle is severed, and your bone is bruised. You have two broken ribs, though, and the doctor says that you are supremely lucky neither pierced your lungs. He tried to give you morphine, but you reacted adversely, so he tried laudanum, which worked even less than did the morphine. I'm sorry, but you're going to have to live with the pain for a while."

Eleana blinked languidly, the only movement she

felt strong enough to make, and licked her lips, a sudden thirst coming upon her. Henry tipped a cup to her mouth and Eleana took a few mouthfuls before turning her head away. She took a deep breath and returned her gaze to Henry.

He pressed his lips together but continued his story, "I had word sent to Richard as soon as the doctor had no further use to me, but I'm afraid we've heard nothing from him. His solicitor's office is closed this late in the afternoon and I sent a footman around to his club, but we've heard nothing. I'm sorry, Eleana. I know you would much rather him here than me."

Eleana furrowed her brows, the realisation that Richard did not even know she had been injured striking her. Henry was right. She wanted him there, to tell her everything was going to be alright. She was fiercely independent by nature, used to relying on herself for everything, from living at Belleview to exploring the city on her own. Just this once, though, she wanted to be weak and to depend on Richard. Yet he was nowhere to be found.

She consoled herself with the thought that he would be there as soon as he got word of what had happened and looked once more at Henry, hoping that he would be able to read her well enough to realise what she was asking. She was not so lucky and could not move to communicate further. A whine outside the bedroom door caught her attention. Henry stood and walked to the door, opening it enough to order Hunter to be quiet before returning to Eleana's bedside.

"Hunter is unhurt, but Smoke suffered severe injuries. He broke both left legs and got a pretty bad blow to his spine. I'm sorry, but he's dead," Henry said, keeping his tone soft and gentle. Eleana felt her resolve wavering and though Henry had been liberal in applying the poultice, pain flared through her. She screwed up her features in a picture of despair and arched her back, a silent cry on her lips. Her eyes were closed but tears still managed to escape, falling down her cheeks to land on the pillow.

Henry looked helplessly at Eleana but knew he could do nothing for her at the moment. He stood and went to the door, opening it wide enough to let Hunter in, before closing it behind him. Eleana's faithful hound leaped to the bed and settled himself at her feet, mindful of her injuries. He rested his sad brown eyes on her and guarded her while Eleana was in the throes of pain and grief, sleeping only when his mistress slipped off into unconsciousness.

Eleana woke again some unknowable number of hours later. The curtains in the room were drawn close, a slim beam of light the only evidence to the time of day. Hunter slept peacefully on the bed, so either very little time had passed, or someone had let him out and fed and watered him while Eleana was asleep. She guessed the latter.

Her shoulder and side no longer burned viciously but they were painful, nevertheless. She could feel whatever herb in the poultice that had numbed her wearing off and kept still and relaxed so as not to incite further pain. Eleana was only mildly sleepy, so she simply laid there, listening to the clatter of horses and wheeled vehicles moving through the street outside, the sound barely audible through the closed window and curtain.

"Where have you been?" Henry's voice rang out harshly through the door and Eleana's interest was excited immediately. His voice was not loud through the closed door, but the words were clear and precise. He probably thought her still asleep.

"How is she?" came the response. Eleana's breath hitched. It was Richard. Surely, he would open the door, no matter if she were asleep or awake and come see her. She wanted to see him.

"She's sleeping, which is good since I can give her nothing for the pain," Henry said, his voice sharp and angry, which confused Eleana. Why hadn't Richard opened the door yet? Was he waiting until he got the full story out of Henry? She was careful not to move, but she wanted to signal Hunter to make noise to indicate she was awake. Instead, she lay there, still and unmoving, listening for the turning of the doorknob.

"I heard what happened from the doctor," Richard said, his voice pained. The sound was louder, indicating he was very close to the door and Eleana waited in anticipation. "Henry let me pass," Richard growled. What? Why wasn't Henry letting him through to her?

"No," Henry said flatly, his voice coming from directly outside of the door. "No, Richard, you do not deserve to see her. Do you have any idea what time it is?"

"Morning," Richard snapped. "I know I should have been here earlier, but I was held up. Let me pass!"

"You should have been here earlier? You should have come home in the fastest cab you could possibly find the moment that you received word at your club! I have confirmation from the footman I sent that you were there, that you initially ignored his message because you were busy conversing with some people about the school," Henry snarled.

"I did not know," Richard begged. Eleana blinked, understanding dawning upon her. Henry had told her that there had been no word from Richard, that his whereabouts were unknown, yet here he was saying that Richard had been at the club and that the footman had delivered the message. And if it was morning, the following day, then Richard had been gone all night.

"No, you did not," Henry said, his voice sharp with anger. "But you finally took the message and what did you do? You should have come here as quickly as possible, to help the doctor, to put poultice on her wounds. Damn it, she's half-naked in there and it should have been you who had to see that, not someone who barely knows her. Yet I was the one who helped the doctor, who treated her, who, despite the fact that she's an unmarried woman, went in there when she was covered with a sheet alone, and treated her wounds. So, answer me this, Richard Byrns, where were you?"

Richard faltered, "I was, ah—"

"Have you been drinking?" Henry's voice was wrought with disbelief and anger. Eleana heard the movement of bodies outside her door and she held her breath, straining to hear, too afraid to think. "Answer me," Henry said, his tone harsh and cold.

"I—yes," Richard said, his voice so quiet that Eleana barely heard him through the door. She was stricken, her breath sharp with shock. Tears, unbidden, gathered in her eyes and she desperately blinked them away, her chest tight.

"Why?" Henry asked, some of the anger gone from his words, replaced with horror and confusion. "You haven't touched a drop for ages," he said so softly that Eleana had to guess at the words.

"I know," Richard replied. "And I had refused every drink that I've been offered here. I hadn't touched a drop until I got that message. I wanted to come home as soon as I had heard, but the only thing I could think was that I should have been there."

"You're right," Henry said flatly. "You should have been."

"But I was not!" Richard replied, his voice just as sharp as Henry's. "And do you want to know why? Because I told Eleana I could not go out with her today to explore the city. You were the one who pointed out what people were saying, what they would think, and I couldn't put her through that. It would only get worse if they saw us together and so I went to my solicitor's office to finish up some menial matters and then went on to my club. I was not there with her because I did not want her to get hurt and yet, somehow, none of that matters because I was not there. I was cowardly and selfish, wanting to keep her reputation clean when I've already ruined it. I wanted to be the white knight, but I was the one who asked her to town. I did not realise the cost until you pointed it out to me, until I saw the faces of people I passed, and so to fix my mistake, I turned to cowardice when I should have defended her. I should have explained to anyone who asked what she meant to me instead of leaving her to fend for herself. And then *this* happens, all because I was a coward, a fool. I couldn't come home, not after that. You have to understand!"

"So, what, you went out and drowned your sorrows just like you always have?" Henry asked. "Richard, I'm your friend. I've been your friend for nearly your entire life and even when my sister died, leaving you heartbroken, I did not think you were wrong for turning to the drink. But this, *this lunacy*, is too much. You say you're a coward? You're right. You say this is your fault? Absolutely. You don't deserve to come home after what you've done and expect things to continue as normal. Eleana needed you and you abandoned her to nurse your own wounds. Stay away from her until she's healed, and you can reasonably explain to her why you weren't there. And for what it's worth, Richard, I hope that Eleana is more forgiving than I."

Richard let out a strangled sound and Eleana heard no more. She was staring up at the ceiling, her mind reeling with the knowledge of what Richard had done, why he had kept himself distant from her and why he wasn't there, as Henry said, when she needed him. Her chest tightened into a pain sharper than that in her shoulder and Eleana let herself cry, realising that she agreed completely with Henry.

CHAPTER 17

*E*leana cried herself out. She lay still on the bed and cried, turning her head aside when Hunter crawled forwards, tentatively licking her cheek. She didn't know how much time had passed, but when Henry came in bearing some broth and a clean cloth with which to treat her wounds, she was out of tears. The pain in her shoulder could not match the sharp throbbing in her chest and, not bothering to engage Henry in conversation, Eleana barely even flinched when he touched and cleaned her wounds.

In a moment of clarity, Eleana realised that, while she thought she had not loved Richard, she cared about him enough for this hurt to feel like heartbreak. And she knew what heartbreak felt like.

Henry finished dabbing the poultice on her and carefully dipped broth into her mouth, his face set and grim. Eleana watched him leave the room, her eyes already drooping with weariness. Henry looked back at her and saw what he had feared most.

Eleana knew. She had heard and so she was silent, asking no questions, seeking no information. Henry closed the door behind him and Eleana closed her eyes, gratefully slipping into unconsciousness, escaping the pain which no poultice could numb.

She woke when Hunter climbed off the bed, going to the opening door and slipping out. In Hunter's place, Richard appeared, his clothing dishevelled and his hair sticking up at all angles. In the half-light of the room, he looked tired, his eyes sunken, his skin pale. Eleana made no motion except to follow him with her eyes, her expression carefully blank.

Richard smiled weakly. "How are you?"

Eleana made no answer.

Richard sat by the side of her bed and reached for her hand. Ignoring the pain it brought, Eleana pulled her hand from his grasp, turning her gaze past Richard and towards the ceiling. Still, it was impossible to miss the flash of deep-rooted pain across his face. He stood and walked towards a painting hanging on the opposite wall, taking deep breaths to control himself.

"You heard us, didn't you?" he asked softly. He didn't have to look at Eleana to know her answer. Richard ran a hand through his hair and chuckled drily, without humour. "Then there's no redeeming myself. I can only tell you I'm sorry and that I wish, with every fibre of my being, that I had done things differently. I'm a coward and a fool and a drunken man too set in his ways to change," he said. Richard turned and looked into Eleana's eyes, the green depths which were so closed off from him. He broke away, fearful of seeing his own pain reflected there.

Richard walked slowly to the door, as if he hoped that Eleana would signal him to stay. She did not, though he stood in the open doorway for many minutes.

"I will make arrangements for your immediate return to Belleview. I still have business here in town, so I will be staying on for two weeks more," he said, his tone clinical and removed. Relief flooded Eleana; she would finally be returning home. She wouldn't have to stay in this grand city house, the only thing to occupy her time being thoughts of a conversation she had overheard.

She pretended not to see the pain in his face.

He swallowed the pain and turned, hand on the doorknob so he could close it behind him. Then, his voice low, "I only hope that you can bring yourself to forgive me someday." He closed the door and left Eleana alone in the room which now felt like a stifling prison.

Eleana discovered that she hadn't cried out all the tears in her. For Richard, for the pain he felt and the pain that Eleana felt, for the mistakes they both had made—her in trusting him more than he deserved, he for turning to cowardice—for herself, Eleana cried.Within two day, the doctor deemed Eleana well enough to travel, provided that she didn't exert herself and she rested properly at Belleview. She returned home immediately, staying at an inn one night on the road and driving up to the house before luncheon the next day. Eleana opened the door of the coach and stepped out carefully, Hunter at her side. There came an excited bark and Colonel raced up, his stumpy tail wagging. Eleana smiled half-heartedly and signalled a greeting, unable to crouch and pet the dog. She looked around for her father.

Joseph appeared from around a corner, smiling lightly at the sight of his daughter and his dog. When he saw the bandages on her shoulder and the sling her arm rested in, he frowned and hurried forwards.

"Eleana," he exclaimed, helping her stand up straight and looking at her in alarm. "What happened? Where is Lord Byrns? I wasn't expecting you home so soon, and especially not alone? Are you alright?" He held Eleana at arms' length, careful of her injured side. To his surprise, his daughter's eyes welled with tears and she lunged forwards to wrap him in a one-armed hug, holding on tight enough to make it seem like she would never let go.

Theo appeared to take care of the horses and paled slightly when he saw Eleana and the state she was in. When she turned her head slightly, catching his face, he saw the tears gathered there. Her lip trembled and he didn't have to say anything to know that Eleana was telling him he had been right. Richard was not who she thought.

"Come," Joseph said gently, leading his daughter away from the coach, Hunter and Colonel following along behind. "Let's go back to the cottage and get you something to eat. You can tell me all about it there," he said. Eleana nodded and, with the support of her father, started walking across the yard to where the kennels were. Theo took charge of her trunk and followed along behind, stoic and silent.

Her gestures were jerky and slightly difficult to understand, even for her father, but she made do with the use of one hand and her ever expressive face. Joseph would occasionally ask a question, clarifying a point or seeking out some detail she did not mention, but overall, he simply sat and listened. Finally, with luncheon cold and mostly untouched, Eleana finished her story and looked hopelessly at her father, posture slumped and good hand resting on Hunter's head, which sat in her lap.

"Eleana, my child," Joseph said and moved closer so he was able to brush a strand of hair behind Eleana's ear. He kissed her forehead gently and Eleana leaned into his shoulder, her tears flowing freely. "Hush," he murmured, rubbing circles on her back, "Everything will be okay. Shhh, shh." Eleana nodded, her father's words of comfort more meaningful than any apology. She let herself be soothed and then, when her tears had turned to silent hiccoughs, she helped her father clear the table. She followed him out to the kennels, greeting the hounds she had left and trying to hold in her pain.

Joseph, over the next week, made no mention of returning to his home in the village. He helped Eleana with her hounds, doing what she could not do with her injured arm and ribs, letting her relax and shouldering some of her burden so that she could recover and take time for herself. She accepted his help thankfully and let herself wander over the grounds when he worked and she needed to be alone, often stopping in the forest at the sight of her mother's and her lover's graves.

She meditated, reflected, and healed. Hunter followed alongside as faithful as ever, his silent presence comforting Eleana. Her shoulder was healed and her ribs, while still sore, were well on the way to healing as well. She was still cautious with her arm, but slowly she began to take back some of the burdens of her work. Her father made no move to leave, which in itself was a relief to Eleana.

At the end of the week, she wandered over to the stables, sure to stay far, far away from the horses, and watched Theo work. He was playing with the foal of the brood mare, acquainting the creature to human contact and subtly training it as well. He spotted Eleana standing near the padlock and halted in his work, the foal stopping as well to see why his play companion wasn't playing. Theo murmured soft words to the horse and led it to its mother, closing them in before jogging over to Eleana.

"Eleana," he said, stopping a few feet from her, not

quite sure what to say. She smiled slightly and reached out for his hand. She took it and squeezed it tightly, revelling in the feeling of his calluses against hers. Here were hands of her own class.

After a moment, she dropped her hand.

"Eleana," he said again, his voice softer and warmer. She stepped forwards and wrapped her arms around him, careful of her shoulder, burying her face in his shoulder, breathing in his scent and thinking that, though he smelled of horses and sweat, perhaps it wasn't so bad.

Theo and Fey and her father were the only friends she needed.

Theo took a breath and pulled back from Eleana a few inches so as to look at her, his eyes questioning and concerned. "Eleana, what happened?"

She sighed and stepped back, keeping her uninjured arm wrapped around Theo's, and started for the kennels where her father was working with some young pups. Theo followed along and when Eleana stopped, disentangling herself and catching the attention of her father, he smiled uncertainly. The two had spoken occasionally in Eleana's absence but with the injured Houndskeeper standing between them, a conversation with Eleana's father made Theo nervous.

To his relief, Eleana signalled to her father something complex which he didn't catch, her back turned to him.

Joseph blinked in surprise, "Are you sure?" Eleana nodded and put her hand on Hunter's head, rubbing his ears, the only sign of anxiety she gave. "Very well," Joseph said and, turning full on to face Theo, he sighed. "Eleana has asked me to explain to you what happened, since I am more familiar with her method of speech. She wants you to tell Fey, Mrs. Graham, and Hayes, but no one else. Listen carefully, because I'm only going to say this once."

"Of course, sir," Theo said respectfully, ducking his head.

Joseph said nothing for a moment, appraising the man standing before him, his features stoic. Then, he started to speak, detailing what had happened to Eleana from the moment of her accepting Richard's impromptu invitation to town to her return to Belle-view. He left out no detail that Eleana had told him and though Theo's jaw clenched in anger at the slights made towards Eleana, Joseph kept his voice calm and his features carefully blank. When he finished, Theo was clenching his fists and grinding his jaw. Eleana touched his arm and he turned to her, prepared to express his anger.

Instead, he saw no anger in Eleana's green eyes. Hurt, yes. There was plenty of hurt. But there was no anger. She took his hand in her own and stared at him insistently. Theo sighed and relaxed his muscles. "You've forgiven him, haven't you?"

Eleana blinked once and nodded, then held up a finger. She touched her chest and brought it outwards then shook her head and put her hand on Theo's chest, her expression grave. The hostler furrowed his brows and looked at Joseph in plea.

"Forgiving," Joseph translated, "isn't the same thing as loving. Nor is it the same as trusting." Eleana nodded and smiled at Theo, her eyebrows pressed together in the middle, creating a single line which bespoke desperation and pleading. Theo stared at her in confusion for a moment before he realised that Eleana was asking for his forgiveness for being so insolent, so disbelieving when he had tried to warn her.

Theo smiled, the gesture surprisingly gentle. He put a hand on her good shoulder. "Think nothing of it." Eleana smiled, though that gesture was not quite as cheerful as before. She pointed to Hunter and shrugged. "That's alright," Theo said. "I…I have to talk to Fey. And then I must return to work. I'll see you at supper."

The week passed and Eleana found herself able to do all her normal duties, albeit a bit more slowly than normal. She shared her work with her father, not yet thinking of sending him back to the village. Nor did Joseph intend to go back to the village, not until he had seen the face of the man who had so hurt his daughter. He knew Eleana could take care of herself, but it was a matter of fatherly pride to be able to look into the eyes of the cause of her pain and strike fear into his heart. Eleana was simply content to have her father near, lending his silent support while she worked and also as she spent time with Theo and Fey. She even sat with Mrs. Graham one afternoon and shared a cup of tea while the woman clucked over her foolishness in encouraging Richard.

MRS. GRAHAM and Hayes were the most affected by Eleana's plight, having had such high hopes for Richard and the lovely Houndskeeper. They made sure that Eleana was treated well in her time of recovery, having the kitchens prepare her favourite foods for supper and having lemon cake delivered to the cottage twice. They even went so far as to ensure that no rumours of Eleana's plight left Belleview grounds. Yet, for all their attention, the housekeeper and butler couldn't but feel pity for Richard.

That is, until his coach pulled into Belleview one morning.

Mrs. Graham immediately ordered the servants to have everything made ready and she went out to meet the master when the carriage stopped in front of the house. She stood, hands pressed together in her skirt, a practised expression of neutrality gracing her face. She nearly dropped the expression when Richard climbed out of the coach, a defeated man. He had lost nearly half a stone and his skin looked sallow and seemed to hang off him. His eyes were bloodshot and sat amidst dark circles which expressed exhaustion. His clothes were loose and not properly done up, his cravat tied improperly, his jacket buttoned with the wrong button, his boots scuffed and dirty.

He watched in complete silence as the footmen came to take his trunks into the house then he met the eyes of Mrs. Graham. Richard smiled wanly, the gesture cynical and knowing. "I guess you've pieced together what happened," he said, his voice hoarse. He coughed slightly then frowned and reached into his jacket pocket to pull out a flask which he opened and pressed to his lips for a good few seconds. The relief on his face was immediate and, while Mrs. Graham was horrified that he was drinking again, she couldn't help but feel pleased that he had found something to numb the pain.

Her anger towards him all but melted away and, in a motherly gesture, she stepped forwards and put one hand on his shoulder, the other under his arm, to lead him into the house. Richard did not protest when she brought him to his bedroom rather than the library or study and he sank into the wing-back chair situated beside his window. Mrs. Graham fiddled with his trunk and various knick-knacks for a moment and when she could do no more without making it obvious that she was keeping an eye on Richard, he spoke.

"How is she?" he asked softly. Mrs. Graham sat on the edge of the bed and sighed.

"She was hurt, physically and emotionally, when she came back," Mrs. Graham said truthfully. "And I wish I could say that she was still hurting, still waiting for someone, for you, to come and make everything alright again, but she isn't. Eleana's always been strong and she's pieced herself together again. She still hurts, but not as much. She has her father and Theo, and all the rest of us to look after her, as well."

Richard frowned and looked out the window, upon the great lawn of Belleview without seeing a single thing. "I guess that means that I've lost her."

"I don't know," Mrs. Graham replied. "Eleana's strong and she's turned to other people to fill what you created. But only you can figure out whether she still has the capacity to love you. And you will never know unless you try."

"Don't you realise what I've already achieved by trying?" Richard snarled. He kept his gaze fixed on the window but there was an obvious flash of anger in his visage. Mrs. Graham understood, though, that his anger wasn't directed at her but at himself.

"You made a mistake," she said sternly.

Richard turned his head sharply to glare at her, his mouth opened to make a response.

"You made one hell of a mistake," Mrs. Graham continued, cutting Richard off. "Luckily for you, making mistakes is what we humans do. You make a mistake, you get the opportunity to make it right. You may not fix everything, or even mend much of anything, but you get to *try*. So, don't you tell me that you've already tried with Eleana, that you're just going to sit there and give up. You get to try again. Because you well know that if you don't, you're going to lose her. You apologise, m'lord, or you'll not only lose her, but all of us."

Mrs. Graham rose from the bed, her cheeks tinted

with red at her frustration with her master and especially with his stupidity. She didn't wait for a response but simply strode out of the room, closing the door briskly behind her, thus leaving Richard to his grim thoughts. He watched the door for a moment, shocked at Mrs. Graham's reaction, then returned his attention to the window.

There were figures out on the lawn, he noted. He stood and walked over to the window, searching for the figure which he wanted most to see. And there she was, with loyal Hunter standing beside her, and someone else. Theo. They were walking, side by side, facing the house. Richard couldn't see if they were talking or if Eleana was smiling, but he wasn't quite sure he wanted to. The sight of her was enough to make his chest tighten in agony and he knew that no pull from his flask would set that right.

If he didn't try to mend his mistake, he would lose her. That was what Mrs Graham said. Lose her? Richard already felt as if he had lost her and he wasn't sure that this pain wasn't going to kill him. Eleana was gone from him, had pushed him aside, and now she was healed, walking around with Theo, with Hunter, as if the world hadn't changed at all. Richard snarled unintelligibly at himself and turned away from the window, searching for something upon which to exact his anger.

He paused. Eleana had been hurting when she came back to Belleview? Was still hurt, if only slightly? That meant he mattered, at least somewhat. He was sorry that he had caused her hurt, but the fact that he had done so could only mean that she cared about him, for him, even a little. And considering Mrs. Graham's words, she likely cared more than a little. That meant that there was still hope.

He had to fix what he had done.

Richard pulled out his flask and wavered between putting it to his lips and disposing of it. His conscience won out and he deposited the flask on his bedside table, moving towards the door. He walked through the house in a daze, not seeing whether he passed any persons or even really where he was going. He went into the study and cleared aside the accumulated letters on his desk, unstopping the inkwell and cutting his quill afresh.

The image of Eleana and the hope Mrs. Graham had instilled floated in his mind as he wrote, putting his frantic words down on paper. He filled two sheets in this manner and, without bothering to read what he had written, folded the sheets and stuffed them into an envelope, writing her name carefully on the front. Automatically, his hand reached for the bell to call a servant, but he hesitated.

"No," he muttered and stood, walking out of the house, his sunken eyes blazing. He strode across the lawn and half expected Eleana to still be walking with Theo. But she was nowhere to be found, so he pushed onwards to her cottage, rapping sharply on the door, the envelope in hand. To his surprise, it was not Eleana that answered, but her father.

"Lord Byrns," Joseph said coldly, his small dog at his side. Richard faltered under the steel gaze of Joseph, his courage quickly vanishing. Had he been wrong? Just because Eleana was hurt didn't mean that she cared in that manner for him. Perhaps he had truly lost her. He still had to apologise, though.

In the face of Richard's hesitation, Joseph spoke.

"I am going to drop the formality that your title requires and speak plainly. I warned you, when you first came here, not to hurt my daughter. You have done so anyways and so I am now free to take action. However, out of consideration for your feelings towards Eleana, I will be lenient."

"I'm sorry," was all that Richard managed. Joseph narrowed his eyes.

"I ought to beat you to the ground for what you've done," he hissed. "But I will simply say this: if you come near Eleana without her express consent, if you attempt to speak with her, if you *ever* bother her, I will be well within my rights to demand recompense."

"You're right," Richard breathed, startling Joseph. "You ought to beat me to the ground. I deserve it, and I will follow your instructions regarding Eleana with all my heart. I only wanted to give her this." Richard held out the envelope which Joseph took tentatively, his eyes wary. "I *am* sorry for what I've done. I wish with every ounce of humanity I have within me that I could take my actions back. I'm in love with Eleana and I never wanted to see her hurt. I would rather die than cause her injury, but I know that I cannot live without her."

He bowed at the waist to Joseph and turned, walking back towards the house, his diminished figure making a pathetic sight. Joseph sighed and looked at the envelope then back at the man that was Eleana's master and her misery. And he thought that it was every bit as likely Eleana could not live without Richard.

My Dearest Eleana,

I know that you will want nothing more than to dash this letter into pieces and never speak to me again, and you would be well within your rights to do so. I pray that you will read this letter through before you come to any conclusions. I shall not make any applications to you unless you wish it and tell me so, but I hope these words grant me the chance to see you again. To apologise.

When I first came to Belleview, I was a broken man. Instead of facing up to the reality that my wife was dead, instead of coming to grips with that fact and dealing with the pain which seemed to wrack my entire being, I turned to drinking. I wanted to numb the pain and the grief and drinking did just that. It made everything in the world which reminded me of my dear Christina seem to be a dream. A dream that I could ignore, and a reality that I could not. So, I chose to live in a dream. I removed myself from town and any lingering reminders of Christina and purchased Belle-

view. I came with no servants, no friends, no great property but a few garments, my horse, and my dog. I expected to live in quiet solitude, dealing with my dream world in my own way. I did not think of the future, but of the moment. And in that moment, I wanted to be alone.

Then you came. I need not tell you what events befell me, as you were there. I only want you to know that I loved you immediately and completely. My dream, which was a nightmare, became wonderful. I hated myself for it. Who was I, a husband who lived when his wife died, to fall in love? My grief was terrible, and yet with help it lessened. I hated you, or so I thought, for making me love you. I put you through terrible abuses because I suffered. I was wrong.

I learned the depth of my mistakes and so I tried to change. I wanted to be your friend, since I felt that I did not deserve to be your love. I still clung to drinking, though. I was fearful of facing reality on the pretence that I would find it not as my current, glorious dream, was wont to be. My body also craved alcohol, as you well know. So, when we went on that fateful hunting trip, I wanted to run away rather than face reality. I stayed, though, because you were there. Still, I fell into illness, the transition between truth and false illusions. I would have died had you not sacrificed your person to save me.

From our shared injuries, we became friends. From friends, I knew we could become more. I did not want to force my love on you, though. I wanted you to come to love me in your own way. I was, again, wrong.

You learned of my love when I told Henry and so I acted, begging your forgiveness, cursing my stupidity—you know the rest of the tale, up to that terrible day in town, when all I had worked and hoped for was lost. I wish that I would have been there, to protect you and carry you from the street, to take the injury in your place, or if I could not, to tend you as a lover should. I was a coward. I was wrong.

Henry informed me of what gossip would befall you due to my ill-thought-out invitation which I pressed you to accept. You, as an unmarried woman and my paid servant, would be painted as a whore or worse. I wish that I could soften this blow, but I have vowed to write the truth upon these pages. Your reputation would be ruined, and you would never be able to be seen in society again. It was all my fault. So, I did what I thought best and let you go about the city alone, with your dear Hunter and my beloved Smoke, as if you were nothing more than my Houndskeeper, in the hopes that I would stave off the rumours and the gossip that your presence with me would draw. It was for this reason that I stayed away, or so I told myself.

I know now that it would have been better had I stood with you and claimed you as my own, my love, rather than leave you alone and act as if I were ashamed of being seen in your presence. My own folly brought more pain and ruin upon you than my good intentions had prevented. A part of me knew this and yet I stayed away, and for that I am sincerely sorry. I was a coward and a fool and for my errors, I beg your forgiveness.

However, I cannot ask your forgiveness for what happened once I learned of your accident. I do not deserve such reverence. I wanted to run to you should you be seriously injured, but I was assured that you would live, that you would only endure superficial injuries and would heal within a month. Then I realised that your injuries had come about because I was too much the coward to walk the city with you. Had I been there, I could have prevented you from going into the street or gone myself. I knew, in that instant, that I did not deserve you and that, though I love you with my whole being, you stood apart from me as something better. Rather than deal with such a terrible reality, which was enough to cause me terrible anguish, I turned to the only solution I know: drink. In doing so I fear that I have lost you forever.

Even if you would never speak with me again, I beg you to take into consideration that my actions were done out of ignorance and that I take full responsibility for what I have done. I love you, dearest Eleana, and I would never intentionally do you harm. I am sorry. To live without you is torturous and heartbreak can be my only end, and it is no more than I deserve.

With all my mind, body and soul, I am sorry that I have hurt you. Forgive me.

- Richard

ELEANA STRUGGLED through the letter in solitude, leaning against her mother's grave for support while Hunter stood vigil at the edge of the clearing. She finished the letter and despite the fact that it had taken her nearly an hour to read, word by word, trying to piece together those words which she did not know by the words around it, she read it again. And she wanted to scream.

He was right; she did want to dash to letter to pieces, to tear it up and to scatter it to the wind. What right did he have to play so on her feelings? She wanted to blame him, but he already had taken the blame. She wanted to hurt him, but it was obvious he was hurting. She thought that she had forgiven him, but the letter forced her to reconsider and she realised that she hadn't.

Eleana took a deep, shuddering breath, and leaned her head back against the tomb, her hands picking through the grass which grew around it. Eleana looked at the letter again, not bothering to read the words, and lowered it, staring into the sky. She closed her eyes against her burning eyes and one, desperate tear slid down her cheek. *I forgive you*, she thought, clutching a hand to her breast. Forgiveness, though, did not mean she knew what to do next. There was the pain that Richard had caused to consider. There was her father's righteous anger. There was Theo.

Dear Theo. He had been so good to her, so protective and kind. He deserved to be loved, but Eleana knew that she would never feel more than a sisterly affection for him. He had not attempted to renew his attentions to her, not after all she had been through. Eleana knew they both were perhaps relieved at that. He would make a good husband, a faithful one, but she did not love him. Nor, she thought, did he love her.

Eleana signalled Hunter to her side and rose from

the ground. Was she really so foolish as to give up a good and quiet life for one broken man, living half in a dream? Was she really so foolish as to fall in love again, to give her heart again to a man who would much probably hurt her again, intentionally or no? Or was it better to put a stop to this whole affair and not take any further steps which would ensure that she would fall in love with Richard? Theirs would never be an easy life, if they married. They would both have to be sure about their devotion, their love. Better, perhaps to be an old maid, a devoted Houndskeeper, than to be hurt.

She would stagnate like that, Eleana knew. She was one who loved and who needed to be loved in return. That was evidenced by her hounds, whom she loved desperately and who loved her just as much. Hunter, who would not leave her side unless under great stress, who obeyed her every command without question, who had allowed her to tame him, did he not love her? She knew that he did and that she loved him in return. So, why should she not love Richard? Because he was human? Because he was more apt to make a mistake and hurt her? It was not intentional. He had acknowledged his wrong and promised to change. Her disappointment at his fear of other people's opinions was no excuse to deny what she knew she felt.

Eleana walked with Hunter through the woods onto the open lawn of Belleview, her eyes glazed and her thoughts distracting her from what she saw before her. Hunter pressed against her side to warn her and she woke from her reverie to see Theo approaching, a grave look on his face. When he saw her, he straightened and smiled, but Eleana could see it did not reach his eyes nor illuminate his features.

She furrowed her brows and touched his hand tentatively, asking a question. Theo laughed her off, the sound dry and slightly brittle. "There's nothing the matter with me. I was just coming to fetch you. It's supper time," Theo said. Eleana frowned and touched Theo's hand again, this time her expression insistent. The horse master took her hand from his and turned towards the house, walking beside Eleana so that she could not see his face. "I'm alright," he assured her. "You have no need to worry."

Eleana sighed but did not press the matter, instead walking with Theo to the servants' hall and taking her usual seat at the end of the table, slowly letting herself fall back into her thoughts of what to do. She was so engrossed by the thoughts of the task she must undertake that she nearly missed the look Fey cast upon Theo when she passed the serving platter on. It would have been impossible to miss, however, the lingering touch between the fingers of Theo and Fey.

Eleana furrowed her brows and looked at Theo. He caught her gaze and paled, opening his mouth then closing it again for lack of words. To his relief, Fey intervened, "Oh, Eleana, I'm so sorry. We thought that you...you weren't interested anymore, and it was all so sudden and..." She looked sincerely upset by the matter and Eleana could do little more than stare in shock. How had she missed such an understanding between Theo and her great friend?

Theo finally regained his powers of speech and took Fey's hand openly, turning to look at Eleana, "It happened while you were in the city. I... was moping about and Fey took it upon herself to cheer me up. It sort of simply, well, happened. And then you came back hurt and I wanted to tell you. I couldn't bring myself to do so, especially not after you told me what happened. I'm your friend, Eleana, and I wanted to explain, but you were in so much pain already. I'm a vagrant for trifling with you the way I did before. But you know there was nothing—there *is* nothing—between us now...right? I'm sorry, Eleana, really."

She blinked her shock away and, her smile wide, took the free hand of Theo and that of Fey and put them together. Fey smiled. "Thank you."

Eleana nodded and, for the first time since her return from the city, felt a great burden lift from her shoulders. Her friends were happy. She ate, then, more than she had in a while, laughing at some joke one of the others made, bringing attention to Fey and Theo and making both of them blush. When supper was finished, she began for the door, feeling cheerful and all thoughts of how to deal with Richard, for the moment, far from her mind.

Theo caught her shoulder and Eleana turned. "You still love him, don't you? Lord Byrns,"

She nodded, her worries regarding him now

coming back, her shoulders slumping with no slight fear.

"I wish you all the greatest happiness," he said. He put his hand to her chin and lifted her face so that their eyes met. "Don't go too hard on him. He has made a mistake, yes, been a fool, yes, but he loves you. He is a good man. Just bear that in mind," Theo murmured, then left Eleana to her own devices.

Eleana walked across the yard to her cottage and let herself in, looking about for her father. He seldom ate with the other servants, claiming that he was far happier to cook his own food and eat in peace and quiet, but Eleana guessed that it was as much to let her have something of her own. She found him sitting at the table, petting old Colonel, smiling pleasantly.

"How was your day?" he asked, looking up when she entered and pushing a chair from the table with a foot, even as he leaned back in his own. "You were gone for quite a while, so I fed and watered the hounds and put your mating pair into the larger kennel, separate from the others so the bitch does not drive the other dogs to madness."

Eleana nodded her thanks and sank into the chair, digging in her trouser pocket to pull out the letter Richard had written and which Joseph had delivered. She hesitated for a moment, wondering whether she ought to let her father read it, then chided herself for being silly. She handed the papers to him and waited nervously while he read the thing through.

At the end of his reading, Joseph set the letter on

the table and took a deep breath which he released slowly. "He certainly waxes eloquently," he murmured, watching Eleana carefully.

She was startled for a moment but nodded in agreement, her eyes showing her apprehension. Joseph studied her before chuckling, the sound quickly deepening and turning to laughter. Eleana frowned.

"You love him, don't you?" Joseph said at last, folding his arms over his chest and looking at his daughter with a great grin. Eleana blinked then ducked her head in assent. Joseph shook his head. "I guessed as much," he said. Eleana frowned and her lower lip slid out in a confused pout. "Hush, daughter," Joseph teased. "How could I not notice when you wander about the grounds, pining away and nursing your hurts? You tried to replace him with Theo, but I could tell that neither of your hearts were really in the matter. Theo loves that blonde maid, doesn't he? Fey, right?"

Eleana nodded sheepishly and touched her heart before reaching out and ruffling the hair of an imaginary child. "Of course you think of him more as a brother. He's too much like you to be anything else. The real question is, what have you decided to do about Lord Byrns?" Joseph asked, leaning forwards, his gaze earnest.

Eleana frowned then lowered her eyes and shrugged, the movement pitiful and frustrated. She threw her hands up in the air and put her head in them, showing her annoyance at herself and at her indecision. Joseph understood completely.

"You don't want to go to him now, because it's too soon after injuries. So wait, love. But don't wait too long or there will be a breach between you that neither will be able to mend," Joseph said. Eleana licked her lips nervously and happily went to the open arms of her father. He petted her hair and kissed her forehead. "It's going to be alright," he murmured.

Eleana waited, working with her hounds and thinking every day how she might go about relaying her feelings to Richard. She even marched up to the house a few times, determined just to have out with it and losing courage as she reached the door to the library, where Joseph assured Eleana that Mrs. Graham said he was spending his time. She spent nearly a week in this manner, fighting between indecision and spurts of bravery, reading his letter nearly every chance she got and considering the option of sending her own. And every day that she waited was another pain to Richard.

RICHARD WAS SPENDING his days in the library, feeling too listless to deal with business in his study. He buried himself in his books, picking up a volume in the morning and spending hours reading it before growling in frustration and tossing it aside, only to pace back and forth for an hour or so, nursing his broken heart and regretting his letter. He wondered whether Eleana had even read it or whether she had simply tossed it aside and pursued Theo or just worked with her hounds.

The image of Eleana kissing Theo all those many weeks ago haunted him.

Mrs. Graham brought Richard his luncheon on a tray, but she would not permit him to have his breakfast and dinner in the library, but rather forced him to sit in his dining room. The largeness of the room and its loneliness drove Richard to fits of anger and annoyance and, no matter where the meal was held, he ate very little. He drank water, determined that, should Eleana come to him, she would find him sober and genial. For this, he suffered bursts of frustration and was abrasive to anyone that came near.

Every morning, he would turn on Mrs. Graham and, though he did not speak of the one thing he wished, question her. She, in turn would give him the trivial news of the house and of the town, reading the morning paper before he did so that she could tell it to him while he paced back and forth. She made no mention of Eleana.

"Well, now, look at this," Mrs. Graham said one morning, sitting in one of the library chairs while Richard walked between the shelves, growling and grumbling to himself. "Miss Martin is engaged to Lord Alistair."

"The two deserve each other," Richard nodded. "Miss Martin was a cunning and selfish woman who wanted only power and money. Lord Alistair was a man with money and power who wanted a pretty woman to be his wife and ignore the way he wandered about."

"That's a pretty thing to say," Mrs. Graham remarked drily. He scoffed.

"Did you know that she tried to get her hooks into me? She would say just what she thought I would want to hear and practically invited herself to Belleview, which, of course, I ignored. Then, she didn't know that I was already in love with Elea—" He broke off, realising the direction of his conversation, and flung himself into a chair, looking desperately at the ceiling. "Do you think she'll ever come to me, tell me that she's forgiven me?"

"I think you should be patient and give the poor girl a bit of time to recover and to figure things out," Mrs. Graham sighed, thumbing through the paper so that she might find something to distract Richard further. She exclaimed in pleasure as she came upon an article concerning some bit of triviality about the new fashions of society and was about to read when Richard cut her off.

"Her father still resides in the cottage beside the kennels?" he asked, trying to keep his tone light, as if he were simply making pleasant conversation. It was obvious, though, that he was strained, and Mrs. Graham might have refused to answer him had not his blue eyes been so wide and despairing.

"Aye, he does at that," she said, then started reading without so much as a 'by your leave.' "This month in the city, there have been startling new fashions, especially amongst the ladies. Shorter sleeves, a slimmer mode of dress. My! Men's fashion, though, remains unchanged, except for the addition of the waistcoat in everyday dress. And the cravats have become—"

"Has Henry sent me any letters?" Richard cut in absently. Mrs. Graham folded the newspaper and sighed.

"Not that I know of," she admitted. "You have letters from your solicitor and from the board you set up for the school, which you asked me to read. There have been professors found for all the positions and a head-master has been interviewed and is waiting your final approval. The staff have been selected, apart from a cook and housekeeper, which the board asks you to apply for and select. Notices regarding enrolment have been sent out to various families in the county and advertisements have been placed in all the well-read papers. Applications will be due in three weeks for the fall term and, if we work hard over the remainder of the summer, everything should be made ready."

"The school," Richard murmured, the look of confusion on his face revealing that he had all but forgotten about his endeavour.

"Yes," Mrs. Graham snapped, throwing down the newspaper to a table and standing. "The school. The school and everything else you've forgotten about while you've been sitting here in the library, pining away and concerning yourself with works of fiction. I understand that you're hurting, that you're heartbro-ken, but frankly, you were of more help when you were drinking!" She turned and, her skirts swirling about her, strode out of the library, her chin high and fire burning in her eyes.

Richard watched her go, slightly surprised by her outburst but not worried or even greatly affected. He was too preoccupied. He turned his thoughts to Eleana and wondered why her father was still with her. Was it because she was still hurting and he was helping her to recover? Or perhaps she simply wanted him to stay. Did Eleana think of him at all? He doubted that, since she had not made any motion to the contrary. He watched her from the windows of the library, occasionally. She worked with her dogs all day, now, no longer taking time out for her injury's sake or walking with Theo.

Had there been an altercation between the hostler and Eleana? Richard hoped so. Then he cursed himself for hoping so, thinking that if Theo made Eleana happy he should not wish her hurt. But if Theo made Eleana happy, there was no hope for himself. His heart ached at that thought and, unable to bear more pain, threw himself on the nearest book he could find, opening it to the place where he had left off and reading furiously. He wasn't sure he comprehended a single word.

Mrs. Graham returned at luncheon time, her anger slackened, bearing a tray with Cornish hen and corn rolls as well as some greens and tomatoes in a vinegar sauce. There were other foods to tempt Richard, sweet meats, sugar rolls, candied fruits and nuts, but his appetite was little. Mrs. Graham put the tray on the table, sweeping the morning paper aside. "You'll eat all that Cornish hen or I'll not leave you alone for the rest of the day," she ordered.

Richard sighed and deposited his book, wandering over to the table and glancing out the window at the same time, hoping to catch a glance of Eleana. He saw her moving towards the house and hope flared within him. Then she paused, hesitated, and turned around and his heart sank. He stabbed into the bird and wished fervently that Smoke were still alive so that he might have someone to talk to. Someone to keep him company who would not judge him. Who loved Eleana.

He had nearly finished the turkey, what little appetite he had waning, when a young maid burst in, her eyes sparkling with excitement, her face flushed from running. She curtseyed to Richard but he ignored her as it was obvious Mrs. Graham was who the maid wanted.

"What is it, Missy?" she asked tiredly, keeping a close eye on Richard while he ate.

The next words had him dropping his fork to the floor in shock and terror. "Theo has been engaged to be married!"

CHAPTER 19

Mrs. Graham hurried the excited maid out of the library with fire burning in her eyes. She wanted to reprimand the girl but calmed herself and put her hands on the girl's shoulders, "Tell me what's happened."

The young maid beamed at the chance to share her gossip, "It was just announced at luncheon a few minutes ago. Theo and Fey are going to be married! Isn't it wonderful?" Mrs. Graham blinked and barely managed a nod. She sent the girl on her way and leaned against the wall for support. Theo and Fey? Not Theo and Eleana? That could only mean one thing.

She turned to go back into the library and tell Richard the good news when he flung the door open and stared at Mrs. Graham, his eyes full of agony and pain. "Is it true?" he whispered, his voice hoarse, his skin pale and his muscles trembling with terror.

"Theo's to be married to—" Mrs. Graham started

but Richard was gone before she could finish. He fairly flew down the hallway, to the stairs, out of the house and across the lawn to the stables. He wanted to look into Theo's eyes and see the truth—no, he wanted to look into Eleana's eyes, those magnificent green depths, but that was not allowed to him—and yet he knew that the man would be at luncheon still.

Mal, to Richard's surprise, was still in the stable, going around to the horses with an oat bucket, murmuring happy nothings to the great creatures. He looked up in surprise as Richard entered. "M'lord! I wasn't expecting to, ah, that is, you didn't have your horse or carriage ordered and, well..."

"Prepare my horse," Richard ordered, then shook his head and walked to the tack room and picked his saddle up, grabbing a blanket and walking back to the stall where his black stallion was housed. Mal spluttered and tried to take the saddle from his master, he who looked so weak and ill, his skin seemingly too large for him, his eyes stormy and sunken. Richard ignored the efforts of the stable master and soon his horse was ready.

He threw himself into the saddle and spurred his horse into action, the black creature snorting in surprise and stepping a few times before lunging forwards, hooves clattering on the hard, stable floor. Richard leaned forwards and rode hard, wanting to get away as quickly as possible. He didn't know where he was going, and he didn't care. Eleana was lost to him and he knew only that he could not survive without her.

So, intent on his flight was he that Richard did not see Eleana walking towards the house, alone but for Hunter at her side. She reached out a hand to Richard as he passed swiftly by, but he did not notice her. She ordered Hunter to bark, but it was too late.

He was gone.

Eleana wanted to run after him, but she knew that she could not dare to hope to catch his horse. She huffed in annoyance; she had finally worked up the courage to go to him and now her chance had vanished once again.

"Eleana!" Mrs. Graham ran from the house, her face flushed and her hair flying from its tight chignon. Eleana went to the flustered housekeeper, her brows furrowed. Mrs. Graham panted for a moment then clutched at Eleana's arm, "He thinks Theo is to marry *you*."

Eleana nearly fell backwards, the breath knocked from her. She shook her head and touched her heart. Mrs. Graham nodded, "I know, but he does not. And I fear he is going to do himself serious harm."

Eleana looked in the direction Richard had gone, towards the town or to nowhere, anywhere, and blanched. She took a few steps in the direction he had raced then halted, knowing it was futile.

She looked at Hunter and wished she had legs such as he did, made for running quickly, for going long distances. An idea struck her and, though her belly clenched with fear, she turned and ran for the stables. Mal was standing there, staring at the empty stall and frowning as he tried to comprehend the recent actions of Richard. Eleana startled him out of his thoughts and pointed desperately towards one of the other horses.

"What? Eleana?" Mal said, aghast. He knew full well the terror of the Hounds Keeper and yet here she was asking for a horse. She repeated her desperate actions and made as if she were running. "The fastest one I've got is that young'un, there, but he's spirited and hard on the best of riders," Mal said, pointing to a yearling with dun coat, whose eyes flashed and whose head tossed. Eleana pointed to the horse and clasped her hands before her. Please.

Mal swallowed uncomfortably but did as she asked, taking the yearling from the stall and saddling him, quickly and efficiently. The horse snorted and tossed his head, pawing at the ground as if in expectation of a race. Eleana pressed her hand to Mal's shoulder in thanks and, using the stall door as a base, climbed into the saddle, sitting uncomfortably and holding the reins as if they were a lifeline. She took a few precious seconds to try and calm her fear before ordering Hunter to seek Richard and digging her heels into the horse's side.

The yearling was off like a shot and Eleana nearly lost her seat on the initial burst of speed. She clenched her knees to the side of the horse and leaned in so she would not lose her balance, fear making her clutch the reins desperately, even as she gave the horse his head.

Hunter, sensing the chase, ran ahead of the horse, barely keeping in front as the yearling galloped along. He soon fell behind, but by then Eleana had an idea of where Richard was going.

His trail led down the drive of Belleview and onto the main, hard packed road. He seemed to be heading towards Hartwell and also to the great crossroads which would lead to other towns or the city, if one chose. She urged the horse onwards though her balance was compromised, and she felt that she would fall at any second. Hunter continued to run after the horse, but he was no match for such speed. Yet he followed his mistress loyally, keeping on her trail though he pushed his muscles to their limit.

Eleana knew the horse master had been right. The yearling was the fastest of the lot and, while Richard had his lead, she was soon catching up. There, in her field of vision, was a rider on a black horse, running swiftly. She leaned further in, instinctively rising in the saddle, her hands on either side of the horse's neck, now blinking furiously as dirt and dust flew into her eyes. The yearling surged forwards.

RICHARD BECAME aware that he was being followed when the dun yearling's hoofbeats sounded above those of his own stallion. He slowed his horse slightly and turned, curiosity outweighing his despair for a moment as he tried to figure out who would be following him. He saw a crouched figure on the horse, brown hair flying behind and he gasped. There was no doubt that it was Eleana, though he was well aware of her fear regarding horses. The bad seat and her determined look gave no chance for him to question it.

"Eleana," he cried, slowing his horse as she drew nearer.

She straightened and pulled on the reins, relief flashing momentarily on her features before fear took over. She had found Richard, had caught up to Richard, but now the realisation that she was on a horse with no idea how to make it stop besides tugging on its reins came into full light. The yearling slowed slightly, but not enough. It passed the stallion and Richard kicked his heels into his horse, determined to keep pace.

"Hold on," he yelled and Eleana hunched her shoulders in response. Richard came abreast of the horse and drew closer, reaching out. "Grab my hand," he ordered and Eleana did so, though it was obvious her instincts were screaming at her to hold onto the horse.

As soon as her hand was clasped in Richard's, he threw himself from his horse, pulling her out of the saddle as he did so. The two fell to the ground and rolled, using the other as a cushion against the pain. Finally, the world stopped moving and the horses slowed to a stop ahead, the stallion nipping at the yearling in annoyance. Richard noticed none of that. He knew only that he was lying on the ground, Eleana in his arms, her head resting on his chest, her eyes squeezed closed.

"Are you hurt?" he asked.

She blinked open her eyes and took stock of her body before deciding that, apart from some bruising, she was fine. Eleana sat up slightly and shook her head, looking at Richard. It was amazing how much better he felt in that moment with her there beside him than he had in weeks past.

"You're trembling," he noted, sitting up as well and drawing Eleana against his chest, his arms wrapping around her shoulders as he comforted her.

She smiled for a moment, letting herself be comforted, then pushed free and glared at Richard. He sucked in a breath, wondering if he had been wrong. Eleana reached out and hit the back of his head then lunged forwards to kiss him.

It was a kiss like none other they had shared. This was passionate and desperate, needy and joyous. This time, there was love on both sides of the kiss. Richard smiled even as her lips moulded to his, then gently pulled away to look at her. Eleana brushed a strand of hair from her eyes and grinned apologetically. "I thought I'd lost you," Richard breathed.

Eleana shook her head and put one hand on her heart, the other on Richard's.

There was no need for translation, but he did it anyways. "I love you."

ACKNOWLEDGMENTS

I would like to thank all the people who helped to make this book a reality. Specifically, Fay over at Fay Lane graphics, who took my wildly vague ideas and turned them into something beautiful. And Ashley Olivier whose edits were precisely what this book needed.

I should also like to thank all my readers over the years. You read the original drafts of this and liked it, which was enough to spur me into doing something crazy—like becoming a romance author. I appreciate every single one of you.

And then there are the people in my life without whom I wouldn't be writing at all. You know precisely who you are and I thank you for it. Your support has gotten me through a lot.

Thank you, everyone.

Best wishes,

Evelyn

ABOUT THE AUTHOR

Evelyn Grimald is, as well as a romance author, fascinated with all things human. She has been exploring the human condition in her writing since she was a young girl. Since then, Evelyn has penned several novels. She chose romance in a desire to show everybody that desire, and love, are in the eye of the beholder. As are our smiles.

Evelyn lives a quiet life reading and writing, which her cat and dog both appreciate. When not writing, she is walking or reading, exploring so many of the worlds which books provide.